MURDER IN DEVIL'S COVE

Melissa Bourbon

Devil's Cove

North Carolina

MURDER IN DEVIL'S COVE

A BOOK MAGIC MYSTERY

MELISSA BOURBON

Print ISBN: 978-0-9978661-1-7

ASIN: B088J48JY8

Published by Lake House Press

Art by Dar Albert, Wicked Smart Designs

To Laura Valerius, the truest sea captain I've ever known. Thank you for your stories, your inspiration, and sharing all your boat knowledge.

And to

Wendy Lyn Watson for your brilliantly creative mind. Without you, my friend, the Book Magic Mysteries would not exist. Thank you for sharing.

The Lane Family

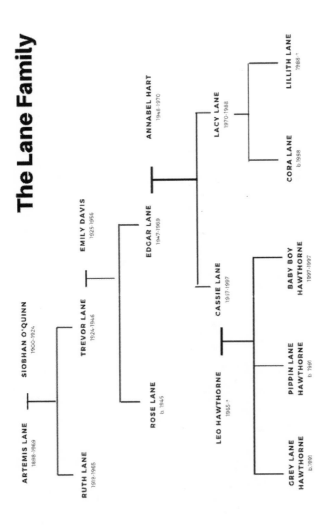

ARTEMIS LANE
1898-1969

SIOBHAN O'QUINN
1900-1924

RUTH LANE
1918-1985

TREVOR LANE
1924-1946

EMILY DAVIS
1925-1956

ANNABEL HART
1948-1970

ROSE LANE
b.1945

EDGAR LANE
1947-1969

LACY LANE
1970-1988

CORA LANE
b.1988

LILLITH LANE
1988-?

LEO HAWTHORNE
1965-?

CASSIE LANE
1967-1997

GREY LANE
HAWTHORNE
b.1991

PIPPIN LANE
HAWTHORNE
b.1991

BABY BOY
HAWTHORNE
1997-1997

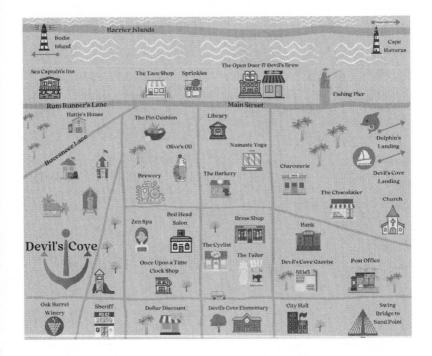

MURDER IN DEVIL'S COVE

PROLOGUE

"Some places speak distinctly. Certain dark gardens cry aloud for a murder; certain old houses demand to be haunted; certain coasts are set apart for shipwreck."
~Robert Louis Stevenson

*C*assandra Lane Hawthorne stood on the main fishing pier in Devil's Cove staring out at the harbor, grasping the pendant she wore around her neck. The breeze blew across the Sound, whipping her hair into her face. The same feeling of foreboding she'd had since the day she'd met her husband filled her. Her insides were a dry sponge slowly expanding with water. "You're not going to take him," she said. Her voice was carried away on the breath of wind. She spoke again, louder this time. "You won't take him!"

"Take who, Mama?" Cassie's six-year-old daughter, Pippin, tugged at the fabric of Cassie's dress.

"Nobody." She took Pippin's hand and squeezed. "It's cold. Come on, let's go home."

They walked along the wooden slats of the pier, Cassie's

white canvas sneakers silent next to the *slap slap slap* of Pippin's sandals. The irony of her daughter's name wasn't lost on Cassie. Leo was a Tolkien fanatic. He and a group of friends had called themselves The Fellowship all through college. And when it came time to name their children, he'd longed for names from Tolkien's classics. Their son, born seventy-three seconds before Pippin, they'd named Grey, after Gandalf the Grey. And their daughter had been named after Peregrin, one of Frodo Baggin's best hobbit friends. Pippin for short.

Cassie had never read the books, but she loved her husband.

She wanted no book that had a past to enter their home, but she'd made concessions for Leo. He kept his personal collection under lock and key in the office of the sea captain's house they'd bought in Devil's Cove when they first married. Cassie would have nothing to do with Leo's books, now more than ever. Her fear about what they could tell her about the future was much greater than her temptation.

Her skirt whipped around her legs, billowing out behind her. This weather...the ocean...the Outer Banks of North Carolina. She loved every bit of it. Everything except waiting for Leo to come home to her. Waiting for the sea to give her husband back to her.

They walked together, Pippin's feet moving in double-time to keep up with Cassie's longer stride. "Library!" Pippin yanked on Cassie's hand and pulled her toward the two-story house that had years ago been converted. The word LIBRARY was spelled across the eaves over the small porch entry. A blue sign with a figure holding a book was secured in the ground at the sidewalk, denoting the building as the town's library.

It was a place Cassie never stepped foot into.

"Another day, lovey," she said to Pippin, pulling her along. She placed one hand on her pregnant belly. Through the fog and straight ahead, the town's bookstore came into view. That was another building she refused to go into.

All books had a history.

All books told stories—those written on the pages, and those between the lines.

Cassie wanted nothing to do with any of them.

The library and the bookstore were on opposite sides of the street. If Cassie took the conventional path, she'd have to pass one or the other. Instead, she marked a diagonal to cross the street, leaving the sidewalk before they got to the library, planning to step up onto the opposite sidewalk a few yards past the bookstore. It was the only way to miss them both.

She muttered under her breath. Only her Aunt Rose thought of their family magic as a blessing. To Cassie, it was a curse. Her mother, and her sister Lacy, had both died in childbirth. Her great-grandfather, grandfather, and father had all been taken by the sea. Cassie had left the west coast and the only family she had, only to fall in love with Leonardo Jay Hawthorne, a bookish fisherman from the Outer Banks. Her destiny to live by the sea was fulfilled. She couldn't escape, that was the truth of the matter.

Cassie grabbed hold of Pippin's hand and hurried on, dipping her head against the cold wind. She touched her swollen belly again. She'd survived childbirth, but would she be able to tempt fate twice? And what about Leo. He'd joined the Lane's through marriage, but had Cassie only transferred the curse to him? Would he be able to escape the fate of the men in her family? For that matter, how could she keep Grey off the water and safe?

An elderly woman, her head lowered, emerged from the bookstore. A cobalt blue scarf covered her hair, its tail whipping behind her. She pulled her woolen coat tight around herself. Instead of staying on the sidewalk, the old woman stepped into the street. Just as Cassie was doing, she cut a diagonal. Cassie looked at the older woman as she and Pippin approached her, gasping when the woman suddenly looked up, her tiger eyes boring into her. A shiver slithered up Cassie's spine.

In an instant, the fog thickened, covering Devil's Cove with a heavy blanket of mist. Something hit the ground as the old woman dropped her gaze again and passed them. Without thinking, Cassie bent to pick up the fallen object. The moment she did, her heart hammered in her chest. She looked at what she held.

It was a tattered copy of Homer's *The Odyssey*.

Cassie cried out. Dropped the book.

It landed on its spine. The pages fell open.

Before Cassie could stop her, Pippin scooped it up and held it out to her, holding it open. "The lady, she dropped it."

Cassie looked over her shoulder. "Wait," she called out, but the fog had swallowed the woman.

A chill swept through Cassie as she looked down at the open pages of the book her daughter held. Her eyes scanned the words and her heart climbed to her throat.

...So ALL THAT has been duly done. Listen now, I will tell you
all, but the very god himself will make you remember.
You will come first of all to the Sirens, who are enchanters
of all mankind and whoever comes their way; and that man
who unsuspecting approaches them, and listens to the Sirens

singing, has no prospect of coming home and delighting

his wife and little children as they stand about him in greeting,

but the Sirens by the melody of their singing enchant him.

they sit in their meadow, but the beach before it is piled with the boneheads

of men now rotted away, and the skins shrivel upon them.

"No. No, no, no." Cassie fell to her knees, unable to hold in her sobs.

Chapter 1

"Home is a name, a word, it is a strong one; stronger than magician ever spoke, or spirit ever answered to, in the strongest conjuration."

~Charles Dickens

The island of Devil's Cove lay between the mainland and the barrier islands on North Carolina's Outer Banks, smack in the middle of four ocean channels. Albermarle Sound was to the north. Roanoke Sound flowed to the east. Croatan Sound was on the west side of the island. And to the south was the inlet of Pamlico Sound. It was connected to the mainland with a single swing bridge. A ferry carted people and their cars back and forth. It wasn't the easiest of the islands to get to, but it was perhaps the most special.

Colorful beach houses overlooked the water. A protected cove was a favorite spot for kayaking and swimming. The quaint town welcomed tourists, but generations

of families called Devil's Cove home. The island drew fishermen, treasure hunters who chartered boats to explore the
Graveyard of the Atlantic, and sun-worshipers.

And now Pippin and Grey Hawthorne, siblings born
seventy-three seconds apart, were back after being gone for
twenty years.

They stood on the sidewalk in front of a decrepit looking
house that sported a combination of Cape Cod and old
Southern Coastal architecture, complete with a million
paned windows, a screened porch on the left side of the
house, a wide sitting porch, and a lookout at the top of the
structure with a view straight to the harbor. A widow's walk,
Pippin thought, where a wife could keep watch as she
waited for her husband to return from sea.

Behind it was Roanoke Sound, Bodie Island with its
lighthouse, and beyond that, the Atlantic.

The house was so much bigger than Pippin remembered, and she remembered it as huge. In its heyday, it had
to have been a spectacular house. Now, it sat neglected,
longing for fresh paint, new shutters, and some tender-
loving care. A shiver passed over Pippin and her hand
moved to her neck. She looked up at the widow's walk. Had
her mother stood up there, staring towards the horizon
while she waited for Leo to come home to her?

Pippin let the thought pass. She was hypnotized by the
overgrown property as much as by the house itself, although
both were in dire need of repair and upkeep. Her gaze skittered over the lawn that was little more than a map of
weeds. Over the walkway leading to the wrap-around porch,
more weeds grew between the red bricks. Over the
flowerbeds that had probably once bloomed with
hydrangeas, hyacinth, daisies, and who knew what other

plants, but which was now filled with an abundance of yet more weeds.

For a moment, she closed her eyes and envisioned what the property could look like. In her mind's eye, she saw it blooming with a perennial garden, annuals tucked here and there for added color and variety. The massive overgrowth of pampas grass behind their father's dry-docked fishing boat could be cleared out and replaced with an enclosed vegetable garden.

Grey could renovate the massive house, bringing it back to habitable. Because right now, from the looks of it, it certainly wasn't.

Grey looked at her with eyebrows raised and chin lowered. "We can't keep it."

She opened her eyes again and gave him a side glance. "We could."

He shook his head. "We can't."

"Oh, but we could."

Grey ran a hand over his face, ending by rubbing the stubble that had recently turned into a beard. Although his hair was chestnut, his Irish came out through the iridescent orange hairs peppered throughout. "Pippin, it's been vacant for twenty years. I can see from here that the porch has dry rot. The place probably has termites. It's not a matter of *if* in North Carolina, it's a matter of *when*. Look. Half the windows are broken. That screen door is hanging on one hinge. And God knows what it looks like inside."

"They left it to us," she said. It wasn't a plea, but a statement of fact. After Grandmother Faye died, Pippin found her parents' will, leaving them the old beach house in Devil's Cove. She and Grey had both thought the place had been sold when their father vanished. Why their grandparents had kept it from them, they'd never know for sure, but Pippin could venture a guess. Faye blamed their mother for their father leaving. She'd held out hope that her son was out there somewhere and that he'd come home. The house and boat hadn't belonged to Pippin and Grey, but to Leo. It was as if holding onto it made it their own lighthouse...a beacon that would guide Leo home.

Only Leo had been gone for two decades. He was not coming back. All this now belonged to the twins. "Nothing's keeping you in Greenville, Greevie," she said.

He didn't respond, but he knew it was true. He worked for a construction company, but it wasn't a career. Neither of them had found their passions. Maybe this house—and coming back to Devil's Cove—maybe these things would help them discover their paths.

Pippin saw movement from the corner of eye. She could just make out a pink nose poking out of the pampas grass. Slowly, it inched its way into the open. A dog. A very mangy looking dog. It was honey colored—and incredibly thin. When was the last time the pup had eaten?

"All right, let's get it over with," Grey said.

Pippin glanced at him, nodding. When she looked back to the yard, the dog was gone. She sighed, hoping it would be able to find its next meal. To Grey, she said, "Maybe it's not as bad as you think."

Her brother shot her a side-eye glance that clearly said he thought it was probably worse than he thought, but he led the way up the brick walkway. "Be careful," he said, pointing to the patches of rotted wood on the steps.

Like all the beach houses on Rum Runner's Lane, the house was built on stilts, pilings, and piers, elevated to protect it from flooding. They walked up the steps to the porch, jigging and jagging to avoid the damaged wood, as if they were trying to avoid cracks in a sidewalk. As Grey carefully took hold of the handle of the screen door, it let out a horrific creak, the last rusty hinge releasing its hold. "Watch out!" he shouted.

Pippin jumped back as the screen door fell. The bottom of it hit the torn-up porch, but Grey caught it and deftly moved it out of the way, leaning it up against the house.

They stood side by side, facing the front door, a haunting feeling coming over her as if this house was going to change things for them. At the same time, she felt like they were in a horror movie in a *too stupid to live* moment. *Don't go in. Bad things will happen. You may never come back out.*

Pippin took a deep breath, swallowing her anxiety. This had been their parents' home. Her home when she was little. An image of her and Grey splashing around in a pink plastic kiddie pool flashed into her mind. A memory of standing next to her mother, the solidness of her leg underneath one of the gauzy skirts she'd always worn. Her mother pacing back and forth as she stared out at the lighthouse on Bodie Island and at the horizon beyond.

Gooseflesh rose on her skin. "We can't sell this house," she said, her voice barely above a whisper.

Grey opened his mouth, looking ready to contradict her, but stopped when he saw her face. "Are you okay?"

"They lived here." She pressed her fingertips against the front door and pushed. It creaked as it swung inward. All she could see was a vast empty and dark room. A room she and Grey had run through and had played hide and seek in. She folded her arms over her chest and looked at him. "*We* lived here."

He turned his back to the house, facing the yard, plunging his hands into the pockets of his jeans. His brow furrowed as he studied the property. "There used to be a fence and a gate, didn't there?"

She tried to remember, thinking back to her childhood before Grandmother Faye and Grandpa Randal had taken them to Greenville. The image appeared in her mind's eye. Grey was right. There had been a white picket fence enclosing the yard. Any remnants of it were long gone. She remembered a distinct clicking sound. "We would go through the gate and walk to the pier sometimes," she said.

"I remember that." Grey cupped his hand against the back of his neck. "She—Mom—used to tell me not to go near the water."

It was true. The house was on the beach, but Cassie hardly let them go out there. Pippin and Grey had given her a run for her money, always escaping and running down the worn boardwalk that led from the house to the sand. Now they fell silent, giving into the memories that surfaced. Grey rocked back on his heels and peered up at the porch ceiling, hands still in his pockets. The traditional haint blue paint was old and peeling. Grandmother Faye had had the same cool blue color on the ceiling of her front porch. "It started with the Gullah communities in South Carolina and Georgia," she'd told Pippin. "The color kept away the haints."

"What's a haint?" Pippin had asked.

"It's a spirit, child. But no need to worry. Now it just keeps away the wasps and other bugs."

"'Cause they think it's the sky?"

"Exactly," Grandmother Faye had said before going back inside to her cool air-conditioned house. Pippin had stayed on the porch, swaying in the rocking chair, and staring up at the blue ceiling. If it wasn't blue, would her mother come visit? From the moment her mother died, remembering her became harder and harder. The color of her eyes had been a vibrant Kelly green, but Pippin couldn't picture them anymore. They'd faded in her mind to a muted version, like a shamrock browned by a fiery sun. Although freckles had dusted the bridge of Cassie's nose, Pippin couldn't picture them. It was only because she could look in the mirror and see her own copper hair that she remembered her mother's. The shade had been the same.

What Pippin *could* bring to mind were the little things. The feel of her hand in her mother's as they walked along the pier. The taste of the strawberry shortcakes she made every summer. The sound of her voice as she hummed quietly to herself when she thought no one was near.

The sound of Grey exhaling chased away the memories. "You're right, Peevie. We can't sell it."

A wave of relief flowed through her at Grey's nickname for her. They had their own way of communicating—including special words they'd formed—ever since they learned how to talk. He called her Peevie and she called him Greevie. They were nonsensical words that belonged to Pippin and Grey alone. She felt her eyes glass over. They hadn't even been inside yet, but this was home. This was where she belonged.

She caught a movement from across the street, but when she looked, all she saw was a curtain falling back into place in the window of the purple and teal house. A shiver wound through her. Someone had been watching them.

"Let's look inside," Grey said.

Pippin took a closer look at the door handle before they stepped inside. "No lock?"

"There was one." Grey pointed to the empty space that used to house a deadbolt. "Wonder how many times this place has been broken into over the years?"

From the broken windows and the evidence right here at the door, she'd guess too many to count.

They spent the next hour exploring the three stories of house. On the widow's walk, she cupped her hand over her eyes, peering out to the sea beyond the harbor and Roanoke Sound. "What about turning it into a little seaside inn?" she said, turning to Grey.

"What, like a bed and breakfast?"

The second she'd laid eyes on the place, she'd started thinking of names. *Devil's Cove Inn* felt uninspired.

The Inn by the Sea didn't feel right because the village was in a harbor in the Sound.

Harbor Inn lacked umph.

She'd land on just the right name for it, eventually. To Grey, she said, "Exactly. We have Grandmother Faye's house. We can sell that to help fund the renovations, plus we have the money she left us." Excitement bloomed in her chest. She could bring the garden back to its glory days and, together, she and Grey could make the house what it once was. And they could make a living by opening it up to visitors and tourists. "Grey, we can do this. We're supposed to be in this house."

Grey chewed his lower lip. "It's a big job."

"You can do it," she said. "*We* can do it."

The consternation on Grey's face lifted. He held up one hand, pinkie extended. Pippin intertwined hers with his and smiled.

He nodded. "We can do it."

They stayed in the house, making plans, leaving only when the sun had set and a chill settled into the darkness.

Chapter 2

"Magic is always pushing and drawing and making things out of nothing. Everything is made out of magic, leaves and trees, flowers and birds, badgers and foxes and squirrels and people. So it must be all around us. In this garden - in all the places."
~Frances Hodgson Burnett, *The Secret Garden*

Their plans came together quickly. Pippin had appointed herself the gardener and interior designer of the project, while Grey was in charge of demo and construction. The house in Greenville went on the market, then into contract. A short time later, Grey rounded up a small crew of three to help him renovate the house. He ordered a dumpster to sit out front and he, Travis Walsh, Kyron Washington, and Jimmy Gallagher set to work. They started with the porch. Piece by piece, the old planks came off and were replaced with brand new pressure treated wood. Once they could safely walk up the steps without danger of a foot crashing through the rot, they started the interior renovations.

Having the men around became the norm. Travis hummed while he worked, talking himself through tasks by narrating his actions. His hair parted in the middle and was long enough to pull back into a ponytail or man bun, depending on the day. He looked to be in his mid-thirties—though acted younger. She'd overheard him talking about surfing and chilling on the beach. Like Peter Pan, he didn't want to grow up.

JIMMY HAD AN EVER-PRESENT smile and twinkling green eyes. He was beanpole thin and stood six feet tall. Pippin couldn't help but notice the enormity of his feet. They could double for water skis. He was the oldest of the group, somewhere in his late thirties, or maybe early forties.

Kyron kept his black hair shorn close to the scalp. He was compact and lean, reminding Pippin of a slightly taller Kevin Hart, complete with the winning smile and love of basketball. His standard work uniform was a short sleeve shirt that showed off his biceps and athletic shorts that revealed toned calves.

They each had tattoos. It made her shiver. The thought of a needle methodically plunging into her skin was enough to turn her blood cold. She'd never be able to get one, which is why she was obsessed with noticing other people's. If someone in her line of sight had one, her eyes sought it out. Which happened a lot. More people than not had them. The edge of a T peeked out from the edges of Kyron's sleeve. Jimmy had Batman's batwings on the back of one calf, and a collection of several other tattoos on both arms. A circle on his clavicle, only part of it visible from under his shirt. A flower, though she couldn't say what variety. Barbed wire. Pippin cringed at the busty woman Travis sported on his arm. He tended toward tanks, so the woman was on display all the time. He had others, but she never looked long enough to see what else he'd inked onto his skin.

Kyron was the baby of the group, closer to Pippin and Grey's age than the other two men. She'd heard him tell Grey that he had one more course to finish his bachelor's degree in business. The men were vastly different from one another, but as a team, they were a finely oiled machine. "Did you all know each other before this project?" Pippin asked them one day as they ripped out the kitchen cabinetry.

Kyron looked up from his crouched position in front of a lower cabinet. "Small town."

She took that as a yes.

Grey had said the guys came recommended by someone at the lumber store. In just over two weeks, they'd already finished the porch, the downstairs bathroom, and had just about wrapped up the demo in the kitchen. Kyron was working on removing the last cabinets while Travis and Jimmy chipped away at what was left of the tile flooring.

Pippin had made checklists, noting everything that needed to be done to the house. The two bedrooms upstairs, as well as the master, just needed cosmetic work done. Each room had its own bathroom, however, and each of them was in pretty bad shape and needed to be gutted. After the kitchen was done, they were next. The top floor had a bunk room and another bathroom, neither of which had ever been finished, as well as two storage rooms, a sitting room, window seats in the dormers, and access to the widow's walk. Finally, the main floor. What had been their father's study, which had its own half bath, was in the back left corner. Off the kitchen was a mudroom, laundry room, and pantry. A bar was built into one wall in the great room. A ten-foot island created a division between the great room and the kitchen. Pippin had plans for new countertops, as well as new cabinets, fresh paint, and shiplap. Lots and lots of shiplap.

A small office sat just to the left of the foyer. Pippin claimed that for herself. It was at the bottom of the renovation list, so she'd cleaned the walls herself, prepped the space by using blue painter's tape to protect the wide baseboards, which were in surprisingly good condition, and painted the space a cream color that made it feel bigger than it actually was, important because, although there were two windows, the covered porch in front and on the side of the house prevented sunlight from streaming in.

She'd found an old table at a secondhand furniture store that she'd stripped and painted white, distressing it. "I don't get it. It was old, you painted it, but then you made it look old again," Grey said as he and Kyron carried it inside for her.

Pippin directed them into the little office. "Yes, but now it's clean. And it's distressed in the way I want it to be. That's the key."

"I get it," Kyron said to her with a wink. To Grey, he said, "Good thing she's in charge of the decorating."

Travis and Jimmy were working upstairs demoing one of the bathrooms. Kyron headed back to the study to sand the wainscoting, and Grey returned to installing the hardwood floor Pippin had chosen for the great room and kitchen. Grey had anticipated the project taking a solid three months. Things were moving along at a pretty good pace and they were ahead of schedule with just a few more weeks to go.

Now, standing just inside the front door, Pippin closed her eyes. She could picture herself sitting next to Grey on the couch watching TV, but instead of the memory bringing her comfort, a feeling of loneliness washed over her. After their mother died, their father had retreated into his head. If he wasn't at the marina working on his boat, or out to sea fishing, he was in his study. After the funeral, he'd tried to act normal. He kept his emotions bottled up, and he never asked Pippin and Grey how they felt. If he did, Pippin thought it would have opened up a floodgate.

He forced smiles that never reached his eyes. He used to take them for ice cream. The three of them would sit on the bench across the street from the ice cream parlor, but the scoop atop his cone always melted in his hand as he stared off into the distance.

She remembered him muttering under his breath, as if he was talking to Cassie. Maybe he was. To her ghost, at least. "I should have been able to protect you," he'd say. "I'll protect them." He blamed himself, she realized, though no one could have predicted the trouble Cassie would have with her pregnancy or that she'd die in childbirth. It wasn't her father's fault.

Pippin and Grey had been sent off to their grandparents when their father was gone on his extended fishing trips, and after he vanished on them, they'd gone to Greenville for good. They tried to push their feelings away. They really did. They made friends with their classmates, but everyone knew they'd been orphaned and abandoned. It was a dark cloud that hovered over them, ready to release a torrent of rain any second. They tried to be normal. To be kids, but it was never the same. The moment Cassie died, Pippin and

Grey had grown up, because how can you still be a child when your mother is gone?

Pippin opened her eyes, chasing away that forlorn feeling that often settled in her. She had to excise it and making new memories in this house was the way to do it.

But deep down, she knew the house had something to tell her.

Chapter 3

"The fishermen know that the sea is dangerous and the storm terrible, but they have never found these dangers sufficient reason for remaining ashore."
~Vincent Van Gogh

*P*ippin had moved on to the garden. She left Grey to the shiplap he was installing in the kitchen and great room, pulled on a pair of work boots, donned her gloves, and hauled the four-tired wheelbarrow she'd bought, a pair of garden shears tossed inside, over to the northeast corner of the property.

She stood back, looking at the mass of pampas grass that blocked the view of the Sound. The grassy foliage had been unchecked for years and almost hid her father's thirty-two-foot fishing vessel. Somehow, the idea of revealing her father's fishing boat and having to figure out how to get it hauled away was more daunting than the renovation of the entire house, but day by day, she'd been cutting the long strands of grass, chopping the plant's white feathery plumes, and bit by bit, she was making headway and getting closer and closer to the boat.

Finally, she'd chopped away enough of the grass to be able to see the dilapidated tarp that had been covering the boat over the last two decades.

Twenty years. When she thought about it in those terms, it was like a mind-blow. That's how long her father had been gone. And her mother had been dead for three years more than that. It felt like a lifetime.

She still ached over the loss of her parents. She had few memories, but the ones she did have were strong and growing more vivid now that she was back in her early childhood home. Sometimes she wanted to chase them away and not feel the loss and emptiness that came with them. Unfortunately, emotions didn't respond to logic. She couldn't just press a button and make them go away. She was learning to live with them. To embrace them, even.

Oddly, she had only a vague memory of her father's boat. She knew from Grandmother Faye that he'd worked on a boat captained by someone else when he'd first left home and moved to the Outer Banks. When he'd finally saved up enough money, he bought a used boat and had captained his own crew. Pippin remembered boarding it as a little girl, but her father forbade it after Cassie died.

Pippin's mind drifted back to the one time she and Grey had left North Carolina. She hadn't thought about it in years, and the story was foggy. It had been just after their father disappeared that Grandmother Faye sent them to Laurel Point, Oregon for a visit. That's when they learned several truths. The first truth was that they had other family. An Aunt Rose, and two cousins, Lily and Cora—twins, just like Pippin and Grey.

Pippin looked a bit like the two girls, what with their massive amounts of ringlets, only Cora and Lily's hair was blonde, while Pippin's was copper. The two sets of twins shared the same gray-green eyes. "Your eyes are the color of an angry sea," Pippin remembered her mother telling her. It was a random memory and one she'd often wondered if she'd imagined. After all, she'd been only six years old when her mother died.

Grey had darker hair than Cora and Lily. It was less red and more chestnut than Pippin's. Still curly, though. His grandmother kept it cut short on the sides with a flounce of curls sitting atop his head. "Your mother's curls," Grandmother Faye often said to him, but not as if it was a good thing. There was always some hidden message in Grandmother Faye's tone when she talked about Cassie, but Pippin and Grey didn't know why...or what it meant.

The newly discovered cousins were three years older than Pippin and Grey, but slighter in stature. Pippin and Grey took after their father who stood six feet two inches tall. Cassie had been five foot five. Her height kept Pippin smaller, but Grey was already shooting up. "You're going to be as tall as your daddy," Grandmother Faye once said. When Grey had asked a question about their father, Grandmother Faye clamped her lips together. It had been one of the rare times she mentioned her son, and once the words left her lips, she looked like she wished she could pull them back. She couldn't forgive her son from walking away from his family. Pippin had heard her grandparents talking about it when they didn't know she was listening. "He'll come back. I know he will. He wouldn't have left his children, not after their mother died," Grandmother Faye said, but Grandpa Randal had shaken his head and grunted with dismay. "There are witnesses," he said.

"People who saw him leave his boat, but he never went home. He walked away, Faye. There's no other explanation."

That was the closest Pippin and Grey had come to knowing anything about their parents. Until they met Cora and Lily. The cousins knew everything about the Lanes. Everything that was lost when their mother died and then when their father disappeared.

One evening during that visit, when Cora and Lily were twelve and Pippin and Grey were nine, the four of them had sat on a mound of rocks on the beach staring out at the roiling Pacific Ocean. "There's Lane family lore, you know," Cora said just as the sun dipped below the horizon, sounding like she was repeating something she'd overheard or been told.

Pippin had looked up at Cora, eyes wide. She used grownup words and seemed so mature. Pippin wished she lived closer to these two mysterious girls who were her only family aside from her brother and her grandparents. She'd only known them for five minutes, and she already hung on every word they said with bated breath. "What does that mean?"

"Our family's *story*," Cora explained.

"What story?" Grey said at the same time she asked the same thing. Being twins meant they often finished each other's sentences and had the same thoughts at the very same moment. Pippin often felt that Grey was an extension of herself. Did Lily and Cora feel that way, too? Was the connection even stronger for them because they were both girls?

The sky grew darker as Cora's voice dropped to a low pitch. She held the flashlight she'd brought to the beach under her chin, the beam of light illuminating her face with an eeriness that sent a shiver down Pippin's spine. "We know the story of our great-great-grandfather."

Pippin and Grey shot a look at each other in the dark. They didn't know anything about their great-great-grandfather. They didn't even know they *had* a great-great-grandfather.

Cora's voice dropped even lower. Lily, Pippin, and Grey had to scoot closer to hear her. She began, sounding like a radio announcer. "Artemis Lane was a fisherman—" She looked suddenly at Pippin and Grey— "Just like your dad."

Pippin sucked in a breath and reached for Grey's hand, fighting the tears. She couldn't think about her dad. "What about our great-great-grandmother?" she asked, turning the conversation.

"Siobhan," Lily said. "She died on the crossing from Europe. Artemis was left to raise his children, Trevor and Ruth, on his own. Like his father before him—"

"Or so we were told—" Lily said.

"—Trevor also became a fisherman."

"Right here in Laurel Point."

Just like Pippin and Grey, Cora and Lily interrupted each other and tagged onto each other's thoughts. Cora continued, "Trevor fought in World War II—"

"He shouldn't have," Lily said. "He was only seventeen. He lied about his age to enlist, but he came back. And when he did, he got married. Had two children—"

"—Edgar and Rose," Cora said.

Lily looked up to the starless sky before continuing. "In 1946, Trevor set off to captain his own ship on his first solo trip."

The flashlight flickered under Cora's chin as she grimaced. "Ruth warned Artemis. *Trevor should not go*, she said. *Something bad is going to happen*."

Lily moved closer to her sister until she and Cora were hip to hip, thigh to thigh. Cora moved the flashlight so it shone on both their faces. "Ruth warned her father and brother," Lily said, her voice ominous, "but they didn't listen."

Grey cleared his throat to interrupt. "Why didn't they listen?"

Cora fluttered her hand in front of her face, as if she were batting away the words. "Artemis was a man of science. He never believed in magic or mysticism. He figured that if Trevor survived the war, he'd survive a fishing trip."

"But he was wrong," Lily said slowly.

Pippin and Grey leaned closer, hanging on every word. Pippin's voice was scarcely a whisper. "Trevor died?"

Lily and Cora nodded slowly. Synchronized. "Ruth spent every day on the beach waiting for her brother to return. She kept his favorite book with her like a talisman. She felt close to him when she held the book."

"What book?" Grey asked.

Cora and Lily looked at each other, then spoke at the same time. "*Moby Dick*."

"Legend has it," Lily said, "that the book foretold her brother's fate."

Once again, Lily picked up the narrative. "The pages told the story of the whale returning to Captain Ahab, who stabs him again. But the harpoon line tangles and drags Ahab into the ocean. Ahab realizes that his ship has become a funeral car as the whale draws him away to his death."

Pippin's breath caught in her throat. She closed her eyes against a memory that bubbled up inside her. She and her mother crossing the street between the bookstore and the library. An old woman. A dropped book. Her mother wailing.

"A storm came," Lily said.

The light shining on the cousins' faces flickered as Cora said, "Trevor's boat was lost at sea."

Pippin gasped. Her hand flew to her mouth. "Ruth was right?"

The sisters nodded solemnly. Lily continued. "Artemis built the lighthouse and called it Cape Misery. For Trevor."

Grey's hand squeezed Pippin's. "That lighthouse?" he asked, pointing with his other hand to the cliff above them.

Pippin's heart slid up to her throat. These people were her family. Her ancestors. "What happened to Ruth?" Her voice caught. "And Trevor's kids?"

Cora spoke. "Ruth never married. She died here at the lighthouse. There's a family burial plot down the wooded lane. She's buried there next to Artemis and Siobhan. There's a memorial for Trevor, too."

"Edgar's our grandfather," Cora said. "He married Annabel—"

Pippin's eyes burned. "Our grandmother."

Cora swung the flashlight to the lighthouse on the cliff. "They took it over, Edgar and Annabel. They're the ones who turned it into a bookstore. And they had two daughters."

Grey moved beside her. "Cassie and Lacy."

Lily nodded. "Our mothers."

Pippin's whole face burned now. Her cousins' voices sounded far away. Her skin felt like it was being pricked with a million pins from the inside out. "What happened to our grandparents?"

"Edgar died—"

"The sea took him," Lily said. That haunting voice again.

Pippin glanced at Grey. His face had grown pale, and she knew he was remembering how their mother had kept them away from the beach when they were little—not an easy feat given the fact that they lived in a beach house. She had a recollection of her mother holding tight to her hand. To Grey's. Why had she kept them away from the water? Why had their father never let them on his boat after Cassie was gone?

"And Annabel..." Cora paused for effect. "She died giving birth to our mother. To Lacy."

Pins pricked behind Pippin's eyelids. Just like their mother had died giving birth to their brother.

"Artemis went crazy," Lily said. "He'd lost almost everyone. He walked into the surf and drowned there. People say he died of a broken heart.

Pippin turned to Grey. "That's why mom was raised by Aunt Rose."

"Our mom, too," Cora said. "Rose never married. Cassie and Lacy were her girls. But your mom didn't want to stay in Laurel Point. She left, but Lacy—our mom, she stayed."

"And Lacy...your mom..." Pippin's voice stuck again. "She...died?"

"Having us." Lily spoke matter-of-factly. Beside her, Cora nodded. They knew this story. They'd experienced all the emotions with it over the years, but Pippin felt like her insides were coming apart. "Aunt Rose raised us, just like she raised our mothers."

That single trip to Cape Misery in Laurel Point had changed Pippin and Grey forever. They'd learned the truth about their Great-Aunt Rose who'd raised their mother. And about the tragic fate of Trevor, Edgar, and Artemis.

Pippin hadn't thought about Cora or Lily in years. Had she blocked their story out of her mind so she wouldn't realize the truth? People said they saw Leo Hawthorne return to the marina, dock his boat, and walk away. A chill swept through Pippin. Just because he'd left his boat at the marina didn't mean he hadn't gone to the pier, or to the beach. He wasn't a Lane, but he'd been married to one. What if the sea had taken her father, too, just like every other Lane man?

Chapter 4

"Human beings need loyalty."
  ~Atul Gawande

*T*he boat in the side yard was an eyesore. A tattered tarp, torn and frayed from years of sitting in Carolina weather covered the vessel, but it had long ago given up actually keeping the water out. Pippin grimaced at the mere thought of what she and Grey might find when they pulled back the covering.

She needed someone to assess the boat's condition then advise them on what to do with it. The marinas, she thought. Surely, they'd be able to recommend someone to her.

The Outer Banks was home to an array of marinas, from smaller outfits that offered inshore or sound fishing, offshore fishing, wreck-diving, and boat moorage, to the larger ones that housed fleets of charter vessels. Devil's Cove, though, only had a few marinas. Pippin sat in her tiny office and did an Internet search on her laptop, looking at pictures of each marina. One, Devil's Cove Landing, sent a spark of familiarity through her. It was a full-service marina at the south end of Devil's Cove, with close access to the Atlantic and to the Gulf Stream, where the warm currents host a myriad of sport fish. It had only sixty slips, whereas the other marinas were much larger. This smaller marina would have been the type of place her father would have chosen. A place where he knew everyone, where he was friends with the dockmaster. Where it felt like a hometown business rather than a big charter marina.

Pippin dialed the phone number and drummed her fingers against the desktop as she waited. It rang and rang and rang, but no one answered. Maybe the office staff was helping someone outside.

She made a split second decision, and three minutes later she was pulling her coral Electra Townie bike out of the garage. Grandmother Faye had bought it for her after high school, as if a bike would have been enough to keep Pippin from leaving Greenville.

She hadn't wanted it at the time, but now she silently thanked her grandmother. The island was small enough and had enough bike and pedestrian friendly streets and paths that she could cycle most places without a car. Grey had replaced the tubes and aired up the tires for her when they first arrived, so it was ready to go. She straddled the bike and placed her wallet in the wicker basket that hooked onto the handlebars. She felt the weight of someone watching her and looked around as she rode down Rum Runner's Lane, but no one was out. Once she left her street and turned onto Devil's Cove Highway, which the locals all called Main Street, the feeling passed and she shook off her apprehension. Her mind was playing tricks on her, that's all. She pushed her worry aside as she rode.

Before long, she pedaled past Dolphin Marina with its signs advertising offshore wreck-diving, inshore and sound fishing, and boat dockage. It was the biggest marina on the island, with its own small fleet of charter vessels. She pedaled past the sun and surf shops that attracted tourists who'd forgotten their towels or sunscreen, or who wanted a new swimsuit or some other Devil's Cove memorabilia. She pedaled past the taco shop with the homemade corn tortillas and the best crab tacos on the Eastern Seaboard.

Then she spotted it. Devil's Cove Landing, a full-service marina. She directed her bicycle onto the paved path leading to the marina's office, releasing the kickstand and setting the bike off to the side.

A boat was being backed out of its slip, two people sitting on the edge of the dock watching, legs swinging, floppy hats on their heads, soda cans in hand. Fishing trips would leave at the crack of dawn, so she'd missed that commotion. Other than a few people milling about on the dock, standing around and chatting, the place was pretty quiet. It was still early in the season, so it wasn't as busy as Pippin was sure it would be in June, July, and August when the tourists started coming.

From what she'd read online, the marina had been around going on fifty years now. From where she stood, it looked like half of it had been upgraded with beautiful docks, new pilings, and wide berths, each that could fit two large boats. Boats of all sizes were moored to the pier, tied to cleats mounted on the docks. White dock boxes, as well as cute white lighthouse shaped covers for the electrical outlets added a quaint touch.

The other side of the marina looked about fifty years

old. The docks were worn and the berths were narrower—no room for the big boats that were on the updated side. The pilings looked old and were lower in the water.

The dockmaster's office was housed in a building that looked like an old house with wide steps leading up to a wraparound deck. The siding was worn from the saltwater, wind, and the occasional hurricane, but the place had the potential to be stunning. It looked like whatever maintenance had been done to the marina over the years had been reserved for the dock itself. The building had seen better days but was still standing.

Inside, safe from the elements, the place didn't look a whole lot better. A large poster was thumbtacked on the main wall behind the information counter, its edges torn. It depicted the shape of the state of North Carolina, inset with the vertical blue and horizontal red and white panels of the state flag. They sold fishing gear, knives, nets, a few sun staples, and charter boat trips, which, along with slip fees, were probably the bread and butter of the operation. Photographs hung haphazardly on the walls featuring boaters, arms around one another, anglers holding their prizes for posterity, and people standing on the decks of their boats waving for the camera. Could her father be up there? Pippin scanned each photograph, searching each face, but her father wasn't among them. One of the photos caught her eye, though. Three men, all of them holding onto a giant fish. It wasn't the triumphant smiles on their faces that caught her attention, though. It was the little girl in a lifejacket standing next to the men, one of her little hands on the fish.

That should have been her. Her father's abandoning of her and Grey had ripped their childhood from them.

"Bluefin tuna," a woman said. She appeared from out of nowhere and now stood behind a long counter.

Pippin looked at her. "Sorry?"

The woman pointed at the picture Pippin had been staring at. "That's a bluefin tuna," she repeated.

"Oh wow! It's huge."

"There's some bigguns out there," the woman said, studying Pippin as if she were familiar. The plait of her long iron gray hair was pulled in front of her right shoulder, hanging down her front. She was as tan as she was wrinkled, which is to say very. Of both. And her voice dripped with honey that was thicker than molasses.

Pippin walked up to the counter. "The new dock looks great," she said.

The woman beamed. "It's been a long time comin'. State of the art floating docks that can accommodate vessels up to 180 feet. Do you need a slip?"

The woman looked hopeful, and Pippin hated to burst her bubble, but she shook her head and launched into the spiel she'd rehearsed in her head on the bike ride over. "No. But I believe my father docked his boat here. It would have been a long time ago. I was wondering if anyone might remember him?"

"Sure thing, hon. What's his name?"

"Leo Hawthorne."

The woman gave a quick intake of breath followed by a low whistle. "I ain't heard that name in ages." She did a double take. "Did you say father?"

"That's right. My name is—"

"Oh my stars! I know who you are, darlin'. If Leo's your daddy, then you're Pippin!" The woman bounded off her stool and circled around to the front of the counter. "Good night. Look at you standing right here in front of me. I knew you looked familiar. You're the spittin' image of your mama. Just beautiful. That woman had to fight the men back. A few from around here, as I recall. I reckon you do, too."

The woman's enthusiasm knocked Pippin for a loop. She didn't want the attention or notoriety that came along with being a Hawthorne in Devil's Cove, but it looked like she was going to get it whether she wanted it or not. "You knew my mother?"

"Well sure I did. Your parents were two lovebirds. She didn't come around here too much. Like I said, too many people in love with her. But once in a while she did, and Lordy did we get to talkin'. Why, when she was pregnant with you and your brother, well I never seen a happier woman in my life. She told me she didn't think she could have another baby after you two, then lo'n behold, there she was—" She broke off and stepped back. "I'm so sorry. I wadn't thinkin'. Of course, that was a tragedy. In this day'n age, no woman should die in childbirth. What a loss."

Pippin forced a small smile. "It was a long time ago."

"That it was. Time passes too quick."

"My dad docked his boat here back then, didn't he?"

"Well sure. Your daddy, now he was one of the good 'uns. He tried to do right by you, you know."

Pippin had been so angry at her father for so long, but maybe this woman could shed some light on where he'd gone. Why he'd abandoned his children. She swallowed down the lump in her throat. "Oh yeah?"

"He shor' did love your mama. Saw him get into more'n one scuffle over her. Then when you babies came, there wadn't a happier man on the planet. When she died, he worked hisself to the bone bein' both mama and papa."

Then why had he left? It would never make sense.

The woman patted her chest. "I'm Bev. You tell me what I can help you with, hon."

Pippin careened her mind back on track. "My dad disappeared a long time ago now."

Bev frowned. "We were all blown to pieces by that. The Leo I knew wouldn't have left y'all—you and your brother. He was downright obsessed with doing right by you both."

Her father had been distracted in the years after their mother died, but Pippin had always known he was there for Grey and her. Until he wasn't. He'd proved her wrong, and she didn't know if she could ever forgive him. Still, she asked, "What do you mean?"

"Leo was single-minded. When he set out to clean his boat, he did it top to bottom, hardly stoppin' for a break. When he lost your mama, I 'member he stuck right to his schedule. Took his crew out and brought back more tuna 'n I reckon he ever had before. He worked 'n went home to you. In fact, all he talked about was making things right for you two. Then that boat sank." Her face fell. "People got to talkin'."

Pippin didn't like the sound of that. "Talking about what?"

Bev's brows rose toward her hairline, her forehead pulling into an accordion of wrinkles. The sun had not been kind to her. She fluttered her hand in front of her. "Never mind any of that, darlin'."

But Bev couldn't put the lid back on the can of worms she'd opened. "What were people saying about my father?" Pippin asked.

Bev ran one hand down her braid. "We don't need to—"

Pippin cut her off. "Please. Tell me."

"Just tell the girl," a man said from the back corner of the office.

Pippin started. She hadn't noticed him there, and she couldn't make out any details. He lay back on a worn couch, sunk down so far that Pippin wondered if he'd ever be able to claw himself out of it.

Bev pressed her lips together before saying, "My husband. Mick."

"Tell her," the man said again.

"They're just rumors—"

"Tell me," Pippin repeated, more urgently this time. She knew almost nothing about her father. Even rumors would be better than that.

Bev released a heavy sigh. "The night before your dad took off, the boat next to his sank. People thought he mighta had somethin' to do with it."

"But you just said that he was a standup guy. One of the good ones. Why would he sink someone else's boat?"

Bev shrugged. "People just thought it was odd that he took off right after." She lowered her voice to secret-telling level. "Some people thought he was aft'r some treasure buried deep in the sea."

Mick scoffed from his sofa. "They're all treasure hunters. It's the lore of the island."

Pippin's mind whirled, trying to formulate a scenario different from the one she'd imagined all these years. She'd never known her father to be one of the many people who wreck-dived, but maybe he'd seen something. Or known something. Pippin suggested the idea. "Maybe *that's* why he left. Maybe it wasn't even about the so-called treasure hunting. "What if he saw who sank the boat and was scared?"

Mick grunted. "Anythin's possible."

Pippin's feelings toward her father were complicated, at best. She'd loved him with all her heart, and then that love had turned to hurt and betrayal. If he'd known something or discovered something and had to run... The idea that he'd had no choice but to leave gave her a sliver of hope. It was as if she'd held onto a piece of yarn at the end of a row of knitting and now that she'd pulled, the entire thing was unravelling. What if everything she'd believed all these years was wrong? Mick had said it. Anything was possible. "So what happened? How did the boat sink?"

Bev's eyes lit up. "A sinkin' boat is a sight to behold, lemme tell you. A sight to behold."

"You were there?"

"Oh yeah, 'course. Happened 'round ten o'clock."

"At night," Mick said.

Bev nodded. "That's right. Ten at night. Your dad had taken a crew out that day. He came in early with a week's worth o' fish. He hung around for a while, went home—we figured to you and your brother. Then he came back later that night to finish cleaning up the boat. That was a bit odd. He didn't usually come back." She shrugged. "But that's what he did, and that's when the brouhaha started. A woman down the dock a ways thought she was havin' a heart attack. Small town 'at we are, out came the ambulance! Out came the fire truck! Out came the chief o' police! Anyone who had a siren on top o' their car, here they came."

"Flyin' out here with all their bells'n whistles," Mick said.

Bev cocked her arms at the elbows and moved them back and forth like she was running. "There they went, barrelin' by me and Mick, the boys, and your dad, out to her slip. It was a ways down from the *Cassandra*."

The *Cassandra*. Pippin had forgotten that Leo had named the boat after her mother. She swallowed the lump in her throat. "Was the woman okay?"

"Perfectly fine. A false alarm. They treated her and

started to leave." Bev leaned back against the counter. "But that's when the *real* commotion started. When those authorities walked back down the dock, they came up to the starboard side of your daddy's boat. Right there, in the next slip. *Glug, glug, glug, glug, glug.* That boat was sinkin'."

"Sinking," Pippin repeated. She felt like she would have remembered hearing about a sinking boat at the marina, but Grandmother Faye had whisked Grey and her away so quickly after their father disappeared on them that she'd never had the chance to hear about it.

"Goin' straight down," Mick said with a whistle. He peered at Bev from his couch. "I cain't remember. What kinda boat was it?"

"Oh, I remember. It was an old steel hulled houseboat. Don't see many of those out here. Not aluminum. Not fiberglass. Steel." She looked at Pippin. "You'd think a boat like that'd take a while to go under, but it didn't."

"Nobody could stop it?" Pippin asked.

"Not a goddamned thing they could do," Mick said. "That thing went down fast."

"Why'd it sink?"

Bev folded her skinny arms over her equally skinny chest. "Now that's the most interesting thing 'bout this whole story. They sent a diver down to check the boat."

Pippin felt her eyes go wide. "Was someone on board?"

"No, no. Not a soul," Bev answered. "We hadn't seen anyone around that boat in a while. But what they *did* find is still a mystery. That boat had two three-inch plugs. Let's just say, those plugs? They are no longer on that boat."

Pippin shook her head, trying to process what that meant. "I don't get it."

"What I'm sayin', darlin', is that those plugs didn't pull themselves free. The working theory is that someone *was* on board, heard the sirens, and sank that boat before the authorities arrived."

"But you just said you hadn't seen anyone around that boat in weeks."

"That's where the rumors started," Bev said. "Your daddy was there. Some people thought he saw something he shouldn't 'ave. That someone was on the boat, but we just didn't know it. They pulled the plugs, swam to another pier, and no one was the wiser. There's also people who think Leo managed to get from his boat to the other one, pull the plugs, then got himself back onto his boat before anyone was the wiser."

"But why would he do that?" Pippin asked. "Why would he sink another boat?"

"Like I said, rumors."

"So what happened?" Pippin asked.

At this, Bev's shoulders lifted and fell with an exaggerated shrug. "The boat's still down there. Over the years, there've been divers who've checked it out, but—"

Pippin interrupted. "It's still down there?"

"Sure," Bev said. "It'd cost God knows how many thousands to float that thing up. Who's gonna pay? Us?"

Mick scoffed. "When they find Davy Jones's Locker, that's when I'll pay to float that houseboat."

Pippin didn't get the joke, but Bev laughed. "Which is to say, never. We have deep water slips. That thing is down too far. It's never coming up."

"So could whoever pulled the plugs still be down there?" Pippin asked, assuming it hadn't been her father who'd done the deed.

"If there's one thing I've learned over the years, it's that anythin' is possible, but probably not. Like I said, divers have been down there, and they haven't found anything,"

Bev said. She stood and came closer to Pippin, placing a reassuring hand on her shoulder. "It was a long time ago, darlin'. I sure didn't mean to stir anything up. You just forget about it."

That was not possible. The seed had been planted and now Pippin would always wonder if her father had anything to do with that boat sinking. Maybe he was on the run because of it. If that were the case, at least it was a reason for him leaving.

"You came here for somethin'," Bev said. "Whatdya need, honey?"

Pippin blinked. "Right. I did. My grandparents had my dad's boat hauled to my parents' house here in Devil's Cove."

"I remember that," the woman said. "They gave it a few months, from what I remember. Hoping he'd come back, I reckon, but in the end, they gave up the slip to dry dock the boat."

"It's been sitting there for a long time."

"It sure has. I go by that house now and again. I've seen the work you've been doin'." Her face lit up. "Why I even saw Travis carrying a load of wood and Jimmy working the table saw out front the other day!"

"You know them?" Pippin asked, but she shouldn't have been surprised. Devil's Cove was a small town. It swelled when the tourists came, but in the off season, it was just the locals. Everyone knew everyone.

"Oh sure. Travis's daddy had a boat he kept here, and Jimmy and my boy, Howie, went to school together. They used to tool around the harbor during the summers." She chuckled. "Got up to no good in the cove. Travis was the odd duck out. Howie was good to him, but Travis was a loner. Never quite fit in."

Pippin had heard of the cove, but she'd never been there. It was a popular swimming hole for locals, but that was all she knew about it. It had been another location on her mother's list of forbidden places. What Pippin did know was that the cove was a small sheltered inlet with a narrow jetty, and it was responsible for the name of the island. It was rumored that a ship carrying Caribbean liquor called "Devil's Rum" had come to the colonies sometime in the mid-17th century. The ship went down in the Atlantic, slipping to the depths of the graveyard. The crew—and the rum —was thought to be lost until two men piloting a single shallop made their way to the Sound and then to the cove with bottles of the lost rum and, legend has it, with some treasure they'd managed to take from the ship. The area became known as Devil's Rum Cove. Over time, as happens, it was shortened to Devil's Cove.

"What are ya doin' to the place?" Bev asked, steering the conversation back to the house.

"It's been vacant for so long. We've had to fix up almost everything. Painting. Carpentry. Replacing rotted wood. Jimmy's been tearing out some of the sheetrock. There's original shiplap underneath in some places. Travis is doing all the plumbing. And another man is doing whatever needs doing inside."

"All your father's stuff is gone?"

As she nodded, she caught a movement from Mick. He had somehow managed to sit upright on the pliable couch, balancing himself on the hard edge of the frame. "You're going to live there?"

"That's the plan," Pippin said. "We're going to open it as an inn."

"Is that so?" Bev's voice rose an octave with her excitement. "Devil's Cove could sure use that. We've had the same ol', same ol' for so long. The tourists keep us afloat, so new accommodations'll be a draw."

"I've watched your progress," Mick said. "Looks good."

"Thank you," Pippin said. "But listen. The reason I'm here is that we need to do something with my dad's boat. Can you recommend someone to come take a look at it and maybe help us figure out the next steps?"

Bev's face lit up. She pointed to a photo of a young seaman standing proudly in front of a boat. "That boat's the Old Salty G," she said, "And that's Old Salty." She circled back to the other side of the counter and sat on her stool again. She stared at Pippin again as if she were studying her. "You really are the spittin' image of Cassie," she said, then she rifled through an old Rolodex, finally landing on the card she was searching for. She scribbled on a Post-it note and slid it to Pippin.

Salty
Shannon

HIS PHONE NUMBER was written beneath. "You call old Salty."

Mick chuckled from his couch. "Oh Salty, he loved your mama. He'll be out to help you in a flash."

Chapter 5

"The Universe doesn't like secrets. It conspires to reveal the truth, to lead you to it."

~ Lisa Unger, *Beautiful Lies*

ippin stood next to Grey as they stared at their father's fishing boat. He had his hands deep in the pockets of his cargo shorts, socks slouched down to the ankles under his work boots, his arms and his light blue t-shirt dingy from sweat and sawdust. From the look on his face, Pippin knew he was just as apprehensive about seeing their father's fishing vessel as she was.

Something rustled the remaining pampas grass and a nose poked through. A dog's nose. The rest of its body emerged. Pippin started. She'd caught glimpses of the pup several times. She'd tried to call it to her, but anytime she drew close, the dog—a girl, she thought—turned and trotted off. She wasn't exactly skittish, but she wouldn't ever stick around. Now Pippin whistled, calling to her. "Come on, pup. Come here."

The honey colored dog looked at her, then at Salty Shannon, the craggy fisherman Bev at the marina had referred her to. Salty grunted as he circled the boat, good and loud. The dog didn't react, but after a few seconds, she beat a hasty retreat, disappearing into the brush again.

"I'll win you over," Pippin muttered.

Salty Shannon came around the bow of the boat, a beat-up mug filled with what Pippin presumed was lukewarm coffee—or possibly rum or some other spirit— in one gnarled hand. He looked at them, dipping his chin in a nod, before continuing his inspection.

Grey leaned in close to her and whispered, "Where'd you find him?"

"I went to the marina where Dad kept the boat. The woman there recommended him."

Grey peered at the seaman, looking skeptical.

Salty was as grizzled as a man could get. With his white beard and bushy mustache, he could have played Santa Claus in any department store, but his bulbous nose sitting atop a face that had seen decades of sun without an ounce of protection left no question that he'd spent his life on the sea rather than at the North Pole. Ancient faded tattoos ran up and down his arms. A woman in a bikini top and grass skirt—a throwback from another era. A rope and anchor, no doubt a symbol of his life on the water. A circle with a face inside, cradled by the letter V. And a ship, sails billowing in the wind. It was an eclectic collection. "The woman said no one knows old boats better than him, and he'd know what to do about it," Pippin said. She didn't have a reason to doubt Bev, but still, she was a tiny bit skeptical about the guy. He looked straight out of an old Popeye comic strip.

It was as if Salty knew they were talking about him. He cleared his throat and said, "I knew your folks back in the day. Your mom, she was a beauty." He looked at Pippin. "You look just like her." He changed tracks. "Now I'm out on Ocracoke. Came up to see ma youngins and their youngins, so I was glad to stop and take a gander." His Eastern Carolina accent was heavy with remnants of Cockney from the original settlers.

"Did you know our dad well?" Grey asked.

Salty shrugged. "He was a solid fisherman. Had a gift, I'd say."

He left it at that and circled back around the boat as a car pulled up in front of the house. Two kids bounded out just as Jimmy came out the front door. He jogged down the porch steps, crouched down, and opened his arms wide. The kids, both boys who looked to be maybe four and six years old, barreled toward him. "Daddy!" they both yelled as Jimmy opened his arms wide. The force knocked Jimmy to the ground, laughing.

The driver's side car door slammed, and a woman Pippin presumed to be Jimmy's wife walked up the steps. She looked at Pippin and Grey, nodding to them and giving a passing wave of her hand. She stopped for a second, frowning as she looked at the boat, then turned to her family when Jimmy called her. "Babe. Camille. Come here," he said. From where Pippin stood, Camille looked a good ten years younger than Jimmy.

Grey touched Pippin's shoulder. Salty was beckoning to them. They left Jimmy to his family and joined the seaman at the bow of the boat. "It's been sitting her for a long time," Pippin said, even though it was stating the obvious.

Salty walked alongside the vessel, trailing the fingertips of one hand along the hull. "It's in purty good shape," he said. "No stress cracks in the fiberglass. The inside'll tell a different story. Thirty-two feet. I reckon it has four bunks, far as I remember. I think your pops ran a crew of four." He scratched the top of his head through his cap. "Maybe five. Can't quite recall. That'd be a mighty tight fit, but possible."

Together, they pulled the worn tarp all the way off, revealing the name Leo had painted on the side of the vessel. Grey tensed beside her, and Pippin felt her nostrils flair. The *Cassandra*.

Leo had loved their mother with all of his heart. That's why, they'd always reasoned, he'd left them. He couldn't cope after losing her. It was the only comfort Pippin had. Any other version of the story—that he just didn't care about them; that he couldn't look at them because they reminded him of Cassie; that he was weak and depressed and gave up—those were stories she couldn't swallow.

The version of the story she chose to accept didn't lessen her anger toward her father, but it took the edge off.

Grey had already followed Salty up the ladder he'd set up and onto the deck. Pippin let go of her thoughts and followed. Once they were standing on the deck of the boat, it was clear that the coastal weather had taken a toll after so many years, leaving tears in the tarp that animals had managed to get through. Squirrels and rats had made their homes inside the boat. Pippin covered her mouth and nose from the smell of the mildewed seats and rotted carpet.

"Transom looks good," Salty said as he looked at the stern of the vessel. "Still, bein' trapped under the cover for so long didn't do the boat any favors."

The three of them poked around for a few more minutes. Jimmy and his wife had buckled their kids into their car seats. Four car doors slammed, and the motor turned over. They drove away, the kids bouncing in their car seats, waving to them. Salty laughed. He took his hat off and bowed to the boys. Behind the car windows, they broke down in giggling fits. In the front passenger seat, Jimmy smiled and waved as Camille carted them away.

"Cute kids," Pippin started to say, but the words stuck in her throat as they made their way below deck.

"Oh, Christ!" Grey pulled the front of his shirt up over his nose.

"Smells fresh as a daisy down here," Salty said to them over his shoulder, his meaning the absolute opposite. It was ripe and rotten, the farthest thing from a sweet-scented flower. They watched Salty as he walked between the facing seats of the dining area that doubled as sleeping bunks on either side of the boat. The table that would have been between the seats had been removed. Salty opened a door on the starboard side to check out the head. Turning to the opposite side with his back to the head, he looked in the small cupboards in the galley, then lifted the lid of one of the three long hatches build into the floor. "Oowee," he said, giving a whistle. "Those rats have definitely been in here."

"What about in the other hatches?" Pippin asked.

"I don't reckon we need to check. They'll all be the same," Salty said, but Pippin already had her finger hooked into the stainless-steel flush latch of the middle floor hatch. She pulled, but the cover didn't budge.

Following the other two down into the cabin, Grey had pulled open a hatch under the port-side dining area seat to reveal an empty but musty and rank hole.

Pippin braced her feet on either side of the stuck hatch, bent down, and gave another yank. This time, the cover popped open like the lid of a coffin. Pippin fell backwards with a thump.

Salty had been standing by the galley sink. He turned at

the sound of her falling. "You okay, Miss Pippin?" he asked as he leaned forward.

Pippin started to scramble up and opened her mouth to say she was fine, but the words froze on her lips as she saw Salty's frozen face. He'd started to move toward her but glanced into the open hatch, stopping short. "Christ almighty," he muttered, stumbling back. He whisked his hat from his head and held it to his chest.

"What is it?" she asked.

Taking a step toward the bow, Grey grabbed Pippin under her armpits and helped her up before they peered into the hole to see what had spooked Salty. They stopped. Stared. The color drained from Grey's face. Pippin staggered back into him, suddenly feeling lightheaded.

There, in the hatch, were the remains—the bones—of a dead body.

Chapter 6

"It has to be him," Pippin said to Grey, but she didn't have to convince her brother. Deep down, they both knew it was Leo's bones in the hatch of the *Cassandra*.

Pippin couldn't fathom who would have wanted to kill their father. The police hadn't said it had been murder, but there was no other explanation for how Leo's body ended up where it had.

She sat on the plastic Adirondack chair she'd dragged over to the boat, staring up at it. The vessel held a secret it would never reveal. The anxious tightening in her chest and the pricking behind her eyelids made her feel as if she was losing her father all over again.

Her father had loved books as much as her mother had

despised them. They'd had no books in the house—with the exception of Leo's study—and Cassie had rarely stepped foot in that private space.

Grandmother Faye's house had had a library, the walls lined with walnut shelves, each filled with books, but the room was off-limits to the twins. As Pippin and Grey hit their teenage years, they'd become bold. They tried to startle their grandmother into revealing why the library in the house was restricted. They'd sneak into the forbidden room, take a random book from a shelf, and plant it right in the center of the kitchen table, or under the pillow of their grandmother's bed, or beneath one of the hydrangea bushes on the side of the old house.

But Grandmother Faye never rose to the bait. The books Pippin and Grey placed for her to find would magically vanish, then reappear on the library shelf from which they'd been taken. The incidents were never spoken of.

At fifteen, Pippin and Grey moved from the forbidden library in their grandparents' house to the library, then to the bookstore in town. Grey chose volumes he wanted to hold onto forever, to read under the sheets with flashlights, to love until the covers were tattered and falling apart, but Pippin chose books with illustrations, reading some of the words but getting more of the story from the pictures. An illustrated children's edition of *The Hobbit* had been her favorite. After years of trying to elicit a reaction from their grandmother, they'd given up. Now they just wanted to escape into another world. To sneak into a secret garden, or slip through a wardrobe and experience the delights of a magical land, or skip down the Yellow Brick Road. Grey flew on spaceships to other planets, fought off the Buggers with Ender, and experienced World War II through the pages of the books he chose.

Pippin's adventures were more limited. The words on the page were mysterious, their meaning elusive. The restriction from books had motivated Grey to become a good reader, but it had had the opposite effect on Pippin. She struggled, and eventually she gave up.

At seventeen, she bought copies of *The Hobbit* and *The Lord of the Rings*. She couldn't count how many times she'd had to explain her name. A thousand times over the years, probably. No one understood it. It wasn't easy to tell the story of how her dad had been obsessed with Tolkien and that she and her brother had been named after two of his favorite characters. Not easy because by the time she wanted to ask him about it, he was gone. All she knew was that he had a passion for these books. They were too challenging for her, and the old directive from her parents, forbidding books, stayed with her, carving out a chasm between then and now, a chasm she couldn't build a bridge between.

Her brother had gotten off easy in the name department. He'd been called Grey, after Gandalf. She'd been laden with Peregrin, one of Frodo's loyal and best friends. Pippin for short. *What kind of name is Peregrin? How is Pippin a nickname for it?* Kids and adults alike asked her, but she couldn't say. They'd both come from JRR Tolkien's mind, and her parents had laid them at their feet, but neither of them were here to fill in the blanks.

"It could be worse," her brother had often reminded her growing up. It was true. She supposed Pippin was better than Elbereth, Tintalle, or Eowyn. And Grey was forever grateful their parents hadn't named him Bilbo, Aragon, or Wormtongue.

For a while after Leo had disappeared, Pippin had imagined that maybe her father was on his own adventure, just like Bilbo had been, then Frodo. But now the image of the body crammed into the lowest hatch of the *Cassandra* had chased that lingering dream away. It would take time for the authorities to definitively determine the identity of the body, but she knew in her heart that it was her father.

The day after the discovery, Pippin left Grey to his shiplap. Overnight, the temperature had dropped nearly ten degrees. She lowered her head against the cool breeze that had picked up and walked the two blocks from Rum Runner's Lane to the town's quaint downtown. Her first stop was the library—a building she'd never stepped foot in. Walking up to the converted two-story house brought a déjà vu moment. She remembered wanting so badly to go inside, but her mother had always refused. They'd give both the library and the bookstore, which sat across the street at a diagonal, a wide berth, as if walking on the sidewalk next to either one would somehow hurt them.

She'd been so young when she last saw the building. She purposely avoided passing through this block since she and Grey had been back in Devil's Cove. Now, staring at it, it was just as she remembered it in her mind's eye. The clapboard house was painted a pale blue with white trim. A sign hung over the porch announcing this as the LIBRARY. Steps led to the porch, but there was also a wheelchair accessible ramp. She stopped at the government sign at the edge of the property showing a figure holding a book. She let the pads of her fingers lightly touch the cold metal. Despite the fact that she and Grey had defied their mother's wishes, and their grandmother's, by borrowing—and sometimes buying —books when they were teenagers, she still experienced a feeling of unease. They had kept Pippin and Grey away from books for a reason. Cassie had kept Pippin away from this building for a reason. The image of her mother falling to her knees in the middle of the road, an open book on the ground before her, flashed in her mind. It was the fear that came from that memory that had kept Pippin from reading and loving books the way she wanted to.

Now, however, she couldn't turn her back.

She made her way up the paved walkway and climbed the steps but stopped at the door. She felt her heart pounding in her throat. In her temples. They were just books, for God's sake. It wasn't as if they were going to reveal some deep dark secret.

She shook loose her anxiety, grabbed the doorknob, and entered.

She was struck immediately by the musty smell—like old carpet mixed with the scent of decaying paper. Was it woody, or was it earthy? Both, she decided. She inhaled, letting the scent enter her body and permeate every cell. Almost instantly, the sense of foreboding she'd felt dissipated. If she didn't know better, she'd say she belonged with books. Or that they belonged with her. She'd never felt this way before, but there it was.

Before she'd taken a full step inside, a woman behind the circulation desk beamed at her with a warmth that seeped all the way to Pippin's chilled bones. The woman's hair was somewhere between the darkest brown and black, but wasn't quite either. It was cut short, but had a few long strands framing her delicately featured face. Combined with her olive skin, hoop earrings, eyelashes that fanned out to either side under pink-framed glasses, and her glossy nude lips, she looked like a pixie. She stood, leaning her head to one side as she looked at her, her smile never wavering. "I know you."

Pippin mirrored the woman by tilting her own head. "I don't think so. My brother and I, we just moved here six weeks ago." She paused. "Moved *back* here, I mean."

The young woman stood and came out from behind the counter to stand before Pippin. She was as petite as her features. Five feet two inches was Pippin's guess. "I'm sure you don't remember, and honestly, I don't know how I do, but my mom and your mom were friends, and we used to play together."

Pippin blinked. Then blinked again. Another memory began to surface. Two little girls, and Grey, splashing around in a hard plastic child's swimming pool. Two women sitting on lawn chairs sipping icy drinks. A name tickled the tip of her tongue. She could picture it. Rose? Holly? Mmm, Jasmine? No, those weren't right. It was on the tip of her tongue. D...Dai... "Daisy?"

The librarian's face lit up. "That's right! Daisy Santiago. You remember!"

Did she? "I remember swimming. And a playground. And playing dress up. Was that with you?"

"Yes!"

"How do you know for sure?" Pippin asked. Her own memories were fuzzy and incomplete.

"My mother is a scrapbooker! So many old photos. You look the same. Same strawberry blonde hair, though it's longer now. Same jade green eyes. Same everything...just older."

Pippin blew out the breath she found she'd been holding. Intellectually, she'd known she and Grey had lived in Devil's Cove as kids, but it was as if her mind had blocked so much of it. But this...this was different. This woman, Daisy, was actually part of Pippin's history.

"It's so good to see y'all working on the old house," Daisy said.

She was hearing that a lot. "It needs a lot of TLC."

Daisy pushed her glasses up as she leaned back against

the circulation desk and crossed one leg over the other. She wore leggings with bright orange Crocks on her feet and a lace-edged tunic. Adorable was the word that came to Pippin's mind. This former childhood friend was adorable. "It's been vacant for so long. I always wondered why it was never sold. I think everyone here wondered, actually," Daisy said.

Pippin had wondered the same thing. Why hadn't her parents wanted the house sold, the money put into a trust for Grey and her? She might never know the answer to that, but her father was explicit in his will. The house, intact, was to go to Pippin and Grey.

Daisy continued. "Of course it is a prime piece of property. I mean, on the beach? Come on! A great view from the widow's walk." She cocked her head and cupped her hand next to one side of her mouth like she was imparting a secret. "I confess, I sneaked in there to poke around when I was a teenager. It was kind of a rite of passage for kids around here. The quintessential haunted house."

Pippin arched a brow. "Haunted?"

Daisy shrugged. "The stories grew, then ballooned until, you know, it was a full on spirit-run house complete with cold spots, hidden rooms, and ghostly sightings. Ridiculous, I know."

"Kids," Pippin said.

"Right. Kids." Daisy clasped her hands and looked Pippin square in the eyes. "You really do look the same, you know. I'll stop by sometime with my mom's old photo album to show you, if you'd like?"

Oh, she'd like. She wanted to fill in the blanks. Surely old photos would help. "Definitely. I'll show you the house. It's looking a lot better now than it probably did when you last saw it."

Daisy stood and made her way back behind the circulation desk. "So, Pippin Hawthorne. You came here for a reason, I presume. What can I help you with?"

Pippin liked Daisy. She was direct, yet approachable. "I don't exactly know."

Daisy pushed up her glasses and gave her an amused smile. "Let's start with the basics then. Do you like sci fi? Romance? Westerns? Mystery—"

"No. I mean yes. I mean, actually, I'm not much of a reader. And I'm not looking for a book like that. At least...I don't think I am." Pippin shook her head, not at all sure how to explain what it was she needed. The memory of her and her mother in the middle of the street, right here in front of the library, wouldn't shake loose from her mind. The odds were slim, but maybe she'd find the answer here. "My mother saw this book once when I was really little. Something in it made her really upset. I have this vague recollection of her telling my father that she'd thought for sure he would never come home again."

"And you're looking for that book?" Daisy picked up a pen and pulled a small pad of paper in front of her. "Tell me what you remember."

Pippin smiled faintly at her, grateful that Daisy didn't think she was crazy for trying to find what was sure to be a needle in a haystack. "Not much, really. A woman was passing us in the street, and she dropped the book. I think it was thick."

"Hardcover or paperback?"

Pippin closed her eyes and imagined the scene, just as she had a hundred times before. "Paperback, I think. I remember picking it up, then my mom saying that no wife would greet him. Or sing to him. Something like that. No children at his knees."

Daisy made a note on her pad of paper. "Got it. What else?"

"It was windy. A storm was blowing in. We'd been at the pier. When the book fell in the street, I remember the wind whipping the pages back and forth. Then they just kind of stopped. That's when my mom looked at the book and kind of freaked out."

"Okay." Daisy didn't look surprised. She pushed at her glasses again.

"Have you heard that story about my mom?"

Daisy shrugged. "Small town, you know."

Pippin waited, letting the silence stretch, hoping Daisy would tell her about the rumors. After a moment, she said, "The story's become...legend. Your mom fell to the ground and started muttering under her breath. Something about someone not coming home, and that the curse was true."

A chill crawled over Pippin's skin. She could almost hear her mother sobbing, saying those words over and over.

"Who do you think she was talking about?" Daisy asked.

Pippin answered without a doubt in her mind, although she didn't understand how or why. "My father."

Chapter 7

"But in a solitary life, there are rare moments when another soul dips near yours, as stars once a year brush the earth. Such a constellation was he to me."

~Madeline Miller, Circe

When Pippin returned to the old house on Rum Runner's Lane, she saw Grey standing outside the crime scene tape that encircled the boat in the side yard. Next to him was a portly man with short graying hair dressed in a navy-blue uniform. And in her peripheral vision, she caught a glimpse of the elusive honey-colored dog vanishing into the bushes.

She wanted to chase the dog, but she couldn't. Her heartbeat ratcheted up and she hurried across the yard to Grey and the officer standing with him. "Have you found out something?"

Grey's afternoon stubble shadowed his face, specks of orange hair peeking through. The second he looked at her, she knew. "Pippin," he said. "This is Lieutenant Roy Jacobs from the Devil's Cove Police Department. He's the officer in charge of the investigation."

She noticed the rectangular gold bars on both sides of his shirt collar. Instead of giving her comfort, that the case was in the hands of someone highly qualified, they made her skittish. Her arms hung by her sides, every nerve in her body suddenly alight. "What have you found?"

"Ma'am," the lieutenant said. "I'm sorry to report to you that the remains found in the boat are those of your father, Leonardo David Hawthorne."

Heat immediately flamed her face, and her heart threatened to pound right out of her chest. She'd known it deep down, of course, but hearing the words spoken aloud made it written in stone. She'd hold onto all the anger she'd harbored over the years if it meant Leo was still alive. Now it couldn't be taken back, and the idea that her father was out there, still living, was a dashed dream. "How do you know?" The words came out sounding stronger than Pippin had anticipated given the fuzziness that filled her body.

"Three things," Lieutenant Jacobs said. "A ring found next to the body, which, based on a wedding photo of your parents, belonged to your father. A set of keys, which includes keys to this house, the boat, and what we believe is a key to the old marina gate."

"That's all circumstantial...or non conclusive...or whatever," Grey said. His arms were crossed over his chest as if they were a barrier to the information the lieutenant was throwing at them. "Right? It still might not be him."

The Lieutenant looked at Grey. "The final confirmation just came in from the medical examiner in Greenville. She was able to use records from the dentist your father went to as a child."

The intermittent sound of a nail gun came from one of the open windows of the house, along with the chatter of Travis, Jimmy, and Kyron, but it faded away for Pippin. She felt her chest start to cave in on itself. Dental records. She'd thought that was nothing more than a TV shortcut, but apparently not. The lieutenant seemed to hear her thoughts. "We can't use them to identify an unknown victim, but we can to confirm an identity. Aside from the fact that this was your father's boat, the other pieces of evidence led us to seek final confirmation that the body is his."

Pippin's emotions spun out of control. All these years she'd thought Leo had walked out on them. She'd sometimes pictured him out there in some unnamed harbor town starting a new life. Other times she imagined him as a captain out on the open sea, caught in a storm, wishing more than anything that he could get home to her and Grey.

She'd maintained hope that he'd come back. Even when Grandmother Faye had finally given up, Pippin had believed it was possible.

But now she knew. He was dead. And not only that. "He was murdered," Pippin said, more to herself than to Grey and the lieutenant. Because how and why would her father have climbed into the lowest hatch of his own boat?

Plain and simple...he wouldn't have.

"A twenty-year-old murder," Jacobs said, sounding like he'd already designated it as a cold case file.

Grey spun to face the police officer, the bands of his neck straining. "But you're going to try to solve it, right?"

Jacobs patted the air with one hand, palm down. "Simmer down there, Mr. Hawthorne," he said, trying to placate Grey with his slow southern drawl.

Grey seethed. "I'm not going to simmer down. You just told us that our father's body has been rotting on his own boat for twenty years. I want to know what you're going to do about it."

Jacobs sighed. "Look. I know you want answers. I'm heading up the investigation, and I'll do my damndest to get to the truth. But I have to be straight with you. After twenty years, the odds of us finding the perpetrator are slim."

Pippin opened her mouth to object, but Jacobs held up his hand to silence her. Like every other man she'd met lately, he had a tattoo, this one on his forearm. It said something, but she didn't see it long enough to read it. He lowered his arm and continued. "That's not to say I'm not going to try. I'll use every resource available to me from the department and town to get to the truth, but I need to be honest. It's going to be a steep hill to climb. Let's assume the body was killed on the boat and placed in the hatch. The boat has since been moved here, to this location. It's been sitting in Carolina weather. Every raindrop. Every gust of wind. Every animal that's passed through has destroyed any piece of viable evidence."

"Do you think he was in there the entire time? Since he disappeared?" Grey asked.

The lieutenant shifted from one foot to the other. "There's no way to know that for sure."

"Do you know how he died?" Pippin asked. Her thoughts had skittered back to Bev and Mick's story about the sinking boat. Her temples pulsed. Was that connected to her father? Could he have been involved? Or maybe he witnessed something.

Jacobs cleared his throat. "Medical Examiner found a nick on one of the ribs. She believes it points to a stabbing."

Pippin's head suddenly felt full of cotton and her chest contracted. Her breath became shallow. "Why would anyone do that to him?"

"Again, after twenty years, it will be difficult to piece together a motive," Jacobs said. His expression softened, the hard lines of his face melting away. "I am sorry. I wish I could tell you more."

Grey had calmed down, but his jaw was tight and his hands were fisted. If he could hit something, Pippin knew he would.

She held her breath for a moment before asking the question burning inside her. "Could it have to do with the boat that sank at the marina? The one next to his?"

Grey's breath shot out in an angry hiss. He clawed his hand through his hair, walking away. Pippin had told him what Bev and Mick had said, but he had chosen not to believe it. "I bet rumors around here travel faster than you can say Outer Banks. It's a story," he'd said. "Nothing else."

But Pippin wasn't so sure. She looked at the lieutenant, waiting.

"That was a long time ago," Jacobs finally said.

"But there could be a motive wrapped up in it, couldn't there? Maybe our dad saw something he shouldn't have."

"It's possible," Jacobs admitted. "Tell you what. I'll look into it. But keep in mind, after this much time, it'll be hard to find anything valuable. Anything related to that boat was hunted down and processed at the time. It's highly unlikely I'll be able to uncover any new evidence."

Pippin forced herself to respond. "I understand."

The lieutenant nodded, closing the door on the topic. He shifted his weight from one foot to the other before asking, "Were any of your father's belongings still in the house?"

Pippin shook her head. She and Grey had searched every room, every closet, every nook and cranny. "Nothing.

Our grandparents must have had it cleared out at some point."

"That's what I figured. Sitting vacant and abandoned for so long, it would have been looted and possibly destroyed in the process if stuff had been left inside. I'll keep you updated on the investigation. I promise."

Lieutenant Jacobs walked across the grass, back toward his car parked alongside the shoulder, leaving Pippin and Grey standing in front of their father's fishing boat grappling with the confirmation that their father had been murdered.

Pippin watched as Jacobs pulled away in his black SUV, Devil's Cove Sheriff's Dept. emblazoned on the sides in a vibrant blue. Another car, this one a zippy lemon-yellow Volkswagen convertible with a black ragtop pulled up. Daisy Santiago popped out and headed toward them. She threw her arm up in a wave. "Hello there!"

Pippin managed to turn her frown to an impassive expression and lifted her hand in greeting before turning to tell Grey who the woman crossing their grass was.

"You remember her?" Grey asked, one brow raised in skepticism. Clearly, he did not.

"I do. Vaguely."

Daisy came up to them. She'd pulled her short hair back with a wide orange headband and looked just as darling as she had earlier at the library. Pippin cleared her throat and swept her hand to the side, palm up. "Daisy, this is—" she started, but Daisy cut her off. "Grey Hawthorne. I'd recognize you anywhere. You look just the same." She laughed and tapped her chin. "Minus the facial hair, of course."

Grey managed a nod, but Daisy had already moved on. She gazed up at the house, shading her eyes from the sun with one hand cupped at her forehead. "It's a helluva house."

"That it is," Grey said.

Daisy pointed to the left side of the house. "Is that Kyron Washington?" Her voice had turned excitedly breathy.

Pippin followed her gaze to the man coming out of the French door from her father's study to the side porch. "Yep. He's one of the guys working on the renovations." Her gaze traveled up to the second floor where she knew Jimmy Gallagher and Travis Walsh were working. The nail gun was still popping. "They're making good progress."

Daisy still had her eyes glued to Kyron. "If you need extra help, I'm game." She flicked her eyebrows up suggestively, and there was no doubt about what kind of help she'd like to offer.

As if he'd sensed they were talking about him, Kyron turned to face them. The features of his face were hidden behind the dark screening, and in the shade of the tall hydrangea bushes next to the porch railing, but his dark skin and bright smile came into focus as he moved out of the shadows. "Everything okay?" he called.

"Yeah. Fine," Grey said. "I'll be there in a sec."

Kyron waved his acknowledgement. Pippin waved back. But Daisy wiggled her fingers coyly, tilting her head to one side. Even from where Kyron stood, Pippin was pretty sure he'd understood the hidden meaning to Daisy's greeting. Subtlety didn't seem to be her strong suit.

Grey turned to Daisy. "Good to see you," he said, before sending a silent communique to Pippin. They'd talk about the bomb Lieutenant Jacobs from the sheriff's department had dropped on them later. She nodded and Grey headed back up the walkway, disappearing into the house.

"Kyron, huh?" Daisy asked.

Pippin nodded.

"He's a cutie. Does he have a girlfriend?"

"I have no idea," Pippin answered. She hadn't had the opportunity or the desire to grill any of the guys about their personal lives, and none of them had offered up the information.

Finally, Daisy redirected her attention away from the house and onto Pippin. "Can you find out?"

"I'll try," Pippin said, a genuine smile coming to her lips.

Daisy gave a little laugh. "That's all I can ask." She pointed to the boat in the side yard. "Your dad's?"

The smile faded away. "Yeah. The police left just before you got here. I'm sure it'll be common knowledge before long. We found the remains of a body in one of the lower hatches. It was our father."

Daisy's pink-lipped mouth dropped open and her hand flew up to cover it. "Oh my God. Are you okay?"

For a while, Pippin would have answered that, no, she wasn't. Her emotions had been spinning. But now she felt oddly removed, if she was being honest. The discovery hadn't instantly erased all the anger and betrayal she'd had buried inside of her all these years. She would come to terms with it, she knew. She just hadn't yet. "I will be," she said.

"Listen," Daisy said. "I've been thinking about the book you were telling me about. Your mom said something about no wife and children greeting him."

"I don't know if she said it, but I think I remember it."

"Did you ever read *The Odyssey*?" she asked.

Pippin shook her head. She'd heard of it, of course, but reading an epic poem was a challenge she'd never taken upon herself.

"Odysseus is gone, fighting in the Trojan War. That's the

story in *The Illiad*. *The Odyssey* is his journey back home to his wife and son."

"Okay. So why do you think that might be the book?"

Daisy's eyes grew larger under the lenses of her glasses. She talked with her hands, moving them as she told Pippin her thought process. "Your mom said something about singing, right? No one would be singing to him. No children to greet him."

That was Pippin's vague memory, but she'd been so young. Only six years old. Maybe it wasn't a memory at all, but something she'd made up in her mind. She just wasn't sure, but she said, "I think so."

"That's the warning Circe gives Odysseus before he sets out to get back to Ithaca. He's being warned about the Sirens."

"Who are the Sirens?" Pippin asked, wishing now that she had read the book.

"They come from Greek mythology. They sang to passing sailors with hauntingly beautiful voices, but really they were luring the men to their deaths." Pippin felt goose-flesh raise on her skin as Daisy continued. "It's the warning that's relevant here. Before Odysseus leaves Circe behind— that's a whole 'other story—she warns him about the Sirens. She's the one who tells him to plug his own ears, and the crew's ears, with beeswax so they won't be lured to their death. The Sirens sing about the past and future truths of the men passing by. For Odysseus, this means the glory he's had, but also the suffering from the battlefield in Troy. They promise to tell him about his future achievements, but Odysseus listened to Circe so he was prepared. He was tied to the mast and then his crew plugged their ears so they were able to escape."

Daisy had grown animated telling Pippin the story. She

stopped for a breath before continuing. "Here's the important part. Circe tells Odysseus that if he succumbs to the Sirens, no woman will greet him and no children will be there for him. It's her warning to him that he'll never return home if he succumbs to the Sirens."

As Pippin listened, her vision grew blurry. "Say it again," she said, her voice low and almost hoarse.

"Circe tells Odysseus that if hears the Sirens' song, he will not make it home to his wife and children."

Pippin's breath grew shallow. She forced herself to slow down. To take deep breaths. Once the heat cleared from her head. "Do you have a copy of the book in the library?"

Daisy shook her head. "We have one, but it's checked out. Try The Open Door Bookshop."

Chapter 8

"Don't you ever mind," she asked suddenly,
  "not being rich enough to buy all the books you want?"
~Edith Wharton, *The House of Mirth*

*P*ippin moved her sunglasses to the top of her head, the arms of the glasses holding back her hair and keeping wayward strands from sticking to her face. She stared up at the sign on the building.

The Open Door Bookshop
Purveyor of New, Used, and Antiquarian Books

IT WAS QUITE A MOUTHFUL. She glanced at the two massive pots of colorful spring flowers flanking the door. She absently yanked a few sprouting weeds, discarding them in a nearby garbage can then opened the door and walked in. The air conditioning hitting her like cool evening breeze off the ocean. She'd taken just one step when her foot brushed against something. She stumbled, losing her balance and barely catching herself before she fell.

She frowned at the longhaired light gray tabby in front of her. "Where'd you come from?"

It gave her a haughty look with its translucent eyes.

Pippin stared right back, not backing down. Her grandmother had had two cats, both temperamental and entitled. The cats had only liked Grandmother Faye. Both Pippin and Grey still had scars from the scratches they suffered at the claws of the two felines.

Finally, the cat turned and sauntered away with a distinct swing of its hind quarters. It leapt up to the display window and found a spot between a stack of children's books and a colorful beach ball. "Ha." Pippin gloated. She'd stood her ground and the cat had blinked first.

She turned away, looking at the bookshop the cat seemed to reign over. A standing fan stood next to the door, keeping the air in the shop circulating. She took in the details of the shop with a discerning eye. A service counter with an old-fashioned cash register was front and center, a few paces from the front entrance. Knickknacks like book plates, book-themed mugs, bookmarks, games based on books, and stationary lined the exposed brick wall behind the counter. Beneath all the goodies was a shelf stacked with rubber banded groups of books, a white sheet of paper folded around each one. Special orders, she guessed.

The store itself was separated into two sections: new books and used books. Every single inch of every single wall was covered. Center freestanding shelves housed even more, divided into categories. In the nonfiction section, there were books on travel, poetry, nature, religion, self-help. On and on it went. In the fiction sections were books grouped by mysteries, romance, science fiction, fantasy, western, and dystopian. The list went on. Bestsellers. Historical fiction. Horror.

The books were small, large, thick, thin. Different colors. Different shades and tones of the same color. The spines of the books created a muted rainbow across the shelves dominated by hues of brown and yellow, black and white, blues and greens, and reds. Pippin marveled at the vastness of the collection. How many stories did the pages of all these books hold? But not only that, what stories did the books themselves tell? Who had held these volumes? Who had loved them, hidden under a sheet, flashlight in hand, to read them into the wee hours of the morning, or screeched from a shocking twist? Imaginary people came to life through the words on the page. Book boyfriends, best friends, worlds in which people wanted to live.

Worlds like the Shire, Pippin thought, the fictional place her father had loved above all others. She started to slip away into wonderings but was startled out of her thoughts when a man's voice said, "Can I help you find something?"

Pippin turned abruptly, bumping her shoulder against a freestanding shelf. She prided herself on being aware of her surroundings. Her grandmother had kept a close eye on her and Grey. As a result, they'd both grown vigilant. They'd learned how to sneak in and out of the house undetected. They knew their grandparents' routines down to the minute. Awareness was an old habit that had stuck with her, but thinking about her father had taken her away from the here and now for a moment. Now she looked at a man who'd started her. He stood at the end of the aisle, a stack of books in his arms. He wore wire-rimmed John Lennon glasses that fit him perfectly. The ends of his dark hair flipped out in a boyish manner, and long lines framed his mouth as he smiled. He looked at her with one eyebrow cocked up in amusement.

She kept her expression level. "I'm looking for a copy of *The Odyssey*, by—

"Homer," the man said, interrupting her with a light chuckle. Or was it a haughty laugh? "I know it well."

Pippin nodded. Of course he did. He worked in a bookstore, and his tone was just as uppity as the cat's demeanor. Two peas in a pod. "Do you have a copy?"

"Pretty sure I do," he said with a very slight Southern accent. He lifted his book-laden arms. "Let me put these down and I'll help you find it."

She started to say that she could find it on her own, but he stopped her with a pointed look. "It's no problem."

He placed the books on the front counter, said something to the girl manning the cash register, and returned to the used book section, rounding the corner to the next aisle and heading straight to the shelves marked CLASSICS. He ran his fingers across the spines of some of the books, stopping abruptly, putting his finger at the top of the book he'd identified, and pulling it out. He held it out to her. "It's your lucky day. Last one in stock."

She took it, feeling its heaviness. Weighted down with answers?

"Do you have a special attachment to *The Odyssey*?" the man asked.

Pippin looked up at him sharply. "Why would you ask that?"

The man's mouth twisted in an amused grin. "Oh, I don't know. Maybe because you're cradling it like a newborn baby?"

Was she? She glanced down at the paperback book in her hands. She'd imagined it being a tattered hardcover, full of history and well-loved. Instead, it was a colorful paperback—brand new and never before read. Pippin didn't respond to the newborn baby comment. Instead, she strode to the cash register, pulled her slim wallet from her purse. The girl who'd been here a moment ago was gone, so Pippin had no choice but to wait for the man to circle around behind the counter to ring up the purchase. "No browsing?" he asked. "Maybe a Kristan Higgins or Kristin Hannah book."

"Why?" she asked, her voice tinged with irritation. "Don't I look smart enough to read Homer?"

He threw up his hands. "Whoa. I did not say that. Spring is here and the Kristans are some of my bestsellers. *The Odyssey*, well, it's a little academic is all. Not exactly light reading."

She pushed the book toward him on the counter. There was no ticking clock. After all, her father's body had been there for years. Still, she felt pulled to the pages of the book the same way a receding wave pulls at your feet, heels rooted in the wet sand. "Just this."

He nodded, that little smile like a permanent fixture on his lips. "A woman who knows what she wants. I like it." He rang up the purchase on a tablet, which was on a handy swivel stand, and she handed over a twenty-dollar bill. He counted her change back to her. "Usually kids read *The Odyssey* for school. You just have a hankering for an epic poem?"

Pippin wasn't about to tell him the truth. She swallowed and said, "Something like that."

She looked around, turning this way and that.

"Something else you need?"

"A chair," she said as she held up the book. "So I can start reading?"

He pointed to an archway that led to another section of the store. A sign above the opening said Devil's Brew Café. "There are a few in the shop, but if you want—"

"The bookshop connects to the coffee shop?" God, what luck. She was dying for a dose of caffeine.

The man chuckled. "Yep. Two separate businesses, but we share a wall. Tell Ruby that Jamie sent you over."

So now she knew his name. Jamie. It fit him. Pippin nodded and thanked him, and a few seconds later, she stopped under the archway between the two spaces. Jamie hadn't been kidding. There were plenty of places to sit, even though the place was buzzing with conversation. Her gaze trailed over the tables and straight-backed chairs, as well as the comfortable arrangements of plush armchairs, one even with a couch in the grouping. An upright piano stood against the wall and framed paintings, some watercolors and others mixed medium, and sketches filled up much of the wall's space. A middle-aged man looked up, as if he sensed Pippin's gaze. He stared at her for a beat too long before giving a slight nod and redirecting his attention to the notebook he'd been writing in. He scribbled furiously, pausing, thinking, then scribbling again. He looked up at her again, but she turned away.

Travis, Jimmy, and Kyron ambled in, plopping down at a vacant table. When there was only one coffee shop in town, it's where everyone came for a break. Kyron noticed her first, gave a smile, and waved. Jimmy and Travis turned to acknowledge her. Their gazes drifted over the other customers before returning to their conversation.

A long exposed brick wall ran the length of the café, just like in the bookshop. The counter in front of the wall held a massive stainless-steel espresso machine, another tablet on a swivel stand for payment, and a glass case filled with cakes, scones, an array of cookies, and muffins. Her stomach growled.

The barista behind the counter, who Pippin assumed was Ruby, was stunning. Her hair was a riot of spirally curls that framed her face like an aura. Bits of highlighted strands were intermixed with the dark brown and her was skin was Halle Berry flawless. She was probably about the same height as Pippin, but Ruby's hair gave her an extra four inches putting her close to six feet. The woman smiled, setting Pippin instantly at ease. Meeting new people—and the inherent risk of becoming friends and then losing them —was always tough. But something about her was welcoming, like a warm summer night.

"Ruby?"

She gave a close-mouthed smile, her hands on her hips. "Let me guess. Jamie sent you."

Pippin held up her newly purchased book. "A place to sit and read."

Ruby gestured to the room at large. "Take your pick. Can I get you something to warm up?"

The late March chill was lingering, not quite ready to give in to warm sunny beach weather so Pippin ordered a latte and a molasses cookie. She thanked Ruby and took her treats to one of the club chairs, choosing a spot where her back was to the man from a moment ago and to the workmen renovating her house. She wanted to concentrate on the book only. She sipped the coffee and broke off a piece of the cookie before setting both cup and plate on the coffee table.

Thanks to Daisy Santiago, Pippin knew she needed to search the book for the section on the Sirens. She flipped through the pages, searching. The text was broken into stanzas. She scanned, page by page wondering what the story of Odysseus could have to do with the life and death of Leo Hawthorne. She couldn't make heads or tails of it. The letters danced on the page, flipping this way and that, mixing themselves up in the middle of words. It had been exactly the same when she'd been a kid. It's why reading frustrated her so much, and why she'd never taken to it.

She went back to *The Odyssey*. What had made her mother cry out and break down sobbing when she'd seen a copy of this book?

Again and again, Pippin skimmed the pages, searching through the different parts of the epic poem. She paused to haltingly decipher the words, then try again, finally dismissing each bit of text as irrelevant. Fifteen minutes passed, then thirty. Her coffee grew cold, her cookie uneaten. Where the hell were the Sirens? Nothing jumped out at her. She slammed the book closed.

Somewhere in the back of her mind she heard conversations going on around her. A few women chattered about their daycare situation, wondering if they should try the brand new facility opening up inland. A man talked on the phone, telling whoever was on the other end that he'd solved the puzzle. A husband and wife had a light-hearted argument about who was the better cook. Pippin blocked it all out, her focus on the closed book in her lap. Her index finger traced the words of the title.

"Still here?"

The voice startled her, and she jumped in her seat. The book slipped from her hand. It landed on its spine and fell open.

Glancing up, she saw Jamie. He waved to someone

behind her, then nodded at her mug and plate. "Something wrong with the coffee and cookie?"

"What?" She followed his gaze. "Oh, no. I got distracted."

"Right. With *The Odyssey*."

She followed his gaze to the book laying open on the floor. Leaning forward again, she started to pick it up, but stopped. The words on the page undulated almost as if they were coming alive. She jolted as a memory shot into her mind from that one visit with Cora and Lily. They'd been in the lighthouse bookstore. Cora had placed a book on it on its spine. Let it fall open. Spun her finger around, finally dropping it to the page.

Pippin didn't know why Cora had done it, or what her satisfied smile had been about, but she held her breath, circled her finger as her cousin had so many years ago, and pressed it down on the page. The words beneath her finger rippled, as if she was seeing them through water. She blinked, trying to bring them into focus, but they shimmied in slow waves, and then part of the stanza seemed to pull free—hovering, magnified above the page.

Jamie sat down next to her, his body turned to face her. "Hey. Are you okay?"

She pointed to the hovering words. "Look," she said, her voice low, practically shoving the book at him.

He read the passage she pointed to aloud.

...*Listen with care*
to this, now, and a god will arm your mind.
Square in your ship's path are Seirênês, crying
beauty to bewitch men coasting by;
woe to the innocent who hears that sound!
He will not see his lady nor his children

in joy, crowding about him, home from sea;
the Seirênês will sing his mind away
on their sweet meadow lolling. There are bones
of dead men rotting in a pile beside them
and fled skins shrivel around the spot.

PIPPIN FELT like the air had been knocked out of her. "How many years was Odysseus gone from Ithaca?" she asked suddenly, but it wasn't Jamie who answered. A man spoke from behind her. "Twenty years."

Pippin turned to look over her shoulder, starting. It was the man she'd made eye contact with earlier. Everyone else in the coffee shop seemed fuzzy to her. She managed a small smile before turning back around. She didn't like that he'd been listening to her conversation.

Jamie watched her, his eyes narrowed beneath his glasses. "That's right," he said. "Twenty years. Ten during the Trojan War and another ten wandering the sea on his voyage home."

Exactly what Daisy had said. Pippin's body went cold. It had been twenty years since her father's disappearance. As they had for her mother, the words lifting off the page in the book were telling her about her father.

Like Odysseus, after twenty years, Leo Hawthorne had come home.

Chapter 9

"People generally see what they look for, and hear what they listen for."
   ~Harper Lee, from *To Kill a Mockingbird*

*P*ippin had slept fitfully. Just as she managed to drift off for what felt like the millionth time, images flitted in and out of her mind, jolting her awake again. The bones in the hatch. The lieutenant telling her and Grey that it had been murder. Standing alone on the beach, staring out at the churning water.

She rolled onto her side, pulling the pale green and white quilt up over her head to block out the streaks of morning light shining through the slats of the plantation shutters Grey had installed on the east facing windows of the master bedroom. She drifted off again, jerking awake to the sound of men's voices. Would they ever be finished? She wanted to be alone in her house. To not walk into a room expecting it to be empty, only to find Jimmy or Travis or Kyron there.

She peered at the square wooden alarm clock on her bedside table. Nine o'clock! The last time she'd looked, it had been six-thirteen. She pushed herself to recline against the pillows, rubbing the sleep from her eyes. Even with the extra hours she'd slept, she still felt groggy.

"Peevie!" Grey's bellowing voice reverberated through the house, sliding into her room from under the door. "Come on! Pippin!"

She scurried from her bed, throwing open the door. "What?" she yelled, matching his volume.

"You need to get out. We're ready to paint."

She pressed the heel of her hand to her forehead. Oh God. That's right. They'd done most of the prep work the day before. Today they'd be spraying. "Give me ten minutes," she hollered back. She wanted nothing more than to slip back between the covers and sink into another hour of sleep. Instead, she went into the bathroom, threw her hair up into a loose bun, took a lightning quick shower, and dressed in a periwinkle blue sundress and her standard white sneakers. She went for comfort, first and foremost. She grabbed a lightweight sweater figuring it would still be cool outside.

Not even a dab of makeup could hide the dark half-moons under her eyes. She'd gotten less sleep than she'd even imagined, by the looks of it, but there was nothing to be done at this point. She slipped on her thin silver watch and a small pair of white gold hoop earrings. A few minutes later, she'd pulled her bike from the garage and pedaled toward town.

~

RESEARCHING anything at a library was not in Pippin's wheelhouse, but visiting the library for the second time, she felt more comfortable. She walked into the little converted house expecting to see Daisy at the circulation desk. Instead, a slightly pudgy young man wearing a sky-blue polo shirt sat there. He looked to be in his mid-twenties but already his dark hair was receding, and he had the firm makings of a double chin. He had a band on his left ring finger and a thin chain around his neck. The badge on a lanyard strung around his neck gave his name as Harold Manatee. He had one elbow propped on the counter, his fist under his chin. With his other hand, he flipped through the pages of a magazine.

From this angle, his receding hairline looked twice as deep. He just had a big head, Pippin realized. "Hi," she said cheerily. "Is Daisy around?"

He perked up when he saw her. Just like her first visit, the place was quiet without a single patron in sight. "Sorry, no. She has the morning off."

Pippin felt more disappointed than she expected to. Even though she wanted to, she didn't know Daisy well enough to call her up and beg her to come into work early on her morning off. Not that she would have done that even if they'd been best friends.

Harold sat up straighter and flashed an amiable smile. "What can I help you with?"

The fact that Daisy wasn't there didn't change Pippin's goal. She was too spooked to think much about what had happened at the coffee shop the day before. Instead, she planned to direct her focus to other things. Namely the sunken boat at Devil's Cove Landing. She'd already scoured the Internet, but she'd come up empty. Twenty years wasn't a lot of time in the scheme of things, yet the Internet had exploded during those two decades. Things available online now hadn't even been imagined then. She'd searched only to learn that Wikipedia didn't launch until 2001 and Google wasn't king yet. She come up empty.

"I hope you can help," she said. "About twenty years ago, a boat sank at one of the marinas in the harbor. I want to see if I can find out anything about it."

"Sure," he said. "We have a microfilm reader. If you know when it happened and if it was reported about, you should be able to find something."

He led her to a desktop computer in a back corner of the library. An old looking machine sat next to it, connected to the CPU. Pippin told Harold the year her father vanished. The young man disappeared into a back room, returning a few minutes later. He turned on the monitor, loaded the film onto the machine, and showed her how to scan through the information. "The local newspaper was a lot more robust back then so there's a lot to scroll through."

"Got it," Pippin said.

"Let me know if you need anything else." The guy was really very accommodating.

"I will. Thanks, Harold."

He gave a little salute with two fingers before he went back to the circulation desk. Pippin sat down, put her purse on the table behind the computer, and got started.

It was tedious work. *The Devil's Cove Gazette* articles were reduced to twenty-five percent of the original size and felt microscopic after a while. She skimmed, looking for keywords. After fifteen minutes, she wished she'd stopped first for a cup of coffee. After another twenty, her fitful sleep caught up with her. She tried to stifle a yawn but couldn't manage it. She scrolled, yawned, scrolled, yawned, scrolled, yawned.

After yet another fifteen minutes, her hopefulness that she'd find anything began to wane. She'd just scooted back in her chair, ready to give up, when her father's picture appeared on the screen. "Oh!" Her eyes widened and she leaned closer to the screen. The accompanying article was written by someone named Quincy Ratherford. A photo of her and Grey when they were about eight years old was there, too. She slowly read, stopping when she figured out that the article advanced the idea that Leo had walked away from them.

Pippin's eyes filled. She couldn't prove it yet, but she knew Leo hadn't willingly left her and Grey. If the police had looked into her father's disappearance at the time... taken it more seriously—a missing person rather than a deadbeat dad, maybe his life could have been saved. Maybe he'd still be here with them.

She shoved the What Ifs aside. They didn't do her an ounce of good, and she couldn't change history. Still, she went to find Harold Manatee, asking him how to print something. He showed her, and she printed out the article. A visit to this journalist, Quincy Ratherford, seemed in order.

The boat sinking at the marina had happened before her father disappeared. Pippin scrolled further back, searching. It didn't take long before she came across a photo of Devil's Cove Landing. Bev at the marina had been right. The sinking had taken place the day before her father had vanished from their lives.

She saw no mention of her father's name in that article. Of course. That would be too easy.

Another photograph accompanying the article showed the empty slip, where presumably the sunken boat had been docked. Next to it was the boat that was now sitting in her front yard. The *Cassandra*. The fact that the boat was pictured didn't mean anything in connection to the article. The focus was on the empty slip, but she printed out the image anyway, as well as the article, which, she saw, was also written by Qunicy Ratherford.

It didn't take long to find the address for *The Devil's Cove Gazette*. The building was located off the beaten track, but still bike-able, as everything in the village was. Pippin thanked Harold, tucked the printed articles into her purse, which she secured in her bike's basket, and once again, headed off. A few short minutes later, she locked her bike in front of a single-story red brick building. She caught a glimpse of her reflection in the large windows. Strands of her hair had come loose and framed her face. The chill in the spring air had tinted her cheeks red. The time she'd been spending in the garden, even though it was only spring, had warmed her skin to a light honey color. The sea air had done her good, she thought. She looked like so many of the other young women who lived in or visited Devil's Cove—windblown, sun kissed, and casual.

She pushed through the door and found herself in a preternaturally quiet office. She'd expected busy. Bustling, even. But this was a small island village, as people kept reminding her, so her expectations had been way off.

A middle-aged man sat behind a desk facing his computer monitor. He'd looked up at the ding of the bell when she'd opened the door. He had ginger hair that was a shade lighter than hers, a ruddy face, thick arms, and he wore his beret like it was nobody's business. As he stood up and came toward her, she raised her brows at his orange and brown plaid pants, a little flare at the ankle, the orange a perfect match to the color of his tucked in polo shirt. He had a little hop in his step. He put his hands on his hips and greeted her with a dipped chin and an enthusiastic, "Good God, but you *are* a beauty, aren't you?"

He wasn't hitting on her. She knew that right away. The tone of his voice. His demeanor. His clothes. No, she definitely wasn't his type. His voice was pleasant and had a little lilt to it. She didn't need to win him over. He seemed thrilled to have her in the office. His exuberance was contagious, and she smiled. "I'm looking for Quincy Ratherford. He used to be—"

The man flung his forearms out to the side, palms up. "Lo and behold, you've found him!"

"Oh. Wow! Okay. You're Quincy Ratherford?"

He chuckled. "Guilty as charged, and at your service."

There was no point in beating around the bush. Pippin pulled the articles from her purse, unfolded them, and held them out. "I'm hoping you can help me with something. I was doing some research at the library and came across these. I see that you wrote both articles."

He took them from her and gave them a good once over. His voice lost some of its buoyancy. "I remember both of these well. They happened so close together, and the strangeness of them, well, they've stuck with me all these years." He ushered her to where he'd been working, pulling a chair from another desk over for her to sit in. "Can I venture a guess?" He continued before she had a chance to even react, let alone acquiesce. "You're Pippin Hawthorne, aren't you?"

She stared. "How did you know that?"

"Investigative journalism at work," he said jauntily. "But seriously, I assumed you were connected to these articles in some way. Plus, my dear, you and your brother are the talk of the town. I've been by to see what you're doing to that house, oh, probably ten times! I saw you outside a few times enjoying that big porch of yours."

Another person keeping tabs on hers and Grey's progress with the house. "Why am I the talk of the town?"

"Oh honey, everyone, and I do mean everyone, is thrilled that you're doing something with that house. You're bringing it back to its heyday glory and, well, we're all excited! Mrs. Pickle gives us all weekly updates."

Mrs. Pickle. That name. It rang a bell in the depths of Pippin's mind. How did she know it?

"She's your neighbor, of course," Quincy said, as if he knew she'd drawn a blank. "Across the street and down one, if I'm not mistaken. She's a character and a half, and she knows everything. If you invite her inside, by the next day, we'll all get a blow by blow of that, too!"

"I don't think that's necessary," she said. Quincy's face fell so she hurried on. "It's going to be an inn. We're going to have an open house as soon as the renovations are completely done. Which should be very soon. Anyone who wants to will be able to come by and see it, inside and out."

He clasped his hands together. "I can do a story on it. That old rum smuggler's house turned into an inn. Brilliant."

Pippin sat up straighter, her interest piqued. "A rum smuggler?"

"Oh yes. You never heard the story—" His face suddenly grew somber. "Of course you haven't, and where are my manners? I'm awfully sorry to hear about your father."

"Thank you," she said. "It was a shock."

"I'm sure it was. Found in one the hatches? That's what we heard."

"That's right." She didn't want to say any more than that, so she pinched her brows together. "Now, what about this rum runner?"

Quincy went back to his story. "He was one of the first to land on our little piece of paradise. After his ship sank, he managed to make his way to the Sound and to our little harbor."

"Wait, are you saying that one of the sailors who named the island Devil's Cove owned my parents' house?"

Quincy's head moved as if he were a bobblehead. "There used to be an historical marker on it. You can read all about him at the Devil's Cove museum. The whole town has been in a funk for the last twenty years what with the house sitting empty and getting worse and worse by the day. You coming back has been like a rainbow stretching across the sky."

With his flowery language, Quincy could have written fiction instead of the dry who, what, when, why, and how journalism required. "What are you calling the inn?" he asked, pen poised above a yellow notepad.

She opened her mouth to say that they hadn't thought of a name yet, but different words came out instead. "Sea Captain's Inn.'" Hearing it spoken out loud underscored how perfect it was. She knew Grey would love it. She smiled, at least one mystery in her life resolved, and repeated, "Sea Captain's Inn." It was perfect.

Quincy asked her a series of questions about the house and the renovations, taking copious notes. When he'd gotten all the information he wanted, he shifted gears and picked up the printed copies of the articles he'd written so long ago. "What did you want to know about these?" he asked.

Pippin considered. She didn't have specific questions. "I guess I'd just like to know what you remember."

Quincy sat back crossing his plaid legs and went into journalism mode, his effusiveness tamed. "Well, gosh. Let me think. The boat sinking was so strange. I mean, who would want to sink a boat in a marina? It didn't make sense to me. I did a little bit of investigative reporting at the time. Tried to find the motive, you know? Because *somebody* pulled those plugs. But why would they? I didn't find anything to lead me to the conclusion that the owners had done it themselves, and the police investigation didn't either. They were weekenders and hadn't been out in a while."

"Weekenders?"

"They lived somewhere else—I can't remember where. Raleigh? Charlotte?—and came down here on the weekends. Lots of second homes out here."

That made sense. "So there was no way they sank their own boat?"

Quincy clasped his fingers together and wrapped them around his top knee. "Not from what I could find. As far as I know, the police never found anything either."

"So who would have done it?"

Quincy gave his head a slow shake. "Honey, that was the big question at the time. There was absolutely no motive. I even went so far as to consider it to be a case of mistaken boat."

"What do you mean?" Pippin asked.

He uncrossed his legs and leaned forward, propping his elbows on his plaid-covered thighs, and pressing his palms together with his fingers under his chin. He dropped his voice almost conspiratorially. "What if it was the wrong boat?"

"The wrong boat," Pippin repeated. This was something she hadn't even considered. The theory led to an obvious question: If it was the *wrong* boat that sank, could the *Cassandra* have been the *right* boat? Her father had been murdered. Whoever had done that could very well have tried to sink his boat, too.

But why?

She looked at Quincy. "When my father disappeared, was his boat searched?"

"I imagine it was given a cursory glance when your father was first reported missing, but conventional wisdom said he'd walked away from his life, so it's unlikely. No one thought a crime had been committed, so there'd been no need to open those hatches." He snorted. "I guess they should have been searched given—"

He broke off, but Pippin finished the sentence in her head. *Given the fact that her father's body was found in one.*

Quincy shook his head in self-chastisement. "Sorry. That was insensitive. It's just that I distinctly remember your father's parents insisting that he'd just walked away. That he needed time to sort things out. With no indication of foul play, the police had nothing to go on. It was assumed that his parents were right."

"It's fine," she said. "I do have another question for you, though."

He leaned back again, resuming his relaxed cross-legged position, hands clasped around his knee. "You can ask me anything, honey."

"The sinking boat and my father vanishing. They happened so close together. Since you thought maybe the wrong boat had been sunk, did you ever think that could be connected to Leo's disappearance?"

Quincy stared at her for a moment before responding.

"You mean your father's boat should have been the one to go down?"

She shrugged helplessly. "I don't know. I'm just asking. I have no idea why it would have been my father's, but what if it should have been?"

His reclining chair jerked forward as he dropped and uncrossed his legs again. "I'll be honest with you. I considered it. As I recall, the names of the vessels were pretty similar." His fingers flew over the keyboard and a minute later he announced, "Yep. Your dad's was the *Cassandra* and the boat that sunk was the *Caterina*. Other than that, I couldn't find any evidence to support the theory that someone had pulled the plugs on the wrong boat, which meant it was dead in the wat—"

He slammed his hand over his mouth, his eyes wide and horrified at his choice of words. "Miss Hawthorne, I am so sorry—"

She fluttered her hand. She didn't want people walking on eggshells around her. "It's fine," she said, then she told him to call her Pippin.

Mistaken boat identity. It was a theory, but it didn't lead her anywhere. She'd wanted to find Quincy Ratherford and have him confirm her suspicions, but how could he? It was unrealistic, and now she'd wasted his time on a dead-end fishing trip. She thanked him and left the offices of *The Devil's Cove Gazette*.

She needed a cup of coffee.

She was just about to get on her bike when Quincy stopped her. "Pippin?"

She held her bike steady with one hand. Outside in the sunlight, Quincy's orange shirt and plaid pants seemed brighter.

"I don't know if this will mean anything," he said, hands on his hips again, "but I thought I'd mention it."

Pippin waited expectantly for him to continue. She'd take any clue, or even a hint of a clue at this point.

"There was a lot of controversy about Devil's Cove Landing back then. The owners wanted to add some floating docks and live-aboard slips. With the coastline and the Inter Coastal Waterways, North Carolina has 5000 miles of waters for boaters. A marina has to be competitive, even in a little island village like Devil's Cove. DC Landing wanted to cancel slip leases and start renovating. The fishermen and their families who'd docked there for generations would have been displaced. From what I remember, your dad wasn't going to give up his slip without a fight."

A ray of dark hope spread through her. Could this fight with the marina have led to his death? It was a potential motive, at least. She gave Quincy her cell number and asked him to call her if he thought of anything else.

"You know I will," he said.

She was hopeful that this man had provided a clue that would lead to the truth.

Chapter 10

"Friends are the family you choose."
  ~Jess C. Scott

*P*aint fumes still lingered heavily in the air, Pippin sat at her little desk in her little office aimlessly sketching logos for Sea Captain's Inn. Her foot shook. She'd hoped that Quincy would remember something else important from twenty years ago, but she hadn't heard from him since she'd seen him the day before. Patience wasn't her strength. She kicked herself for not getting his cell phone number in return for hers.

The sound of women's voices drifted to her through the windows, taking her away from her thoughts. She glanced out to see Ruby and Daisy coming up the front walkway, then climbing the steps. She hadn't known they were friends, but it made sense. One was the head librarian while the other worked across the street at the only coffee shop in town. Of course they knew each other. Ruby towered over

Daisy by almost a full foot, enhancing the feeling that Daisy was a pixie who was impersonating a human.

When they reached the porch, Pippin pushed up from her chair and went to the foyer, opening the door. Ruby's hand froze in midair. Daisy's face lit up with a smile. "Good timing!"

Pippin laughed and pointed to her office window. "Saw you coming."

She wasn't ready to bring furniture into the house, not with the renovations still going on, so she swept her arm wide to encompass the house. "Just painted and no place to sit," she said and stepped out onto the porch to join them.

Ruby handed her a folded piece of paper. "Saw the corner of this under the mat."

Pippin unfolded it and saw that it had been torn from a bound notebook of some sort. Pippin's and Grey's names were printed at the top of the lined paper in tight almost cramped writing. It was as if someone had hurriedly written this on whatever bit of paper they could find. Someone had brought it to the house and left it.

PIPPIN AND GREY,

You are back in Devil's Cove at long last! You do not know me, but I was a friend of your father's. Both scholars, he and I. He was a good man. I have always suspected that his disappearance was more than it seemed. Hard as it is to accept, the truth has brought me peace. I hope to you, as well.

I have seen you here, becoming part of our island village. I almost didn't believe my eyes. Your parents would be so pleased to see you in their old house.

Leo entrusted me with something. It belongs to you. Please meet me tomorrow at noon at the fishing pier near the cove.

. . .

DESPITE THE WARMTH of the day, Pippin's body grew cold. The note wasn't signed. She read it again, looking for hidden messages between the words, but she couldn't find any. It was written by a man, she knew. A friend of her father's. Leo had been a fisherman, but this person called him a fellow scholar. Curious. She glanced up and down the street. "Did you see anyone?" she asked Ruby and Daisy.

"Just Hattie," Ruby said, pointing across the street, but whoever Hattie was, she was no longer there, and there was no way to know for sure when the note was left. It could have been there for days unnoticed.

Pippin willed away the goosebumps on her flesh. She folded the note and slipped it into her back pocket. She'd show Grey later, and together they'd decide what to do about the requested meeting tomorrow.

The three women sat side by side at the top of the porch steps, Pippin sitting between Daisy and Ruby. Ruby patted the curls framing her head, as if she were making sure they were all still in place. "Did you hear the news?" she asked.

Pippin flicked a giant black ant that had appeared on her leg. She turned a raised eyebrow to Ruby "What kind of news?"

Daisy responded, her voice low as if she was imparting a great secret. "They found a body."

Pippin gaped. "Who found a body? What body?"

"Some kids who were tooling around in a skiff this morning," Ruby said. "They went to the cove. There was an abandoned kayak...and the body of a man."

"What was he doing there?" Daisy said, more musing to herself than a question to Pippin and Ruby.

"That's too bad," she said. "Caught in a riptide?"

They both shrugged. "Maybe," Ruby said.

Pippin's throat constricted. She closed her eyes for a second. She was sorry for the man—and for whoever he may have left behind—she was. But she had the murder of her father to focus on.

The three women chatted for a few minutes—about nothing in particular. Pippin updated them on the renovation progress and the open house she wanted to have. Ruby, who it turned out, owned the coffee shop, which just shared a wall with the bookshop, lit up. "I can supply the coffee and the pastries!"

It was a lovely offer, so why did Pippin feel her eyebrows pinch together and a tightening in her chest?

It took her a matter of seconds to figure it out. She'd had superficial friends throughout middle and high school, but she'd relied on Grey, and after she graduated, she knew she needed to figure out how to rely on herself. What did she, herself, have to offer? She'd left whatever friends she had made behind...left Greenville and the safety of her brother... and roamed the northeast. She'd gone into a period of existential crisis. She'd waitressed some, but mostly she'd worked in garden centers and nurseries. She'd bounced from garden center to garden center. Flowers didn't care if you liked to read. She'd come out the other side of her wandering only to find that her father hadn't abandoned them but had been killed. She had the house. And she had these two women, who, for some reason she couldn't explain, wanted to help her.

"That sounds perfect," she said, a little speechless and more than a little unsure what to do with this offering of friendship. "Thank you."

Daisy popped off the steps and stood at the bottom, extending her arm toward them. Ruby cupped her hand over Daisy's. They both looked at Pippin. It took her a full breath in and out to get up the nerve, but finally she did. She placed her hand on top of Ruby's. Daisy dropped her arm, then lifted it. Dropped, then lifted. And after the third lower, she lifted with enough momentum to throw all their hands up. They should have said, "Break!" as if they'd been in a huddle. Instead, Daisy grinned and said, "To new friends."

Ruby echoed, "To new friends."

Pippin's eyes glazed. She absently scratched her head.

"Hey," Ruby said. "You okay?"

Pippin nodded. Maybe a little too vigorously. "I'm fine," she said, but then, like floodgates opening, she told them how it felt to see her father's bones in the hatch of his own boat. She told them about the research she'd done on the sunken boat at DC Landing, and about meeting Quincy and his story about the battle over the marina. Bev and Mick's faces flashed in her mind. They'd seemed harmless, but could they possibly be behind her father's death?

And then there was the letter. It felt like a hot brand in her back pocket. As much as she tried to put it out of her mind, she felt the weight of its words. "It all feels so strange," she finished.

Daisy grabbed Pippin's hand and jumped up. "Come on," she said, yanking Pippin to standing. "We're going on a mini road trip."

"Neither of you are working today?" Pippin asked.

"I have two high school kids work on Saturdays," Ruby said.

"And I have the noon to four shift." Daisy pressed a button on her phone. "Which means I have a little less than two hours."

Pippin resisted. She had things to do. A mystery to solve. "Where do you want to go?"

"To see my dad. He used to work at Dolphin Landing. If there is any *chisme*—gossip—about the boat or your dad, he'll know it."

A few minutes later, Pippin was shivering in the backseat of Daisy's yellow convertible, the back ragtop down. She should have brought a heavier sweater.

Daisy drove and Ruby rode shotgun. Pippin glanced at the two-story house across the street and down one. Like hers, it had siding and a high-pitched roof. It was in good shape. Bright and happy with its lavender and teal color palette. But it wasn't the house itself that caught her attention. It was the face in the window, staring right at her, following the car as it rolled down the street toward the north side of town.

She started to ask Daisy or Ruby if they'd seen the face but changed her mind before the words came out. They would have said something if they had, right? And maybe she was just being paranoid.

"Someday, I'll live on the island," Daisy said dreamily as they approached the swing bridge connecting the island to the mainland. It was a relic, but also historic. Passing over it and Croatan Sound onto Devil's Cove marked the beginning of a tourist's vacation. Going back marked the end. It was a symbol of the island.

As the car rolled onto the bridge, the ruckus of tires against the grooved surface of the bridge gave Pippin an involuntary response. The grating sound brought back her memories of leaving the island for good when she and Grey had gone to live with their grandparents.

The outside of the bridge stirred up just as many memories. The sea foam green steel trusses were marked with splotchy rust spots. The town of Sand Point made no effort to disguise the rust. The canopy of steel was beautiful, rust or not.

Daisy and Ruby were oblivious to the emotions crashing through Pippin, and she was determined to keep it that way. She didn't want to alienate her new friends by bringing them *all* her baggage. Daisy sped across the 400-foot bridge, turning south once she reached the end of the bridge.

Sand Point didn't look that different from Devil's Cove. They were both harbor towns, the only difference being that Devil's Cove was an island and Sand Point was on the mainland, bisected by an intercostal waterway.

"It's beautiful here, though," Pippin said.

"Oh it is, and I love it Sand Point! But there's something about the islands. Roanoke." She sighed. "And Manteo. They have the best bed and breakfasts on Manteo. But there's something about Topsail and Ocracoke and Cedar Island...and Devil's Cove. They're less developed. Well, Topsail's south end, anyway. They're...I don't know...special. And Devil's Cove has always been my favorite."

Pippin remembered her father talking about how much Cassie loved Devil's Cove. "From the moment she saw it, she knew there was no place else she could live," Leo said when he told her and Grey the story. "Your mother left Oregon and never looked back. She had to start fresh, and she ended up here." Leo would always ruffle Pippin's hair at that point. "And thank God she did otherwise we never would have met, and you and your brother wouldn't be here."

After Cassie died, it took Leo a while to get to the point where he could tell Pippin and Grey the story about how he met their mother. It wasn't that he didn't want to revisit those memories, but it was difficult to.

Finally, he managed it, his face taking on a melancholy

expression as he spun his magical tale. "It was a beautiful summer morning. The sunlight draped over our little island, blanketing it with a golden glow. I was at the fish market with the morning catch. I suddenly sensed the air change. Every sound, every voice seemed so far away. And everything turned to slow motion for me. I turned around and there she was. Her hair was a little darker than yours, Pipsqueak," he'd said, using the nickname only he ever called her. "She had it piled on the top of her head, these vibrant red strands pulled loose and framing her face. There was a light breeze that morning. The dress your mother wore billowed out behind her. She laughed, spinning around to catch the fabric, holding it gathered in one hand as she walked through the market. Just like I'd sensed her presence, she said she felt someone's eyes on her. She looked up and saw me. In that second, it was like a bolt of energy flowed between us, drawing us together." He always smiled before continuing with, "I'd never believed in love at first sight, but in that moment, everything changed. I became a believer."

She could recite that story verbatim, she'd heard it so many times, but she also recalled hiding around a corner in their house and overhearing her mother saying to her father that their relationship was doomed. He'd disagreed with her, but she'd been right in the end. The love affair between Cassandra Lane and Leo Hawthorne *had* been doomed.

"Why'd your dad leave Dolphin Landing?" Ruby asked.

Daisy flipped on her turn signal as she approached the harbor. "His dream was always to have a bait and tackle shop. He worked on the island for more than twenty years. He ran charters and wreck dives. My mom works in Sand Point. She's a hairdresser. They saved as much as they could, and finally, about four years ago, he did it. The Tackle Box went up for sale and he bought it. He catches his own bait. Shiners. Snappers. Suckers. Fat heads," she said proudly. "I go out with him once in a while."

Once Daisy started naming fish, Pippin's eyes glazed. Her father may have been a fisherman, but he hadn't passed that love to his daughter. Clearly the same couldn't be said of Daisy.

"That goes to show you," Ruby said as they pulled into a parking spot near the pier. "Dreams do come true."

A sign inside The Tackle Box advertised live bait by the bucket, or by individual fish, but that wasn't all it sold. The place also had lures, hooks, line, and spare rod pieces as well as ocean fishing gear like rods and reels, waterproof waders, and lifejackets. And on a display case near the cash register was a prominent display of something called daisy chains. Ruby pointed at it. "Did your parents name you after a fishing thingamajig?"

Daisy rolled her eyes, laughing at the same time. "I usually tell people I'm named after the flower, but, yeah. I'm named after a fancy chain of plastic lures."

Ruby bit back her laugh as she patted Daisy on the shoulder. "I'm sorry."

"*M'ija,*" a man said coming toward them. He wore khaki shorts, sandals, and a sea green t-shirt with a small The Tackle Box logo on the left chest. He had the same warm olive skin as Daisy and the same big smile, but he was a lot taller than his pixie daughter.

"Pops!" Daisy wrapped her arms around him, hugging him like she hadn't seen him in weeks. Or even years. She released him and spun around. "Pops, you remember Ruby. She owns the cafe on Devil's Cove. And this is Pippin. Ladies, this is my dad, Chavi Santiago."

"*Mucho gusto,*" he said. "Very nice to meet you both."

Ruby gave a little nod. "Good to see you again, sir," she said.

Pippin smiled. Daisy's father had a warm geniality that made him familiar and put her at ease. "Nice to meet you, too."

"Pops," Daisy said. "Pippin is opening up an inn!"

Half of Daisy's sentences were punctuated with enthusiastic exclamation points and she wore a permanent smile. Pippin was still getting used to that. When she needed a pick-me-up, calling Daisy would be first on her list of Things To Do.

"On Devil's Cove?" he asked her. "The place could use one."

"That's what I hear," Pippin said. "It's going to be called Sea Captain's Inn."

"On the water, then?"

"Yes. It's on the south end of the island, just a few blocks from town."

As he nodded, Daisy said, "Pippin is Leo Hawthorne's daughter."

No exclamation point, and for the first time, the man's smile faded. He took a step back, letting the arm that had been draped over Daisy's shoulders drop. "Pops, you okay?" Daisy asked.

"I have not heard that name in a long time," he said.

"He's been gone a long time," Pippin said, "but his name's been in the news lately."

The man half shook his head, half nodded. "Of course. I have seen it in the paper, but..." He trailed off and scrubbed his hand over his face. "You are Leo's daughter." He gave her a pointed look. "And your brother?"

"He's on the island. He's doing the renovations on the house."

"That is good. Yes, that is good. My condolences," he said somberly.

"Pops," Daisy said. "Do you remember about a boat that sank at DC Landing?"

Slowly, he nodded and looked at Pippin. "It was the boat next to your father's."

Pippin's heart raced. Chavi Santiago remembered that. "I have a question, if you don't mind," she said.

Santiago nodded, just once. "Go on."

"Do you think the boat that sank was supposed to have been my father's?"

Chavi Santiago's looked surprised. "Why would you think that?"

She shrugged. "I heard the marina owners wanted to cancel the slip leases and people were upset."

"It is true. Many people were angry. Your father fought against the marina. He wanted the slip leases honored."

"He fought against Bev and Mick?" Pippin asked.

"He did. But Pippin, they would have known your father's boat. If they'd wanted to sink it, they would have. They are not those kind of people. They wanted to improve their marina. To compete with Dolphin's Landing. But if you are thinking they might have killed your father? No. No, they would not."

A flood of disappointment washed over Pippin. It wasn't that she wanted Bev and Mick to be involved in her father's death, but if they weren't, she was back to zero.

Someone called his name and he turned away. Spread across the back of his shirt was the logo for the store—an open box with a detailed fish overlaying it. Chavi Santiago moved away to help the customer with a new reel, returning to the three of them a short while later. "Come with me," he said to them. They followed him behind the register counter and through the door leading to the back. The room was filled with cardboard boxes and plastic bins stacked on the floor, shelving that housed smaller containers, a door marked RESTROOM, and another door marked EXIT. Daisy's father managed to keep the small space well organized.

A tidy desk butted up to the corner walls. An old computer sat on it, a calendar hung over it, and manilla file folders and papers were arranged neatly in a multilevel desktop organizer. A handmade clay dish sat in the upper corner of the desk blotter. Pippin remembered making something similar when she'd been in Kindergarten...or maybe first grade. She'd given it to her mother who'd used it for the earrings and the necklace she wore. So many times, Pippin had wished she had that necklace, but it had gone with her mother into the grave.

Three separate shelves, lined with books, were mounted on the side wall. The majority of the titles looked to be about fish and fishing. Mr. Santiago knew exactly which one he wanted to remove. He pulled the book off, briefly glanced at the cover, then held it out to Pippin.

She took it with both hands, holding it as if it were something valuable and breakable rather than a simple hardcover book. She looked at Mr. Santiago, questioning him with her raised brows.

"Your mother gave it to my wife."

It was a book of poetry. But that couldn't be right. "My mother never—" She stopped. If she told them that her mother never had anything to do with books, she'd have to explain it, and what could she say? She didn't know the whole truth. She'd put the incident with *The Odyssey* out of her mind, but she couldn't avoid it forever.

"She never what?" Ruby asked. She, Daisy, and Mr.

Santiago all stared at her, each with their own curious expression.

"She wasn't much of a reader," Pippin said, returning it to the shelf. She'd wanted Daisy's mother to have it. That was all that mattered.

Mr. Santiago simply nodded. "I am glad you are back. I know they loved that house. They would be happy to know you and your brother are taking care of it now."

Pippin wanted to believe that Leo and Cassie were looking down on her right now, filling her with their strength. With their love.

They turned to leave, but Pippin spotted the corner of a frame sitting on the end of the middle shelf, turned so that she almost didn't see it.

Mr. Santiago followed her gaze, and started. "I had forgotten this," he said, grabbing it and holding it out to her.

Pippin held the framed photo, staring at it. The ocean in the background. A fish. Two men and a little girl. She recognized Daisy, then Mr. Santiago, but her gaze shifted and lingered on the other man.

Her father.

In the photograph, Mr. Santiago had a wide toothy smile, but Leo looked somber. Preoccupied. "When was this taken?" she asked.

Mr. Santiago couldn't hide his sadness. "That photo was taken the day before your father disappeared."

Pippin's breath caught in her throat. "The day the boat sank?"

"Yes," he said, his voice low.

"Did he go fishing with you?"

Mr. Santiago shook his head. "No. That trip was with a couple of friends. Daisy came along. Leo was at the marina when we got back."

Pippin studied her father's face in the photo. There was something about the way he stood. His shoulders were tense. His gaze looked beyond the camera. What had been on his mind?

The picture was familiar, but then again, the ocean was the ocean. She'd seen a hundred photos with the Atlantic or the Sound or the Gulf Stream in the background. She started to hand it back, but Mr. Santiago stopped her. "It's yours. Take it."

She smiled her thanks and slipped the framed photograph into her purse to think about later.

Chapter 11

"Dogs just need you and love, that's all."
~Jennifer Westfeldt

*O*nce Pippin was back in the privacy of her new old home, she withdrew the cryptic note from her back pocket. She tossed her purse aside in her office and grabbed the copy of *The Odyssey* she'd purchased at the bookshop. She slid the note between the pages for safe keeping. Her head swam with her convoluted thoughts. She felt like she'd been keeping secrets from Grey, and now she needed to come clean.

She had learned early on that people left. Her mother. Her father. Her grandfather. And then her grandmother. Anyone who'd cared for her had left her.

Except for Grey. It had always been Peevie and Greevie against the world.

But how would Grey take all she had to tell him? Would he think she was crazy? Barking mad? Maybe she was.

Maybe there had been something in the coffee or the cookie she'd had at the coffee shop the other day...something that had made the book fall open to just the right page, and for her finger to find just the right passage. Something that made her see the words shift on the page.

It didn't matter. She couldn't keep it from him any longer.

"Pippin, come here!"

Kyron's voice interrupted her thoughts. She hurried into the great room. Kyron stood in the little hallway that led to the study. Her father's study. "Come here." He beckoned to her, his voice lowered to an urgent whisper.

She hurried over, book still in hand, and followed him into the study, stopping in front of the built-in bookshelves along the back wall. An image of being in here with her father flashed in her mind. Stacks of books on the floor. A ship in a bottle. A jar filled with seashells.

"Over here," Kyron said. He walked out the French doors onto the screened-in side porch and pointed.

Pippin blinked away the image and peered through the screen, not sure what she was supposed to be looking at. Her father's boat was still there, a haunting reminder of what they'd found onboard. Pampas grass still lined the fence.

"That dog you've been tryin' to get to come to you? There he is under the stern of the boat."

Pippin had gotten a look at the dog's undercarriage. "Pretty sure *he's* a *she*."

"Didn't know you'd been able to get that close," Kyron said with a laugh. His voice was deep and sonorous. She could picture him crooning a melody in a jazz club, leaning into the mic and making the ladies swoon. "Do you see her?"

She looked to the back of the boat and under the trailer. "Oh! There she is! I see her!"

She lay on her side, only her honey paws poking out from the shadows. Pippin straightened up. Would she be able to approach the dog without spooking her? Maybe if she offered a treat.

"Thank you, Kyron."

Pippin started toward the door but Kyron clearing his throat made her stop and turn. "The woman who was here earlier...?" He ran one hand over his head. "She works in the library, right?"

So he'd seen Daisy Santiago. "She does."

He sighed. "Never been much of a reader."

"We have that in common," she said.

"So you know. Doesn't feel right to go to the library when the last thing I want to do is check out a book."

"She might be able to find one you like. She *is* a librarian. That's what they do. They recommend books." Pippin grinned. "You want to get to know her?"

Kyron cocked his head to one side and gave a sheepish shrug. "I wouldn't mind."

Pippin didn't think she was speaking out of turn when she replied. "I got the feeling she'd like to get to know you, too."

His nervous smile broadened. "You think so?"

"I know so."

"Maybe I should make my way down to the library then?"

His nervousness was sweet. He was a good-looking man. The epitome of tall, dark, and handsome...minus the tall part. "They close at four, so you better take off early," she said.

"I'll do that," he said, and when he turned to go back to

the hardwood planks he was sanding, there was an excited bounce in his step.

PIPPIN AND GREY had purchased a few things for the house early on. A washing machine and dryer. A hose and some outdoor tools so Pippin could start getting the garden up to snuff. And a refrigerator they'd stocked with a large water jug so the guys could fill their water bottles, luncheon meats and cheeses, and all the condiments needed for a lunch break. She got a few pieces of turkey and went out to the yard, circling around to where the boat sat. She slowed as she got close to the stern, giving it a wide berth. Pippin was afraid the dog would be skittish. That she'd hop up and bolt the second she got wind of an intruder, but the pup didn't seem to hear her.

That could change as quickly as a deer could decimate a rose bush, though, so Pippin moved as quietly and slowly as she could, finally dropping to her knees to see if the dog's ears would perk up.

They didn't.

She held out the turkey and softly whistled.

The dog didn't budge.

She tried again. Still nothing. For a moment, Pippin wondered if the dog was dead. She held her breath, hoping against hope that that wasn't the case. Finally, she saw the shallow rise and fall of her stomach. The pup was in a deep sleep after a long night of staying alive.

Staying low to the ground, Pippin inched forward. "Come here, girl," she cooed. "Want a treat?"

After a few more tries, Pippin gave up her fear of

spooking the dog. She just wanted her to wake up. She found a pebble and tossed it against the hull of the boat.

No reaction.

She spoke at full volume. "Hey. Puppy!"

No response.

"Can you hear me?" she said aloud.

Nothing.

Realization struck. The dog was deaf.

As Pippin pondered what to do, the dog's eyes popped open. She didn't move her head, but her ears twitched. She emitted a small sound. Not a whimper, but close.

Maybe she'd smelled the lunchmeat Pippin held. She tore off a piece and tossed it. It landed a foot from the dog's nose. She lifted her snout and sniffed, then she scooted forward. Sniffed. Moved closer. Sniffed. Finally, her nose landed on the turkey and she gobbled it up.

"Good girl!" Pippin said. The dog looked at her with her sad brown eyes. Pippin gave a wide smile and tossed another piece. Once again, it landed in front of the dog. Instead of crawling forward on the ground, though, the dog popped up and went right to the treat, then looked up at Pippin expectantly. Her tail was still, but she wasn't acting skittish. Most importantly, she didn't look like she was going to bolt.

Bit by bit, Pippin tossed turkey and the dog moved closer. By the time she was down to the last bit, the dog stood right in front of her. Pippin reached out a tentative hand to gently pet the dog's neck. At the same time, she offered the last of the treat.

The dog sniffed Pippin's hand as if she wanted to be sure it was still the turkey. Once she assured herself that it was, she took it and backed away.

"Hey, sweet girl," Pippin said. There was no collar around the dog's neck. "Do you belong to someone?"

She reached out to pet the dog again, but this time the movement startled the dog and she bolted, disappearing into the pampas grass like it was a portal to another world.

Pippin stood, folded her arms, and stared into the spot that had swallowed up the dog. One way or another, she was determined to build trust with her.

Chapter 12

"... you asked me once if I were superstitious, I remember (as what do I forget that you say?). However that may be, yesterday morning as I turned to look for a book, an old fancy seized me to try the 'sortes' and dip into the first page of the first I chanced upon, for my fortune ; I said 'what will be the event of my love for Her' — in so many words...Well, I ventured, and what did I find ? This — which I copy from the book now —

'If we love in the other world as we do in this, I shall love thee to eternity —"

~Robert Browning to Elizabeth Barrett

"We are definitely going," Grey said when Pippin had shown him the letter the night before, and now, it was exactly noon and they stood against the railing of the main fishing pier in Devil's Cove.

Pippin looked at every person that approached, wondering if that was her father's trusted friend, but time and time again, the men and the women passed them by without a glance.

"Let me take another look," Grey said, holding his hand out.

Pippin had rolled up the sheet of paper and had been clutching it in one hand. She unfurled it and handed it to her brother. He flattened it out and reread the message. "It could have been there for days," he said, not for the first time. He was right. There was no way to know how long the paper had sat under their doormat. Pippin could only assume that no one had been home, and so the note had been hurriedly written and left for them. Had it been yesterday, or the day before? Maybe they were supposed to have met the note-writer the day before. Or the day before that.

They'd talked through the meaning of the letter until both their heads pounded. Without a signature, they had no way of knowing who it was from, or what Leo had entrusted with him, or why it caused fear.

"Let's give it another ten minutes," Grey said after thirty minutes had already passed. They did, but no one sought them out. Nobody came to talk to them. Whoever wrote the letter must have changed his mind.

Grey dropped her back at the house. "I have to pick up some things," he said, but Pippin knew better. The distracted look on his face told her that he needed some time to think. It used to be that she and Grey had been a comfort to each other, but more and more, they withdrew into themselves. Grey, she knew, needed to be on his own.

"Greevie," she started, but he stopped her with a shake of his head.

"I'll see you later," he said, and drove off.

For an hour, Pippin tried to work on the inn's website content, but she couldn't concentrate. The constant crack of the nail gun, the whir of the circular saw, and the hammering grated on her nerves. She'd holed herself up in her little office, but the walls and doors in-between her and the work being done in different areas of the house didn't create enough of a barrier. She tried her earbuds, but they weren't noise cancelling so the sounds penetrated with ease. Finally, with an exasperated sigh, she grabbed her wallet and keys from her purse, *The Odyssey*, and went to the garage, pulling out her bike, dropping it all into the wicker handlebar basket. She looked around for the dog, hoping to catch a glimpse, but their progress the day before hadn't brought the pup back to Sea Captain's Inn. "I'm going to win you over," Pippin said quietly, as if her words could travel on the breeze and circle around the dog.

She pedaled down town. The library was on the right and The Open Door Bookshop was on the left, and Devil's Brew Café right next to it. She could sit quietly and think in either spot, but in the end, she opted for the library. She wasn't ready to talk about the book magic she'd witnessed at The Open Door in front of Jamie, the bookshop guy. Once she'd seen the floating words, and read the passage about the sirens, she'd grabbed the book and run. She didn't know if Jamie had seen what she'd seen, but she wasn't ready to explain it if he had. How could she when she didn't understand it herself?

She'd started to tell Grey about it the day before but changed her mind at the last minute. What if she really had imagined it? No, she needed to see if it would happen again.

She locked up her bike and went into the library, disappointed to see that Daisy wasn't at the circulation desk. Harold looked up from a catalog he'd been reading and greeted her with a smile. "Morning. Can I help you with something?"

She held up her copy of *The Odyssey*. "Can I just sit for a while and read?"

He waved a hand. "Yeah, of course. That's what we're here for."

"Great, thanks," Pippin said. She looked left, then right, not sure which way to go.

Harold pointed to Pippin's right. "Armchairs are in that corner. Private study rooms upstairs. A few tables in the back."

Pippin thanked him and headed for the armchairs. She found them behind freestanding shelving that housed books for sale, courtesy of the Friends of the Library. The chairs were dark gray with single needle stitching around the flared arms, seats, and backs. The soft fabric made them look rich and inviting. She sank into one of them, dropping her purse on the floor by her side. She crossed her legs and opened the book on her lap.

Her heart pounded and her hands shook. She held the book out in front of her and closed her eyes. "Show me something," she whispered, as if some force could hear her and would give her all the answers she sought.

She opened her eyes, opened the book, and studied the page. Nothing happened. No words undulated. The letters didn't darken.

She tried again, repeating the actions of holding out the book in front of her, closing her eyes, and whispering, "Tell me a secret."

Once again, she opened the book to a random page, and once again, she couldn't make any sense of the passages she read. She slammed it shut. Maybe she really had imagined it.

"Hey! I didn't know you were here."

Pippin started, dropping the book on her lap. Daisy

smiled at her and sat in the armchair opposite. "I forgot to even ask! You found a copy at The Open Door?" she said, nodding toward the open book.

"Yeah. I got the last copy."

"Jamie keeps pretty good stock. He pretty much meets everyone's needs. He's got used books, new books, old records and vintage games, plus he has a whole separate room in back for rare books and documents. He does a lot of business online. Whatever you need, if he doesn't have it, he'll find it for you." Daisy glanced at *The Odyssey* again. "Do you think that's the book your mom had? Well, not *that* book, but you know, the book?"

Pippin glanced down at the book in her lap. It had fallen open when she dropped it. Instantly, her eyes zoomed in on a particular passage, the letters lifting slightly from the page as if they were hovering just above it. She gasped before she could stop herself.

"What is it?" Daisy asked. "Are you okay?"

Pippin didn't take her eyes off the page. When she spoke, her voice was low and hoarse. "Do you see that?"

Pippin could feel Daisy staring at her, could imagine her mouth gaping, could hear the puzzlement in her voice. She left her chair and perched on the table, gently laying one hand on Pippin's shoulder. "See what?"

"That." She pointed to the passage. She swallowed as she started to read. The letters jumbled and the words came out slowly, as if she was sounding them out. "The rest of you...who are...my eager...comp..." she began, but then stopped and shoved it closer to Daisy, who finished the passage aloud.

The rest of you, who are my eager

companions, wait here,
while I, with my own ship and companions
that are in it,
go and find out about these people, and I
learn what they are,
whether they are savage and violent,
and without justice,
or hospitable to strangers and with minds
that are godly.

"I DON'T KNOW what it means," Pippin muttered.

"What *what* means?" Daisy asked. "That passage?"

Pippin looked up at her. She spoke hesitantly. Nervously. Daisy was going to think she'd lost her mind. Her new friend would probably become a former friend, but she had to ask. "Did you see the words? Did you see them peel off the page?"

Daisy gave a slow blink, cocking her head. She held the back of her hand against Pippin's forehead. "Are you feeling all right?"

Pippin knocked the hand away, gaining conviction. "I'm fine. Daisy. Did you see the words lift off the page?"

Slowly, Daisy shook her head. "It's just a book. I saw the section you pointed to."

Pippin exhaled, her breath shaky. "No. It's not just a book. It's trying to tell me something. I don't understand it, but I know it's true."

Daisy returned to her chair, but the concern was still clear on her face. "What's going on, Pippin?"

Pippin's mind reeled. Should she tell Daisy? Rumors in small towns ran rampant. Did she risk being known as the crazy lady in the haunted house if it got around that she thought a book was trying to communicate with her?

Once again, Daisy leaned toward her over the table between the chairs. "You can trust me."

The fact was, Pippin wanted someone to confide in. She made up her mind. She was going to trust Daisy.

DAISY LISTENED with rapt attention as Pippin told her the story Cora and Lily had shared so long ago, the story she'd been remembering more and more of. Artemis and Siobhan Lane, crossing the Atlantic from Ireland to America. Trevor dying at sea. Ruth knowing it was going to happen.

"Wait." Daisy stopped her. "So you're saying you're destined to die in childbirth and Grey is going to drown in the ocean?

Pippin shrugged helplessly. "If it's true." She placed her hand on the open page of the book. "Which it seems it is."

"So you can never have kids, and Grey can never go on a boat."

Pippin's thoughts shot back to her mother and her insistence that Pippin and Grey never go on Leo's boat. And then to the fact that Cassie had died giving birth to their little brother who hadn't survived.

"It's a curse," Daisy said.

Pippin looked gratefully at her. "You believe me, then?"

Daisy's hand covered her mouth and she tapped her index and middle finger against her cheek. She glanced around before settling her attention back on Pippin. "There have always been rumors about your mom. About your family."

Pippin's heart climbed to her throat. "What kind of rumors?"

As if she'd made a sudden decision, Daisy jumped up and said, "Come with me."

Pippin just managed to tuck the copy of *The Odyssey* into her purse when Daisy pulled her up out of her chair, then hurried through the stacks and past the circulation desk. "Harold, I'll be back in a little while. Hold down the fort!"

Harold stared wide-eyed at them and nodded as Daisy grabbed Pippin's hand and careened through the door, down the steps, and across the street.

"What are you doing?" Pippin asked, managing to pull back, a counterweight to Daisy's forward motion.

"We have to talk to Mr. McAdams," Daisy said through a panting breath.

"Who?"

"From the bookshop."

Pippin's mind whirled. What did Jamie have to do with her mother?

She didn't have time to ask before Daisy barreled through the door of the bookshop. Ruby leaned against the checkout counter. Pippin thought Daisy would stop there to ask where Jamie was, but she passed it right by, dragging Pippin behind her.

Pippin managed a quick look, seeing Ruby's copper honey eyes going wide as she stared after them. At the same time, Pippin caught a glimpse of Jamie shelving a book from the stack he held in his arms. "There—" she started, but stopped as Daisy plunged through yet another door, this one leading to a storage room. A flight of stairs led up, which Daisy took two at a time. Pippin scrambled to keep up. "Where are we going?" she asked. "Jamie was out there."

Finally, Daisy slowed as they reached the top. She

stopped in front of the first of three doors in the short hall-way. "We aren't here to see Jamie," she said, catching her breath.

"Then who—"

The door suddenly swung open, and the words froze on Pippin's lips. An elderly man stood before them, his blue eyes alert and clear, not a hunch in his shoulders or a tremble in his hands.

"Mr. McAdams," Daisy said. "Sorry to barge in."

The man gave Daisy a bemused smile. He spoke slowly. Deliberately. "Not at all, Ms. Santiago. Is everything all right?"

"With me? Yes. Perfectly fine. But I brought someone to meet you."

She pulled Pippin forward so they stood side by side facing the man in the threshold of the door. His eyes angled down on the outsides and were mere slits. Pippin couldn't say if they made him look sinister or contemplative.

"This is Pippin Hawthorne," Daisy said. "Pippin *Lane* Hawthorne."

Pippin's eyes shot over to Daisy. Why the emphasis on Lane?

Whatever it meant, it had the desired impact on the man. Mr. McAdams gave Pippin a long, hard look. After a moment, he stood back and opened the door wide. "I've been waiting for you. Come in."

Pippin breathed in the fresh scent of the man as she passed by him. It was like the ocean breeze after a hearty rain. It was familiar and set her at ease. She glanced around at the living space. It was a large room that had been converted into a flat with a framed opening between the living area and the bedroom. A collection of black and white photographs hung above the full-sized bed that was covered with a dark gray bedspread. It was simple and sleek. The symmetrical room had windows over two small nightstands on either side of the bed that faced the Sound. The color scheme carried throughout the entire flat with a modern gray couch, low profile white chairs, a black coffee table, and black open-backed bookshelves against one entire wall, the shelves filled with books and the occasional knick-knack. Mostly old books, Pippin noted.

A small kitchen was in the back corner with a table and two chairs up against the wall under the open window that faced the public library. A feeling came over her...a feeling that she'd been here before.

"Have a seat," Mr. McAdams said, gesturing to the couch. "Something to drink?"

"I'm good," Pippin said.

Daisy shook her head. "No thanks."

"Straight to business. Right. What can I do for you?"

Pippin couldn't place the man's age. He was dapper and poised with his snowy white hair and distinguished, closely shaved goatee. His receding hairline revealed a forehead marked with horizontal lines. Puffy half-moons hung under his eyes, but he smiled and spoke in a smooth tenor. He wore a black sweater with a three-quarter zip and collar. Yes, Pippin thought, dapper was definitely the word to describe him.

He perched on the edge of one of the chairs, his gaze intent on Pippin. He drew his faded brows together as he studied her and before Daisy could say whatever it was she'd planned to, he spoke. "You look just like her."

Pippin felt a sudden pulsing in her temples. In her gut, she knew what the answer to her question would be, but she asked anyway. "Like who?"

"Cassandra Hawthorne né Lane, of course. You are her daughter, I presume."

Pippin drew in and expelled tremulous breaths and her mind worked. She had so many questions but settled for the obvious one. "You knew my mother?"

"I knew her quite well, actually. Her time came to an end far too soon. But then that is the curse of the Lane women, is it not?"

Pippin stared. "You know about...us?"

"I do," Mr. McAdams said. "Your parents told me everything. They thought I could help stop it from happening to your mother, and to you and your brother. Alas, I could not. The power of a curse is very strong. Very strong indeed."

That single word rattled around in Pippin's head. *Curse. Curse. Curse.* It's what Cora had said so long ago, and now this man was confirming it. Maybe it was all true.

"I was very sorry to hear about the discovery on Leo's boat," Mr. McAdams said. "Quite a shock, I'm sure, after so many years."

His comment struck Pippin as odd. Almost as if it was an afterthought. "It was," she said, then pivoted back to his words before his condolence. "How would you have been able to stop the...the curse?"

He glanced to the side, as if to gather his thoughts. After a moment, he looked back at the two women. "I don't know that I could have. I am an historian, and I dabble in genealogy, you see. That's all. I helped Cassandra trace some of her ancestry. We thought that if we knew where or how the curse started, we would have a better chance at stopping it."

Once again, Pippin's cousins and the story they'd told her about their great-great-grandfather came to mind. The years had faded so many of the details. "What did you find out?" she asked.

"Your parents kept the information we found. I don't know what happened to it after...after they passed. It was a lot of years ago." He tapped his temple. "I have an old man's mind. I don't remember things like I used to. As such, I do not recall many specifics."

Pippin paid attention to language. The fact that Mr. McAdams had used the word *many* was telling. "But you do remember some things?"

"There were rumors about your mother here in Devil's Cove," he said. "It was said that she could tell the future. That she had a magical gift."

Pippin stared at Mr. McAdams. "Surely you don't believe that."

"Why wouldn't I believe it?" he asked, his eyes narrowing more than they already naturally did. "Do you know the meaning of the name Cassandra?"

She knew the meaning of her own name—foreigner or stranger—but she'd never thought to look up her mother's name. "No, I don't," she said, feeling woefully ill-informed about her own family. Why hadn't Grandmother Faye shared any of this with her?

"In Greek mythology, Cassandra forewarned people about tragedy, doom, and disaster," Mr. McAdams said. "She could see the future but was cursed so people didn't believe her prophecies. She couldn't say whether or not her parents —Annabel and Edgar, if I'm not mistaken—?"

Pippin nodded.

"—whether they knew the meaning of the name Cassandra."

"It could have been a coincidence," Daisy said, speaking for the first time since they'd come into Mr. McAdams's flat.

Mr. McAdams slowly shook his head. "I do not believe in coincidences, Ms. Santiago. I believe that Annabel and

Edgar Lane bestowed Cassandra with her name to reflect her gift—or curse, as the case may be." He looked at Pippin. "I suspect it was a reminder of the power your mother held."

Pippin thought back to that day on the street and the open book. Her mother's sobs echoed in her ears. "That book told her something," she said, her voice low and tentative.

"Ah yes, Homer's *Odyssey*. That was the day I knew your mother was a bibliomancer."

Heat flooded Pippin's head as she looked from Daisy to Mr. McAdams. "I'm sorry, a biblio-what?"

Daisy spun to face Pippin on the couch. "A bibliomancer. The gift of bibliomancy dates back centuries. It is the practice of foretelling the future or discovering hidden truths using a divine book."

"*The Odyssey* is not a divine book," Pippin said, yet if she was to believe what Mr. McAdams had said, Homer's book had held information for her mother about Leo, and it had also conveyed something to Pippin. Just like Odysseus, her father had returned home after twenty years. The only difference was that her father had been dead and had no wife or children to reclaim.

"No, but bibliomancy is similar to stichomancy," Daisy said. "Stichomancy dates back to the 17th century. It's divination by random lines in a book. The prophecies don't have to come from divine books."

Pippin looked at Daisy wide-eyed as if to ask, *How do you know all this?* In response, Daisy put her open palm to her chest, gave a sheepish smile, and shrugged. "Librarian."

"So being a bibliomancer, it was like my mother's superpower?" Pippin asked Mr. McAdams.

"That is one way to put it," he said. "Would I be correct in saying it is yours, as well?"

Pippin leaned back on the couch, resting the back of her head against the hard edge of the cushion. "I don't know."

Mr. McAdams kept his gaze on Pippin, unwavering and intense. "Tell me what has happened."

She held up her copy of *The Odyssey*. It felt hot in her hands. She didn't know if it was genuinely hot or if she imagined it. "I'm pretty sure this is the book my mother saw that day."

"Well not that exact copy—" Daisy interjected.

Mr. McAdams nodded sagely. "Of course not." He rotated a finger in the air and said, "Continue."

"My memories are blurry," Pippin continued. "I remember the air turning cold. My mother pulled me across the street. She always went at a diagonal, so we didn't walk on the sidewalk next to the library or the bookshop. A woman crossed and a book dropped. It fell open. My mom read something on that page, and then she started crying and saying, *No, no, no*. Over and over again. I remember feeling scared. I didn't know what was happening."

"I saw it happen from here," he said, pointing to the kitchen table and the window above it that faced the library. "I'd come up and poured myself a drink. The weather underwent a rapid change. Fog rolled in. That's when I saw your mother and you on the street. I saw the woman pass, the book drop, and your mother's reaction. I went down to her immediately. She was very...out of sorts, shall we say? I brought her up here until she calmed down."

Pippin's eyes went wide. Her eyes darted around the flat again, that feeling of familiarity overcoming her again.

Mr. McAdams chuckled lightly. "Yes, my dear. You've been here before."

"Oh my God, you sensed it, didn't you?" Daisy said. Her

voice dropped to a whisper. "*Ay dios mio*," she said, and she made the sign of the cross.

"It was, indeed, a copy of *The Odyssey* your mother saw that day. Good deduction on your part."

"It was Daisy," Pippin said, finding her voice.

"No, no," Daisy said. "We figured it out together. Your memories and my book knowledge."

"Whatever the case," Mr. McAdams said, "here you are." He pointed to the book in Pippin's lap. "Tell me about it. Surely not your father's. His things must be long gone."

Pippin swallowed, the hairs on her arms standing up, a chill niggling at the base of her head. She'd been questioning whether what she'd experienced was actually real. Now here this man was, telling her it was. "I bought it downstairs," she said. "And I, um, I saw the words lift off the page."

"Twice," Daisy said, and Pippin nodded. "Right, twice."

Mr. McAdams's brows reached toward his far away hairline, crinkling the lines on his forehead. "The words lifted off the page, you say?" Pippin nodded, and he said, "Interesting."

"Is that supposed to happen?" she asked.

"There is no *supposed* to. It isn't as if there are studies on bibliomancy. It's widely believed to be along the lines of mythology. That is to say, not real."

"But you said bibliomancers use divine books. Like the Bible? The Koran? The Torah—"

"It is true. The idea of bibliomancy is that a divine book guides one. With stichomancy, as Daisy so eloquently put it a moment ago, the book need not be divine. I believe you— and the Lane women—have the gift of both. But how do you use it? Must you have a worksheet? Do you write down a question, open a random book to a random page, run your finger across said page, and like the roll of the dice, this passage will guide you toward the answer to your question? No! Certainly not.

"It's true that any lay person could use this method to reflect and seek an answer. Robert Browning did before marrying Elizabeth Barrett, for example. But your mystique is more than just aleatory guidance. Your gift—for I do believe your bibliomancy is a gift and not a curse—delves deeper into truths."

Pippin's heart raced as she listened. She zeroed in on one of the ideas Mr. McAdams presented. "How can it be a gift, and not a curse, if it results in the deaths of the men and women in my family?"

"The bibliomancy itself does not cause the deaths. It simply reveals what will be. We must find the secret behind it," Mr. McAdams said. "This is what your parents sought. It is what I was helping them with."

"Helping them how?" she asked. "What did you find out?"

"We traced some your mother's ancestry."

Pippin processed what he was saying, but she was missing something. "Are you saying that someone or something started this curse?"

Mr. McAdams nodded slowly. "That, my dear, is exactly what I am saying."

Chapter 13

"From now on, it is our task to suspect each and every one amongst us."

~Agatha Christie, from *And Then There Were None*

*P*ippin hadn't been able to hear any more from Mr. McAdams the day before. She'd needed to think. He'd asked her to meet with him at Devil's Brew Café the following morning. Daisy had offered to go with her, but this was something Pippin had to do on her own. She dressed quickly in a floral spring dress and her white sneakers. She pulled her hair into a bun, grabbed a banana, and was heading out to the garage to pull out her bike when the doorbell rang.

Another lookie-loo, she thought, this one bold enough to actually come to the door. She couldn't even count the number of people who drove by so slowly, staring at the house through their rolled down windows, or the passerby who stopped to stare. The old abandoned house had come to life in the last few months, and everyone on the island of Devil's Cove was watching the ugly duckling turn into a swan.

The doorbell rang again just as Pippin reached the landing. She pulled the door open, pasting a smile on her face. A man stood there, hands in his pockets, head tilted back so he could look up at the porch roof. He looked at her and grinned, his round face crinkling, crow's feet sprouting from the outsides of his eyes. He was about her height, but stocky and with brown hair which was solidly gray at the temples. "Fine job you're doing here," he said, his voice full and loud. He spoke like he was talking to invisible people in the back of a room. "I pass by nearly every day. The transformation has brought it back to its former glory."

The man looked vaguely familiar, but she couldn't place him. From the library or the café, perhaps? She opened her mouth to speak, but he chuckled and carried on before she had a chance. "Sorry. You're probably wondering who I am. Jed Riordin," he said, bowing his head as if she were royalty. "And you're Pippin Hawthorne, if I'm not mistaken."

Jed Riordin. It wasn't a name she recognized, but then again, why would it be? It was the strangest feeling, to be known by complete strangers in a town you hardly remembered. "I am," Pippin said.

"I knew your parents."

She'd heard those four little words so frequently lately, but they still made her breath catch. Anyone who knew Leo and Cassie felt like a gift. They could help round out her image of them. Another thought came to her and her heart raced. Could this be the mystery man who'd left the letter for her and Grey?

"When I heard they found your father," he continued, his voice quieting, "I'd planned to stop by. Offer my condolences. But I didn't want to disturb. It was a blow. I never did understand why he'd just vanished. Now, I guess, it makes sense."

"Does it?" Pippin asked. Her father's death still made no sense to her.

Jed blinked. "Ah. I take your meaning. No, his death certainly doesn't make sense. What I meant was, Leo never struck me as the type of man who'd shirk his responsibilities. You. Your brother. His crew. This house." His eyes softened, as if he was remembering some moment he'd spent there. "Your mother's legacy."

What a strange choice of word. "Her legacy?"

"You know. The way she..." He trailed off, waving one hand around almost apologetically. "Your father spent so much time researching. Trying to figure it all out."

Pippin stopped her jaw from dropping open. This man knew. He knew about her mother's gift. About her father's efforts to understand it. She checked her watch. She'd be a little bit late for her meeting with Mr. McAdams, but it couldn't be helped. She stepped back, opening the door wider. "Would you like to come in?"

His face lit up again and he followed her inside. When he spoke again, she could almost hear his voice bouncing off the walls. "I would love to see what you've done with the place."

Pippin led him through the downstairs on a tour, talking through the renovations she and Grey, and their team of three, had done. She ended with the empty room that had been her father's study.

He scanned the room. "Everything's gone?" he asked. "The books? The ships? The bottles? The maps?"

So Jed Riordin hadn't been one of the many people who'd snuck through the broken windows to check out the abandoned house. If he had, he'd know that the place was empty. She didn't understand why he'd be so aghast. It had been twenty years, after all. "My grandparents had the house emptied out not long after we moved in with them."

Jed frowned. "He had some classic books, from what I remember. What a shame."

She couldn't agree more, but something about him asking at all bothered her. First the sheriff. Bev and Mick. Mr. McAdams. And now this guy. Why did so many people comment or ask about her father's belongings? The few memories she had of Leo always featured books or boats. Once the boat was hauled off, there would be nothing left of Leo Hawthorne.

Her brain stuck on the word research. "What about his research?" she asked.

"He was a passionate guy. Half his life was spent in books," he said. "Funny since your mom wasn't much of a reader, from what I remember."

The hair on the back of Pippin's neck went up at that comment. "How did you say you knew my dad?"

If he caught the suspicion in her voice, he didn't let on. Instead, his face lit up again, like a lantern turning on from the inside, the light slowly flowing outward. "From the marina. My boat was docked a few slips down from his. Of course, *I'm* just a recreational boater. Your dad was the real deal. A sailor meant for the sea. He had this collection of little boats." He raised an eyebrow. "All of it gone?"

Pippin tried to call up a memory of the bookshelves in her father's study, but it was elusive. Just out of reach. "All of it," she commented, unable to summon up any other response. Her memories of her father were few, and they faded with each passing year. She knew he loved boats because he'd been a fisherman and had owned one. She knew he'd grown up sailing with his father. She knew he loved books because she remembered him sitting in his study, reading. She knew he loved Tolkien because of her name. But these were more facts than memories, and they felt hollow.

"Did my father give you anything?" she asked, thinking about the letter from the front door. She regretted it the second she'd spoken. It was reckless. This man hadn't mentioned the letter. Hadn't given any indication that he wanted to pass something of her father's to her and Grey. And if he wasn't the person who'd asked to meet them at the pier, she'd just played a card in her hand. She'd revealed that she thought her father and given *something* to *someone*.

Two deep vertical lines formed between Jed Riordin's eyebrows. "Like what?"

Pippin thought quickly. "Like I said, my grandparents got rid of everything. If any of my father's old friends have anything of his, well, I guess I'm just hoping I can get them back."

It wasn't a lie. Jed's face softened, those vertical lines leaving only a faint indentation. "Sadly, no. You might try Bev and Mick at the marina. Devil's Cove Landing. Never know. They might still have something laying around."

"Good idea," she said. She didn't tell him that she'd already been to see Bev and Mick and neither one had mentioned having any of her father's things.

"What are you going to do with the place?" Jed asked. "It's a big house for one person."

Pippin was glad for the change of subject. "Sea Captain's Inn," she said, feeling the way the words sounded on her tongue. The more she said them, the more right they felt. "The goal is to open in a month or so, just in time for the summer tourists."

"Brilliant! You'll make a killing." His eyes opened wide the moment that last word left his mouth, as if he realized it was in poor taste. "Mmm, it will be in high demand, I have no doubt."

She hoped he was right. The money they'd put into the renovations didn't compare to the sweat equity they'd invested, especially Grey. Her brother trusted her vision. She didn't want to let him down. "Thank you, Jed," she said. "I hope you come back to the open house. I'll be posting flyers about it to get the word out."

He grinned, his mouth stretching wide. "I'll be on the lookout," he boomed. "Now, I'd best be on my way and leave you to your day. Thanks for the tour."

"Nice meeting you, Jed," Pippin said, and she found that she meant it. Sometimes she felt as if she were connected to a chain, and on another chain, far away, were her parents. Each person she met who'd known Leo and Cassie felt like a link that would eventually bring the two sides of the chains together.

MR. MCADAMS SAT at a four-top table in Devil's Brew, a steaming cup of coffee in front of him. He looked just as débonnaire today as he had the day before. He wore a dark gray sports coat over a lighter gray collared shirt. The open neck revealed a tuft of white chest hair. He was a good-looking man now, so Pippin imagined that in his salad days, he'd been a real ladies' man.

A little girl, maybe five or six, sat at a table across from Mr. McAdams, a crayon in her hand. Sweet. She was so focused on her coloring, nothing was going to bother her.

Jamie suddenly appeared next to Pippin. "Oh. Hello," she said.

"Hello to you."

With his wire-rimmed glasses and his button-down chambray shirt, the sleeves rolled up over his forearms, he looked like the quintessential college professor that all the girls fell for. A scene from *Raiders of the Lost Ar*k came to mind—the one with the girl in Indiana Jones's classroom blinking, the words *Love You* written on her eyelids. Just like Indy, Jamie seemed unaware of his good looks and the way every woman in the café stared at him.

Mr. McAdams waved them both over. "Have a seat, Ms. Hawthorne," he said.

Jamie pulled out a chair for her next to the wall and directly across from Mr. McAdams. "Ms. Hawthorne," he said.

"Um..." What was going on? She looked at Mr. McAdams, eyebrows raised.

The man gestured to Jamie. "My grandson, Ms. Hawthorne."

Pippin drew back. "Oh."

Jamie sat and turned his chair slightly so he was angled toward her and she noticed the amber rim around the irises of his brown eyes. "So. Your name is Pippin," he said.

Why was Jamie even there? She looked at Mr. McAdams for an answer, but the elder man didn't offer up an explanation. "It is," Pippin said.

"Was it your mom or your dad?"

"Was what my mom or dad?" The words came out with the force of driving a shovel into the ground.

He lifted his glasses up with his thumb and forefinger, closing his eyes and pressing his fingertips into the corners of his eyes. "Sorry," he said. "That was insensitive."

She sighed, giving her head a little shake. Giving him a break. "It wasn't really."

Jamie let his glasses drop back into place and adjusted them. "I just figured with you named Pippin and your brother Grey that either your mom or your dad had to be a Tolkien fan."

"You'd be right," she said. "It was my dad. He would spend hours reading all these old books in his office. He was always passionate about them, but more so after my mom died. It was how he dealt with it. Tolkien was a comfort for him, I think."

"Please excuse my grandson," Mr. McAdams said to her. "He is also a Tolkien fan. Has been since he was in elementary school."

"Middle school, actually, and then it was only *The Hobbit*," Jamie said. "Waited till high school for *Lord of the Rings*."

Mr. McAdams threw up his hands in mock surrender. "I stand corrected."

"I guess that's why you work in a bookstore," Pippin said.

"I *own* a bookstore."

Mr. McAdams cleared his throat. His head tilted to one side and his forehead furrowed.

Jamie wagged a finger between him and his grandfather. "*We* own the bookshop."

"Jamie is a scholar of Irish literature," Mr. McAdams said.

"*Medieval* Irish," Jamie corrected.

Pippin cocked one eyebrow. Was this guy being pretentious, arrogant, or just factual? Mr. McAdams didn't miss a beat. "Sadly, there is not a robust job market for people with Jamie's expertise," Mr. McAdams said, answering her question.

"No, I guess there wouldn't be." Pippin looked at her watch, then around the café. It was half full with people sipping their flat whites and cappuccinos, chatting with friends or reading.

Jamie adjusted his chair again, giving himself room to cross his legs. He leaned one forearm on the arm of the chair and held his heavy white mug of coffee with his other hand. "My grandfather asked me to join you. Are you okay with that?"

Pippin couldn't fathom what a bookshop owner and scholar of medieval Irish Literature could tell her about her parents, but she nodded her assent.

"Let the girl get a cup of coffee first, my boy." Mr. McAdams raised his arm overhead. "A moment, Ms. Perkins, if you please."

Just like that, Ruby appeared. She was just as stunning today as she'd been every time Pippin had seen her. Her hair was pulled back with a wide head wrap, her spirally curls like a halo around her head. She wore loose jeans that sat at her hips, a cream-colored peasant blouse, and sandals. Outside it was chilly, but inside Ruby made it seem like it was already summer.

"What would you like, Ms. Hawthorne?" Mr. McAdams asked.

What Pippin *wanted* was information—specifically whatever information the elder Mr. McAdams had about her parents.

"To eat or drink," Jamie said, as if he could read her mind and knew her thoughts had strayed away from the café's offerings.

"A caramel latte," she said, ordering the same as she had last time."

"And one of your blueberry scones," Mr. McAdams said.

"My treat."

"You got it." Ruby said. She gave Pippin a pointed look. "Lemme know if these guys give you any trouble." Then she winked and sauntered away.

"That is a smart one," Mr. McAdams said, nodding at Ruby's retreating figure. "She could help you get good and connected here in Devil's Cove."

"I heard that!" Ruby called over her shoulder. "And he's one hundred percent correct on both counts."

Pippin laughed, feeling just a touch more at ease than she had been a moment ago. A moment later, Jamie spoke up. "I grew up in Wilmington, so obviously I wasn't around when your parents lived here—"

"Obviously," Pippin said dryly, but at least they were getting to the point. And she felt there had to be a point.

"—but my grandfather filled me in on what he remembered about them when you showed up."

"He told me some of it yesterday. About someone—or something—starting the curse my family is burdened with."

"That's what we think, although we don't know for sure," Jamie said. He glanced over at the little girl who was still coloring. She sensed his attention on her and looked up, grinning and fluttering her fingers in a little wave. She held up the coloring book to show him her progress and he gave her a thumbs up and a wink.

He knew her. Oh! Pippin felt slow to make the connection. He was the little girl's dad. For some reason, she felt a pang of disappointment. She wasn't interested in Jamie. She didn't *do* relationships. But now he was definitely off-limits, because where there was a little girl, there was a mother.

Mr. McAdams cleared his throat again—a habit he had when he had something to interject. "This is why I wanted

Jamie here. In this instance, his knowledge of the very obscure medieval Irish literature may be an asset, you see."

Pippin looked from one man to the other. How in the world could medieval Irish literature be an asset to anything? "I don't understand."

In response, Mr. McAdams withdrew a folded sheet of paper from the inside pocket of his coat. He placed it on the table and slid it over to her just as Ruby returned with a white cup and saucer, a ribbon of steam reaching toward the ceiling, and on a plate a triangular scone.

"Thank you," Pippin said to her, but as she stared at the unfolded paper in her hands, her appetite vanished.

"Sure thing," Ruby said, but she didn't budge. Instead, she looked over Pippin's shoulder at the paper.

"It's a family tree," Pippin said. "*My* family tree."

"It is indeed," Mr. McAdams said. "Your mother told me the story of your great-great-grandparents' passage to America, your grandmother Siobhan's death in 1924."

Pippin traced her fingers over the names as Mr. McAdams mentioned each person. They were the same people Cora and Lily had told them about when she and Grey had been nine years old. These people had been important enough to Pippin's mother that she'd told this man. Sought his help.

"Do you know why Artemis and Siobhan Lane left Ireland, my dear?" Mr. McAdams asked.

Slowly, Pippin shook her head. "My mother never mentioned them. I visited my great aunt and my cousins in Oregon only once. That's the first time—the only time—I've ever heard anything about them."

"Apparently your mom thought they left Ireland because of the curse," Jamie said.

She looked at Mr. McAdams for confirmation. He nodded. "That's correct."

Ruby plopped down in the chair next to Mr. McAdams, propping her elbows on the table, her fists under her chin. "That's why they left, or that's what Pippin's mom thought?"

"Have a seat, Ruby," Jamie said, his tone droll.

"Thanks, I will." She smirked, once again giving Pippin a quick wink.

"Cassandra *suspected* that it had to do with the curse. She had no proof, however. Leo was determined to find that proof." Mr. McAdams directed his steely gaze to Pippin. "Those old books your father spent his time reading? I believe that had everything to do with his research."

Jamie uncrossed his legs and leaned toward her. "Do you have his books?"

God, how she wished she did. "There's nothing left," she said.

Jamie heaved a disappointed sigh and sat back in his chair. Mr. McAdams pursed his lips. Ruby shrugged. "Bummer."

"That does sum it up, doesn't it?" Mr. McAdams mused.

A middle-aged couple and their teenage children entered the café. Ruby stood reluctantly and scurried away to help them. A moment later, Pippin said, "I still don't understand what medieval Irish literature has to do with any of this."

Mr. McAdams drummed the pads of his fingers on the table. "Cassandra remembered overhearing a conversation between her Aunt Rose and some unknown person. She didn't recall the details, only that there were Lanes who used the books of Chaucer."

Pippin shrugged, feeling ignorant and helpless. "Chaucer?"

"Geoffrey Chaucer, the father of English literature?" Jamie said. Pippin shook her head and frowned, so he continued. "He was an English poet in the Middle Ages. Circa 1400. He wrote *The Canterbury Tales*. Buried in Poets' Corner in Westminster Abbey."

"It's the verbiage that is important," Mr. McAdams said. "Your mother remembers your aunt saying the Lanes *used* the books of Chaucer. One could surmise from this phrasing that the Lanes used the books as a guide."

"Like a bibliomancer," Pippin said.

Both men nodded. "Like a bibliomancer," Mr. McAdams said.

The words hung between them. Hung over Pippin, pressing down on her. This lore surrounding her family wasn't some made up legend. It was real. A chill swept over her body. She reached for her coffee cup to warm her, but her hands trembled. Coffee sloshed over the edge of the cup and onto the saucer.

"Hey." Jamie touched her forearm. "Are you okay?"

Was she? "I don't know." It was the most honest answer she could give. Her family was truly cursed.

Finally, Mr. McAdams spoke again. "There is one other thing."

Pippin expelled the breath she'd been holding. "What's that?"

"Your mother had a letter. It was written in some sort of code. Your father showed it to me. It looked to be Old Irish. This was, of course, before Jamie was here and educated in his field."

Pippin's gaze fell to Mr. McAdams sports coat. Was he going to pull this letter from the inside pocket as he had the family tree?

Mr. McAdams clucked. "I don't have it. I wondered if you'd unearthed it amongst your father's things."

Her thoughts immediately shifted to the mysterious note she'd received. Her father had given that person something. Could it be this letter?

"We don't have any of my father's things," she said again. "Everything's gone."

Ruby came up to the table holding two fresh mugs of coffee. She set them down, sliding one to Mr. McAdams, the other to Jamie. "Maybe the letter told about a buried treasure," she said.

Mr. McAdams chuckled. "Ah, if only it were so simple, but I fear not. Real life rarely follows the plot of a blockbuster movie."

"If I find the letter, or document, or whatever it is, I'll let you know," Pippin said. She needed a little time to process her conversations with the McAdams men.

"You're leaving?" Ruby asked.

"Yeah. I need to go. There's a stray dog I'm trying to woo."

Mr. McAdams nodded. "We'll talk again soon."

Ruby grabbed her coffee and scone. "Let me get this to go for you." She disappeared behind the barista counter, returning a minute later with a fresh latte in a disposable cup and the scone in a small paper bag. "Let me know if you need anything," she said so only she could hear. "The McAdams boys can be intense."

"Thanks," Pippin said, thinking she just might take Ruby up on that.

Chapter 14

"There is nothing so far removed from us to be beyond our reach, or so far hidden that we cannot discover it."

~Rene Descartes

*D*aisy and Ruby showed up the next afternoon bearing gifts. Ruby held two disposable cups of coffee. Daisy held her own, as well as a tote bag slung over her shoulder.

Pippin greeted them at the door, but a movement at the lavender and teal house across the street caught her eye. Once again, she'd swear there was a face in the upstairs window, but just as she was about to ask Ruby and Daisy if they saw it, the curtain dropped back into place. God, she needed to get a grip.

"Where can we sit?" Daisy asked. She withdrew a yellow book from her tote. It was covered with illustrations of happy looking flower boxes, friendly bumblebees, and cartoony butterflies.

Everything else left Pippin's mind for the time being. "You brought it!"

Daisy bounced on the balls of her feet. "I brought it!"

Pippin led them through the house and to the back deck, which overlooked the Sound, just beyond the barrier islands. She'd bought a few pots, some potting soil, and had planted basil, cilantro, flat leaf parsley, as well as a few flowers. She had more she wanted to do, but had reined herself in. She had to work a little bit at a time.

Ruby and Daisy oohed and awed. The three of them stood at the railing for a minute, breathing in the salty air, looking down at the sandy beach and the clear blue-green water beyond.

"Breathtaking." Ruby seemed to sigh the word as she tilted her head back and took a deep breath. "I'd live my life right here if I could."

Pippin felt the same way. The Outer Banks was a sanctuary she was only starting to appreciate. Her grandparents had kept them away from the OBX, so her experience was limited. She hadn't been to Nags Head, or the Bodie Island Lighthouse. She hadn't seen the wild horses or the Wright Brothers museum. She hadn't been over to Topsail Island at the southern end of the Outer Banks. She would get to it all eventually, but right now she had Devil's Cove and it was enough.

They sat down side by side on the hanging swing Grey had put up, once again with Pippin in the middle. Daisy placed the book on Pippin's lap. "We were pretty cute kids, I have to say." She reached over and flipped the pages, stopping on one she'd marked with a Post-it Note. Underneath the plastic overlay on the open spread were eighteen pictures. They depicted various scenes from a birthday party. "This is when I turned six," Daisy said. Her finger landed on a photo of her holding a plastic bat, mid-swing, a Disney princess piñata, the intended victim.

Pippin scanned the pictures, looking at each face in the groups of kids. Once again, Daisy's finger touched the page. "That's you, isn't it?"

Pippin peered down at the little girl with the plump cheeks and strawberry hair, a goodie bag clutched in one fist, a cupcake in the other. She did love a good cupcake. "Yep, that's me."

Daisy pulled out another album from her tote, this one thin. She opened it up, flipping it to the page she'd tabbed so Pippin could see the photos there. In one of them, two little girls—not more than two or three years old—raced toward the receding tide of the ocean as if they could catch it.

"That's us right there," Daisy said softly, pointing to the beach.

A series of images flashed in Pippin's mind. Two little girls making sand angels in the wet sand. Building sandcastles. Latent memories surfacing. Happy memories.

Another photo showed two women on chaise lounges on the sand. They sipped from glasses of what looked like iced tea, the brims of their floppy hats obscuring their faces. Pippin's breath caught. She didn't need to see the entire face to know that the woman on the left was her mother.

Ruby reached over and gently touched Pippin's knee. Pippin wanted to jump back. To dislodge the hand. It was her instinct to block people from knowing her, but Ruby and Daisy had shown up. They'd called each other friends. She exhaled as Daisy reached into her tote again. It seemed to be as bottomless as a carpetbag you could step into and descend into the depths of some unknown world. Her hand came back out with a third album, this one about half the size of the first. She opened it up to the marked page and handed it to Pippin. In the photos on the pages, the two girls looked to be about seven or eight. They sat hunched over a game board on the floor in Leo's study. A bit of Leo's back as he sat at his desk was in the frame, the bookshelves in the background.

Pippin fluttered her fingers over his form, the backs of her eyelids pricking with new emotions. She blinked, forcing herself to look at the rest of the photo. Just like Jed Riordin had said, there were some books and miniatures of boats dotting the shelves. She counted five in all. Would the books have been a magnet for Cassie, like a bag of cookies in the pantry of someone who was dieting? Or was she able to completely ignore them like Pippin had all these years? That was a question she'd never have an answer to.

Leo's study had a different feeling than the rest of the house. The dark wood of the built-in shelves, the dark wood flooring, and the matching window frames helped create a feeling of warmth and coziness. It hadn't changed. Kyron had refinished the wood, and now it looked just as it had in the picture. Pippin had always loved spending time in there with her dad, especially when she'd snuggle up with him on the leather recliner under the sea foam afghan her mother had knitted. A sliver of green edged the photo, the memory of her mother sitting on a wicker chair on the front porch, knitting needles clicking together in a soothing rhythm.

Where was that afghan?

The next photo showed Pippin, open-mouthed and with fire in her eyes, yelling at whoever manned the camera. It had to have been Grey. Leo's face was visible this time. Her heart hammered. A barrage of emotion hit her. It looked like he'd leaned back in his chair at the commotion, but instead of the anger or frustration Pippin had expected to see on his face, she saw the edge of a smile.

"I'm sorry," Daisy said quickly, reading Pippin's face. "I didn't mean to upset you. I just...I thought you'd like to see—"

"I did...I do." Pippin scrambled to express what she was feeling, but she couldn't put it all into words. She felt the loss of her parents, the new connection with Ruby and Daisy, for her father that she'd suppressed all these years, thinking he'd abandoned them. It was too much. She started to close the book but stopped.

Something in the photo caught her eye. A trick of light? The bookshelf... It looked like...but it couldn't be. Could it?

She peered more closely.

It definitely was.

She dropped the album as she jumped up and ran inside.

～

PIPPIN STOPPED short at the doorway to her father's study. Kryon had finished sanding the floor and it was ready for staining. Thankfully he hadn't started that yet. She breathed in, conjuring up the familiar scent of the room. Her father's books. His papers. Him.

Behind her, she heard Daisy's voice. "Pippin! Wait! What are you doing? Pippin!"

She turned as they skidded to a stop, her words coming fast and furious. "Let me see that picture."

"What?" Daisy looked around, puzzled, as if whatever picture Pippin wanted would materialize. "You mean the album?"

"We left it outside," Ruby said.

"I'll get it," Daisy called over her shoulder, already on her way.

Pippin and Ruby stepped onto the dusty floors. "Cool room," Ruby said.

"Yeah," Pippin said. "It was my dad's."

"So what's the deal?"

Instead of answering, Pippin walked straight to the bookshelves. She moved to the right corner where the shelving met the perpendicular wall. She placed her open palms against the vertical piece that ran from the ceiling to the floor, then she moved to the left, studying the shelving.

Daisy barreled back in, her tote slung over her shoulder, the bulky photo albums cradled in her arms. She dropped the tote and albums to the floor, except for the last one they'd been looking at. That one she flipped it open to the page with the pictures taken in this room and held it so Pippin could see. "What is it?"

Pippin looked at the photo—the one of her scolding the photographer—then at the built-in shelves. She started feeling the wood again, looking for...something. A lever? A button?

"Does it open?" Ruby asked.

"It looks like it, doesn't it?" Pippin spoke over her shoulder, her hands still moving. She remembered asking her grandparents about the rest of her father's books. "Where's the Tolkien collection?" she mused.

Everyone, in fact, seemed interested in his books. As if he'd had more than what he'd actually left behind. Grandmother Faye thought there had been more. They'd cleared out the house of all her parents' belongings, but what if...

Her mother had refused to have books in the house. It was a rule only Leo could break, but they'd been allowed only in this room. His space, and a room where Cassie had never stepped foot in as far as Pippin could remember. Now she understood why. Cassie hadn't wanted to tempt fate. If she steered clear of books, they couldn't tell her anything.

The book had found its way to Cassie, though. How wrong Cassie had been, and Leo's fate had been foretold.

Ruby moved next to her. Started scanning the shelving. "So you think he created a secret space? Amazing."

Daisy studied the photo. "It's to your left," she said. "It's hard to tell, but I think it opens out like a door."

"I don't see any hinges." Pippin stood in front of the vertical trim that divided two sections of shelving. She curled her fingers around the edges and pulled. It didn't budge. She tried again. Nothing.

And yet... She looked more closely, running her fingernail down a razor-thin vertical line in one of the beveled groves of the wood. "It has to open," she said, more to herself than to Ruby and Daisy.

"Try the other side," Ruby said. "Opening on the right."

Pippin stepped to the side then curled her fingers around the right edge of the shelf. She exhaled, expelling all the breath she had in her. She rooted herself and with her next inhale, she pulled with all her might.

The shelf swung open. Easily. Pippin stumbled backward, bumping into Daisy and Ruby like she was a bowling ball and they were the pins. They caught her and righted her. With Ruby holding onto her left shoulder and Daisy holding onto her right shoulder, the three of them crept forward with synchronized steps. Pippin felt like they were part of the Scooby Doo gang, heading toward some supernatural killer.

The door had swung towards closed again, revealing a faint sliver of light—just as it was in the photograph. How had she never registered this when she was a child? Had she simply blocked it out, or had her father kept the secret door closed, protecting whatever lay inside?

She grabbed a hold of the door, opening it slowly, as if a goblin might have crept just out of sight and was waiting to jump out at them. None did, of course. She didn't know what she'd been expecting. A bookshelf behind the book-shelf, perhaps? She peered in and saw a narrow staircase leading up.

"Where does it go?" Ruby whispered.

She lowered her voice to match. "Let's see."

Daisy's fingers clawed into Pippin's shoulder. "I don't know…"

Pippin turned her head and saw the anxiousness written on her friend's face. "You don't have to come. You can stay down here."

Daisy looked instantly relieved. She released her hold on Pippin and nodded. "I'll keep watch."

"For what?" Ruby asked, her laugh breaking the tension. "It's Pippin's house. It's not like we're breaking and entering." She pointed up the stairs. "Plus anything spooky is probably up there."

Daisy's mouth twisted. "Holler down if you need help."

Ruby cocked one eyebrow. "If we do, you'll come to the rescue?"

Daisy waggled her head. "No, but I'll dial 911."

If it hadn't been for the fact that Leo's remains had already been discovered, Pippin might have been wary of what they'd find. As it was, she was more curious.

They were still standing at the base of the hidden stair-case. "Did your grandparents know about—" Ruby waved one hand around in a circle— "this?"

That was a question Pippin would never have the answer to. "I have no idea."

Ruby gently nudged her forward, throwing a casual, "Put 911 on speed dial," over her head to Daisy.

Daisy blew an anxious raspberry. "Oh, it's there."

Ruby blew her a kiss. "Love ya, Dais."

Pippin started up the stairs as Daisy called out. "Let me know what you find!"

If they found anything. Pippin thought the stairs probably led to a hidden door upstairs and she and Ruby would spill out into the landing up there. More a Shoots and Ladders passageway than stairs to a destination.

How wrong she was.

At the top, they stepped onto a small bit of flooring and faced a wall. Pippin turned. A U-shaped railing guarded the stairwell opening. A narrow bit of floor was the only way to get from where they stood to the open space on the other side. She held onto the iron railing, making her way to what looked like her father's second study. The room was half the size of Leo's study beneath them. A single rail-backed chair sat in one corner. Two freestanding bookshelves stood against the one wall. Opposite them was a map pinned to a large beige rectangular bulletin board, as well as what looked like a family tree created on a large sheet of paper. She moved to it, her fingertips lightly touching the letters. She knew immediately that it was her father's hand that had written the names. She didn't remember it, exactly, yet she recognized it.

Her own name, as well as Grey's was at the bottom on the left, the children of Cassandra Lane and Leonardo Hawthorne. On the right, on the same line, were her cousins, Cora and Lily, the children of Lacey Lane and some unknown man. Above that, her grandparents, Annabel and Edgar, were listed, and above that two more generations. The top level, where it all started, listed Artemis and Siobhan, Pippin's great-great-grandparents. There were spaces above Artemis for more family members to be added, but they were blank. Vertical lines in black marker had been drawn, leading up to the top of the page and a single word —Ireland.

This was a life-sized version of the family tree Mr. McAdams had given her. His story, then, was true. Her father had been trying to trace Cassie's ancestry.

"Your dad's secret lair?" Ruby said, her tone hushed.

"Yeah. I guess so." She looked around, trying to fathom how she and Grey, or even Travis Walsh, Jimmy Gallagher, and Kyron Washington hadn't figured out that there was space in the house that wasn't accounted for.

In a flash, Pippin dashed down the stairs, raced past Daisy, and plowed through the French doors. She tilted her head back and peered at the porch ceiling, which covered the entire screened porch. What she needed was to see it from the outside. She retreated back through the study, went through the great room, and out the front door. She hurried down the porch steps and rounded the side of the house. She cupped her hand over her eyes and peered up. There it was. A faux window dormer. A faux window. The wall she and Ruby had faced at the top of the stairs—on the other side of it was that bedroom. She walked along the side of the house, trying to work out where the hidden study stopped and where the bedroom behind it began.

A few feet before the bedroom window, she reckoned. She smiled and shook her head. "You clever man," she said aloud.

Had her father built this room, or had it been here when her parents bought the house? She could imagine it being the old sea captain's secret hideaway.

Of course, the sea captain was really her father, wasn't

he? She closed her eyes and imagined him here, in this room, surrounded by the books he'd loved the most. The private collection he'd kept separate from the rest. She went back through the French doors to her father's downstairs study. Daisy wasn't there. Maybe Ruby had convinced her to go up. Back in the hidden room though, only Ruby was there. They stood side by side looking at an elaborate sailing ship enclosed in a glass bottle displayed on a stand.

A few steps brought Pippin to the opposite side of the small room where she ran her fingers lightly across the spines of the books there. Some were gilded, others had dark muted colors. The majority of them looked old.

"Jamie would flip seeing this room," Ruby said to her. "He's a rare book nerd. That doesn't sound right. A nerdy guy who loves rare books."

Somehow that didn't surprise Pippin. She hardly knew him, but she could picture Jamie McAdams in a room just like this, lost in a mountain of books. She brought her attention back to the shelves. She tilted her head to the right so she could read the spines, starting with the top shelf. "Tolkien." She chuckled to herself. "Of course."

There were editions of Shakespeare's complete works, Chaucer, that medieval poet Jamie had told her about, a copy of *The Martian Chronicles* by Ray Bradbury, a green spine with gold lettering—*North of Boston*, by Robert Frost. "I think these are first editions," Pippin said.

"What's going on up there!" Daisy voice drifted up to them.

"Where'd you go?" Pippin called.

"Bathroom break," she said.

Ruby leaned over the rickety railing and called back, "All's clear. Come up!"

There was only a moment's hesitation before the clickity

clack of Daisy's quick footsteps sounded. A few seconds later she was at the top of the steps doing a U-turn and scooting along the edge of the stairwell to join them. "Wow."

"Very big wow," Ruby said.

Just like Pippin and Ruby had, Daisy spun around, taking in the small hidden room.

"I have to get Grey," Pippin muttered aloud.

Daisy held up her hand looking like a student wanting to answer a question in class. "I'll do it." Before Pippin could even thank her, she'd scurried over the narrow walkway to the steps and disappeared.

Pippin went back to her examination of the shelves. Three framed family photographs sat on one of the shelves in front of a collection of binders—one of her as an infant with Cassie, their noses pressed together; another was of her mother with her arms stretching up to the sky holding Grey, his face in elation as Cassie suspended him in the air; and a third was of the twins, with Cassie kneeling around a sandcastle they'd built on the beach. Her father had to have been the photographer in each, preferring to be behind the camera rather than in front of it.

A framed photo on a different shelf caught her attention. It was turned so it faced the books rather than the room. She picked it up and flipped it around. In it, an adoring Leo stood behind Cassie, his arms wrapped around her, resting on her belly. Her pregnant belly, Pippin realized. Cassie had her hands atop Leo's. She leaned on him, the back of her head resting against his chest and turned so that her gaze was directed at him. The love between them was so clear. So...present. A lump formed in her throat, and for the first time in a long time, the feeling of loss inside her felt visceral. Deep, like it had when she was a child, rather than the dull emptiness that their absence had later morphed into.

"You look so much like her," Ruby said.

Pippin drew her head back. People said that, but she'd never really thought so. She'd always seen Cassie as just her mother. A person completely separate from Pippin. But now she zeroed in on her facial features. A dappling of freckles across the bridge of Pippin's nose mirrored Cassie's. And their green eyes, bright like a field of clovers. Their copper hair, almost the same.

The sound of footsteps click-clacking and clomping towards them interrupted her thoughts. Daisy appeared, rounding the corner and scooting alongside the railing and back into the secret room, Grey on her heels. Behind him were Kyron and Travis.

"What the hell..." Grey stared. The other two men stopped abruptly behind him. There was barely enough room for Pippin, Daisy, and Ruby. Adding Grey made the space feel cramped. The only way Kyron and Travis could fit was if they stood stick straight and shuffled around each other.

They didn't bother. Instead, they staggered on different levels of the stairs turned to face the room with Kyron at the top and Travis just below him. "Whoa," Travis said, while Kyron gave a low whistle.

Ruby jumped up, turning her body so she could slip by Grey. "We should go downstairs," she said, ushering Daisy toward the stairs.

Travis whipped his ball cap off his head and scratched his scalp with his fingertips. He looked like he'd just panned for gold and had ended up with a solid handful of nuggets. "You don't see shit like this in real life."

He wasn't wrong. In a million years, Pippin wouldn't have thought there'd be a secret room in her parents' house.

The two men, followed by Daisy and Ruby, descended the stairs, leaving Pippin and Grey alone in the study.

"What the hell is this?" Grey said, slowly turning to take it all in.

"Dad's secret lair," Pippin said. She pointed to the top shelf. "Tolkien."

"Hmph," Grey said with an upward flick of his eyebrows. "Of course."

"Other stuff, too, though." Pippin said.

They spent the next fifteen minutes in silence, each examining the room and the shelves. Aside from the Tolkien collection, Leo had had a decent number of other classic fiction novels. Still, the vast majority of the books were nonfiction. Ancient languages. Mythologies. Histories of Europe.

Leaning up against the shelf was an old atlas that looked like it had come from another century. It had, she realized. It was dated 1875 and was titled *McNally's System of Geography for Schools, Academies, and Seminaries*. The cover was worn, with the edges of the hard cover lifting up in the corners, but overall it seemed to be in good shape. Especially for a book that was a hundred and fifty years old.

She carefully turned the pages, revealing the opening section, which gave basic definitions and lessons in geography. Next came maps, each beautifully shaded in pale blues, greens, and corals, of the western and eastern hemispheres. Next was North American, denoting Canada and British America, showing the United States as a whole, then broken into regions and showing areas that had now become states and the territories they once were. South America and Europe. Asia. Each illustration, hand drawn and colored, was beautiful. It had taken great skill and attention to detail to create a book like this.

At the end were maps showing elevations and mountains. One, which based on the ease to which the book fell open at this section was a favorite of Leo's, depicted the oceans and continental basins. Pippin smiled to herself. Her father, the seaman, had lived and breathed the ocean, even so much as to study the ocean currents in such an old book.

Cartography in the twenty-first century was a completely different art than it had been in the nineteenth century, that was clear. At the end of the book were pages giving a step by step guide to the process of making your own maps. Another turn of the page revealed a sheet of paper with a crude map of Ireland drawn on it. Leo, it seemed, had been practicing his own map making skills. He'd written notes in pencil, his straight and contained writing faded with time but still legible. *Reachraiin. Artifacts — Roman? County Dublin.* The map itself was of an island, the body of water around it labeled as the Irish Sea.

"I didn't know he was so into maps, did you?" she asked Grey, pointing to the one on the wall. It was a representation of a map of Ireland, circa 400 AD, Arrival of Christianity. It had arrows pointing to Wales and Cornwall and Devon. How did the hand drawn map from the atlas connect to this?

"Nope," Grey said. He held out a miniature book that fit in the palm of his hand. It was tattered with age.

"Is it real?" she asked, her fingers hovering over it, but not quite touching it.

Grey carefully opened it revealing yellowed pages filled with writing. "What language do you think that is?"

His guess was as good as hers. Whatever it was, neither one of them could read it. The writing reminded Pippin of calligraphy but using letters that were not part of the English or Latin alphabets. Lots of horizontal lines on the tops of the letters, a few accents here and there, and long words with only intermittent spacing made the whole thing look like gibberish to her.

"I didn't know he was so obsessed with Ireland," Grey said.

Pippin moved to stand in front of the family tree. "He was trying to trace our ancestry."

Grey came to stand beside her. "Looks like it." He scraped his fingers through his hair. "What other secrets are we going to unearth?"

That was an excellent question.

Pippin went back to the bookshelves while Grey flipped through the Atlas again. Leo had kept a small collection of old books, most written in the same unidentifiable language as the miniature book Grey had found. Many were history texts about the Roman Empire and their sweeping rule of Britain for more than 400 years. *The Agricola. The Rise and Fall of the Roman Empire. Iron Age Hoards in Britain.* Her eyes stopped on a white spine. *Tracing Your Irish Ancestors.* She pulled it off the shelf and held it out to Grey.

He glanced at it, then back at the family tree on the bulletin board.

They looked at each other. Had Leo Hawthorne's search for their mother's history led to his death?

Chapter 15

"There is so much more to a book than just the reading."
~Maurice Sendak

*L*ater that night, Grey and Pippin sat across from one another in a booth at Amberjack Grill, a little hole in the wall seafood restaurant a mile or so past the fishing pier. Grey nursed a draft beer, the mug no longer frosty, and Pippin sipped on a light rosé. They'd ordered—Pippin the fish tacos with a zesty slaw and avocado cream and Grey the grilled triggerfish and potato salad—but Pippin wasn't sure either of them would have the appetite to actually eat the food.

They both put their drinks down at the same time and looked at each other. Grey sighed, heavy. "I don't know if I can do this, Pippin."

She raised her eyebrows in a question. Even now, as adults, they often experienced the same emotions or had the same thoughts at the same time, but she wasn't sure what he was talking about at this moment. What couldn't he do? Find out the truth about their father's death? Finish the renovations on the house so they could open it up as an inn? Stay in Devil's Cove?

"I'm tired."

"Tired of what?"

He threw his arms up. "Of all of it. The house. The secrets. Not knowing anything about our parents. Our father had a secret room, for Christ's sake. What is that about?"

She shrugged helplessly. She didn't have any answers, but she understood Grey's reticence. Unearthing their long-buried emotions about losing their parents meant facing truths they'd been able to deny until now, like why had their grandparents cleared out all their parents' belongings, not saving anything for them. She wanted the quilts her mother had made, the blankets she'd knitted. The necklace she'd always worn. Her journals. Pippin had memories of her mother writing in journals. Where were they now?

That led to another question. Why had Grandmother Faye disliked Cassie so much? Both she and Grey had felt that from her throughout their teenage years, particularly Pippin. "You look so much like your mother," Grandmother Faye often said. Her voice conveyed the disdain she felt about that little fact. "At least Grey looks like Leo," she'd overheard her grandmother say to her grandfather once, driving home the feeling that Pippin was an outsider in her own family, such as it was.

"Greevie," she said, reaching across and cupping one hand over his. "We know more now that we ever have before."

"Yeah," Grey muttered.

Their food came. The waitress flashed a comely smile at Grey as she set his plate down in front of him.

Bold, Pippin thought, since the young woman had no idea that she was Grey's sister. What if she had been his girl-friend or even his wife? After all, they didn't look alike, and Pippin had her hand on Grey's.

Maybe the waitress, whose name tag she now saw said Brittney, had overheard them talking and had put it together. Pippin would give her the benefit of the doubt rather than classifying her as the type of girl who'd openly flirt with a guy who was sitting with another woman—a future homewrecker. "Let me know if you need anything else," Brittney said, glancing at her before dragging her gaze back to Grey.

Grey smiled back. "I'll do that, thanks." His eyes followed her as she sashayed away to help another table.

Pippin snapped her fingers in front of his face.

He cracked another smile. "She's cute, eh?"

"Yeah. Adorable. Can we focus here?"

Grey dug into his food, his mood visibly lifted. She could thank Brittney for that, anyway.

She squeezed the juice from a lime wedge over the cabbage slaw in her fish taco, spooned on some of the creamy avocado sauce, and took a sloppy bite. She grabbed her napkin to catch a dribble on her lip and held the drip-ping taco over her plate.

Grey was hunched over his plate. Apparently, they'd both gotten their appetites back. He lifted his eyes to her as he stuck another forkful of fish in his mouth. He took a hefty bite of potato salad, then lifted his hand to flag down Brittney. When she looked his way, he held up his nearly empty mug. He glanced at Pippin, but she covered the top of her wine glass with her fingers. "I'm fine."

Brittney gave him a thumbs up and disappeared behind the counter, returning a moment later with a freshly chilled glass of draft beer. "Thanks, Brit," Grey said. There was no questioning the flirtation in his voice.

"How'd you know I go by Brit?" she asked with a giggle.

Grey draped his left arm across the back of the booth, turning his body in her direction. "Lucky guess."

Pippin rolled her eyes. Grey's way of dealing with things was to tuck them into an imaginary compartment to think about at some later date. Or not. Whatever angst he was feeling just a little while ago was safely hidden away thanks to Brit.

This time the young woman sauntered away with a flirty swing of her hips. Grey's eyes obligingly followed for a few seconds before turning back to Pippin.

"The guys and I have been working our asses off on the renovations. Your inn'll be ready to open in a few more weeks," he said.

He was right, of course. Grey, Jimmy, Kyron, and Travis had been working round the clock and the place was almost ready. It would be up to Pippin to finish furnishing each room. She planned to set up local ads advertising the inn, and she needed to finish the content for the website designer she'd hired. The site would come complete with booking and payment capabilities. All she needed were the photographs once the place was furnished. She was planning the opening just before Memorial Day for the three-day weekend.

"And it looks amazing," she said. It really did. They'd put shiplap on a few of the focal walls in the kitchen and bedrooms, and even in the bathrooms, black wood-framed mirrors completing the rustic look. They'd found someone to fabricate a slab of white marbled quartz for the kitchen and bathroom counters. They'd laid wide planks of hard-wood flooring and she'd found area rugs to add warmth and define spaces. Pippin had found a long farm table made of reclaimed maple wood in need of some love and care. Kyron, it turned out, loved working with furniture—both building and refinishing. He'd sanded the table, removing years of abuse, and stained it a warm honey color. He'd then had gone a step beyond and found a hand-hewn maple mantel. Pippin fell in love with it instantly. It was perfect.

Something hit her at that moment. "You said *my* inn will be ready. It's *our* inn."

He picked at one of his fingernails, not meeting her gaze. "Grey?"

He let out another sigh and raised his eyes to her. "I'm going to start a different venture."

She couldn't help it. Her jaw dropped. "What does that mean, a different venture?"

"My own business."

What was he saying? "What do you mean? What about Dad...and the inn--" She broke off. She'd finally told him everything about her experiences with *The Odyssey*, and what Mr. McAdams had told her about Cassie and the copy of *The Odyssey*. "—and my book magic?"

He pushed his plate out of the way and leaned forward, resting his forearms on the table and lacing his fingers together. His voice took on an angry tinge. "I can't help you with that. It's your gift, not mine."

"It's more of a curse," she said in an effort to placate him. Neither of them knew why only the women in the Lane family had this so-called gift of bibliomancy. She'd just discovered it...didn't know how to use it...but she was stuck with it. She looked at him. "Dad was trying to learn about it. To figure out how to stop it. He wanted to help Mom."

"Maybe, but he didn't, did he? She still died, and so did he."

She remembered his reaction when Lieutenant Jacobs had confirmed that the remains were their father. "Don't you want to know why?"

Grey lowered his voice to a whispery growl. "Of course I do, but if there was physical evidence, it's gone now. Jacobs said it was a long shot."

She and Grey rarely disagreed. Their connection ran deep, but where they used to have the same thought at the same time, or finish each other's sentences, she now felt them separating from one another. Going off in their own directions. That wasn't necessarily a bad thing, but it felt... odd. He sat across from her, but she already felt a hole inside of her heart. "What venture?" she asked, trying to keep her voice even.

For the first time since Brit left the table, he smiled. "Custom furniture." She waited for him to elaborate and after a few seconds, he did. "I rented a house. There's a shop already on the property. Kyron and I are going to do it together. He'll do more of the finish work, and I'm going to design and build."

She wanted to be happy for him. She *was* happy for him. She'd found her inspiration in the old house they'd inherited, but it clearly wasn't *his* inspiration. She nodded, making herself smile. "Sounds perfect."

"I'm not going anywhere, Peevie. I'll be ten minutes away just doing my own thing."

"I know. I'm happy for you. I really am." Her voice cracked. "It's just—"

"We've always been together," he finished.

She laughed through her tears. "Exactly."

He stretched his hand across the table, laying it on top of

hers. "But look. You traveled after high school. I stayed in Greenville. Even when we're apart, we're still connected. You know that."

She steeled herself against her emotions. She wouldn't let them get the better of her. Of course he was right. They were adults. They had their own lives to live. They'd always be there for one another, but that didn't mean they had to want to do the same thing with their lives. She had the inn. He'd have his business. Maybe one day, if they were lucky, they'd have families of their own. "It sounds great," she said. "Really great."

He sat back again, the ghost of his smile still lingering. "It will be."

"So," she said, looking at him most earnestly. "Can I be your first customer? I need built-in bookshelves in the great room."

He cocked an eyebrow. "For actual *books*?"

She smiled, genuinely this time. "You better believe it. I'll move some of Dad's collection onto it. And who knows, maybe I'll even get a few books of my own."

Chapter 16

"The language of friendship is not words but meanings."
    ~Henry David Thoreau

The police had restricted Pippin and Grey from moving the boat until they'd released the crime scene. Despite Lieutenant Jacob's promise, Pippin knew it was a cold case. He and Grey were right. Whatever physical evidence might have once existed was long ago swept away by the elements.

Finally, Jacobs had called giving them the all clear to haul the boat away. Pippin promptly called Salty Shannon. "I can come on up tomorrow, if'n that's alright with you," he said.

She agreed and went outside to look at the boat one last time. The sky was blue. A chilly breeze found its way through her knitted sweater, but it was tolerable. She sat in the Adirondack chair she'd left on the grass and stared at the vessel. She didn't feel any sentimentality towards it, but the fact that it would be gone after tomorrow still made her feel a little bit melancholy. She looked at the hull of the boat, trying to imagine it as it was when she and Grey were kids. "If only your boat could speak," she whispered. A minute passed. Then two. At the end of a third, she sat up suddenly. "But your *books* can."

She flew out of her chair to head inside but stopped short when a snout poked out of the pampas grass. Instantly, she dropped to her knees and softened her voice. "Hey, pup." She extended her arm and tapped the ground.

To her astonishment, the dog inched forward, slowly emerging from the grass—first the head, then the front legs, followed by the torso.

"Good girl," Pippin cooed. "Come on."

The dog stood frozen, her hind side still hidden.

Somewhere behind her, a door slammed followed by the rat-tat-tat of someone descending the porch steps. Pippin turned to shush whoever was coming, forgetting for a second that the dog couldn't hear.

A rustle pulled her attention back to the pampas grass. The dog was gone.

"Everything okay?"

She pressed her hands against the ground to push herself back to standing, turning to see Jimmy looking at her. "Yeah, fine. That stray dog was just here."

"You're really trying to catch it?" Jimmy asked as he lit a cigarette.

She looked back at the pampas grass, hoping to catch another glimpse of the pup's nose. "Trying, but no luck so far. She's skittish. Taking a break?"

Jimmy held up his burning cigarette. "Smoke break."

Pippin hadn't spent much time with Jimmy, and now she

was glad of that. Sparking conversation was not his strength. "Okay then. See you later." She waved and disappeared into the house.

Ten minutes later, she'd talked with Ruby, then Daisy. Both were ready to drop everything to come over and hear what Pippin had to say. Daisy said she could come immediately. "Harold can watch the library for a little while."

"Jamie went out to run an errand. I need thirty minutes," Ruby said.

"Perfect. I'll see you then." Pippin hung up, fixed herself a glass of sweet tea, and headed back to the porch. She sat on one of the new rocking chairs. A sound drew her attention to the side yard. The dog! She set her glass on the little table she'd found at a thrift store and raced down the steps, rounding the corner.

What she saw wasn't the dog returning, though. It was Jimmy climbing down off the boat. What had he been doing up there?

Before she could ask him, a horn beeped, and Daisy's zippy little Turbo Beetle pulled up in front of the house. Pippin waved at her but turned back to the boat.

She felt a pang of unease. Jimmy was gone.

A FEW MINUTES LATER, Ruby, her legs pumping the pedals of a red bicycle as she road up the street, arrived. She dismounted at the sidewalk and walked up the front brick path. She leaned the bike up against the porch railing before mounting the steps and reaching for the glass of tea Pippin had prepared for her. "Just what I need," she said. "Got any ice?"

"Yep. Come on." Pippin headed inside to the kitchen, Ruby and Daisy hot on her heels.

The two friends stopped short and gaped at the new farm table that filled the dining room space opposite the kitchen. "Wow," Ruby said. "*That* is my dream table."

Daisy surged forward, stretched her arms wide, and laid her upper body on it like she was hugging the wood. "I want to take it home."

"Did you see the mantle?" Pippin asked. Grey and Kyron had brought it all in the night before.

They'd been so single-minded about their iced tea that they'd all sped through the great room, not even glancing around. Now Ruby and Daisy raced around the center structure that divided the great room from the kitchen and dining area. Pippin heard them gasp and smiled. That was the reaction she was going for.

"This place doesn't even look the same." Ruby spun around taking in all the details of the kitchen and dining room. The shiplap on the backside of the fireplace was a backdrop for a farm style hutch Pippin had found. Two plush chairs sat catty-corner against the right side wall, a round coffee table with a reading lamp on top between them. And then there was the table and the twelve color-fully mismatched—yet compatible—chairs placed all the way around. "You have a gift, Pippin."

She smiled to herself. She wanted everyone who entered the house to feel welcome, and she wanted the kitchen to be the heart of the home. From the expressions on Ruby's and Daisy's faces, she'd succeeded.

"What's the emergency?" Ruby asked after filling her glass to the brim with ice and joining Pippin and Daisy at the table.

"Book magic."

"What about it?" Ruby sounded so casual, as if it was an ordinary thing.

"I'm going to use it to find out what happened to my father."

Ruby and Daisy looked at each other, then back at Pippin. Ruby arched a brow. "What do you mean?"

Pippin wasn't entirely sure how the book magic thing worked, exactly, so what *did* she mean? "I haven't gotten that far yet," she admitted. "And I guess it might not work, but— I'm going to start calling it a gift instead of a curse—it told my mother that my father was going to die, but it also told me that he'd come back after twenty years."

"Like Odysseus," Daisy said.

Pippin touched her forefinger to her nose. "Exactly. Like Odysseus."

Daisy gave a serious nod. "So if it told you that, and told your mom about your dad, you think it can help you solve your dad's murder?"

It had sounded so sane when the idea came to her. Saying it aloud made it sound a little crazy. But Daisy had seen it. Jamie had seen it for that matter. Ruby had heard the discussion. And Mr. McAdams believed in it. It was real, and she was going to figure out how it worked. "Yes," she said.

Ruby stretched her arm out, her hand in the center of the table between them. Daisy grinned and put hers over it. Pippin laid hers on top. "To Pippin's Book Magic," Ruby said.

Daisy's grin grew bigger. "To finding out the truth,"

The one thing Pippin hadn't expected when she and Grey had come back to Devil's Cove was forming friendships. She looked at the two women who sat across from one another, each with their own stories to tell. It had been the last thing she'd expected, but here she was. "And to new friends," Pippin said.

They echoed each other with a "Hip, hip, hooray!" and released their hands.

Ruby took a sip of her tea and looked at Daisy and Pippin. "So. When do we get started?"

Chapter 17

"Your visions will become clear only when you can look into your own heart. Who looks outside, dreams; who looks inside, awakes."

~C.G. Jung

*T*he three women sat on the floor, cross-legged, in Leo's secret room, Pippin's copy of *The Odyssey* on the floor between them. Pippin had her back to the staircase leading to the study, Daisy had her back to the bookshelves, and Ruby was angled and leaning against the armchair.

"So how does it work?" Ruby asked.

"Oh my God, it's so cool!" Daisy gestured with her hands when she spoke. "The words just lifted off the page. Of course, I didn't actually see that part. Only Pippin can since she's the bibliomancer, but from what she said, they just lift up."

"So you just open the book and some of the words will float?"

The truth was, she didn't really know. When she'd been in Devil's Brew Café, she'd placed one finger randomly on the page and that had been the passage that separated from the rest. At the library, she'd asked the book to tell her a secret...and it had. "I'm not really sure if there's a *method*," she admitted, using air quotes.

"Let's give it a go," Daisy said, giving the book a little shove closer to Pippin.

Pippin couldn't say why she felt a little bit nervous. If she believed her cousins in California, this was her destiny as a Lane woman. But did that mean it could help her solve a crime that was twenty years old?

She took a bolstering breath before picking up the book. She opened it to a random page and let her gaze drift over the words. She looked for any ripple...any movement.

"Anything?" Ruby asked.

Pippin shook her head.

Daisy's shoulders had slumped as she'd watched Pippin with complete attention, but now her spine straightened and she snapped her fingers, her forefinger pointing at Pippin. "You said you pressed your finger against the page at The Open Door."

That was true. Jamie had interrupted her, she'd dropped the book, and then she'd touched the open page with her finger, revealing the passage about the Sirens. "I'll try it," she said.

She fanned the pages of the book and let it fall open naturally. Setting it down on her lap, she closed her eyes and started to rotate her finger in the air, but she stopped, cracking open one eyelid. "I feel ridiculous. Like I'm trying to cast a spell or something."

Ruby reached over and gave Pippin's knee an encouraging squeeze. "You're among friends here," she said. "Just see what happens."

Pippin blew the air from her lungs, closed her eye, and did the rotation thing with her finger again. After three air circles, she dropped her finger to the page, opened her eyes, and looked down. The passage under her finger told about Odysseus telling the Cyclops that his name was Nobody. She read it aloud.

"Maybe your father gave a different name to someone," Daisy said.

Ruby pursed her lips and thought for a moment. "Or it could mean that the person who killed your dad has only one eye," she said.

Daisy snapped and pointed, this time at Ruby. "Right! Maybe he wears an eyepatch."

"The one-eyed killer." Ruby shook her head. "Sounds a little farfetched."

Pippin stayed focused. "Both times, the words hovered. It was like they actually separated from the page."

"But that's not happening?"

"No. Nothing."

Where Daisy was curious and boisterous, Ruby was quiet and contemplative. Daisy drummed her fingers on her knee, wriggling her upper body as if she was ready to break out into a dance. Ruby sat still, her gaze lifted to the ceiling as she thought. "Take us through the two times it happened," she said.

"The first time was in The Open Door. Actually, no, I was at the coffee shop," Pippin said. "I'd just bought the book—"

"This same book?" Ruby asked.

"Yes. It was the only copy the store had."

Ruby rolled one finger in the air. "Okay, go on."

"I was flipping through the book, reading sections,

looking for the Sirens."

"Why the Sirens?" Ruby asked.

Daisy bounced and raised her hand as if she wanted to answer a question in a classroom. "Pippin told me about the old lady dropping a book in the street and her mom freaking out. Her mom read something from the book, something about a wife and children not being there to greet him."

"Him meaning Leo?" Ruby asked.

Pippin nodded. "Right."

Daisy continued. "I thought about it and it came to me. Odysseus was warned by Circe not to listen to the Siren's song. Any man who did, never went home to see his wife or children."

"So I went to the bookshop and bought a copy," Pippin said.

"Got it." Ruby looked like she was taking mental notes. "What happened next?"

"I was reading, then Jamie came up. He startled me. I dropped the book, and when I picked it up and put my finger down, the passage was there, just like Daisy had said. It was the passage that my mom saw, I'm sure of it."

"Interesting." Ruby tapped one finger against her lips. "And in the library?"

"I was sitting in one of the reading chairs."

"I came up to her and..."

Pippin and Daisy looked at each other, then spoke at the same time. "The book dropped in my lap."

"The book dropped," Pippin said again. "Both times, the book dropped." She grabbed for the book, opened it to a random page, then dropped it. She bent forward and peered at the open pages, sitting up a moment later, frustrated. "Nothing."

"Okay, okay," Ruby said. "Let's think about this. The book dropped both times."

"Right."

"And it was open to a specific page when it dropped?"

Pippin thought about this, replaying the scenes in her mind. "I was at the café sitting in one of the club chairs. Jamie came up. He startled me and I dropped the book."

"Had it already been opened to a page?" Ruby asked again.

Slowly, Pippin shook her head. "I don't think so. I'd been flipping through it, but I couldn't find anything that seemed like the right passage.

"So it dropped, and then..."

"I started to pick it up and the words just stared dancing, then the section about the Sirens popped up."

"And what about at the library," Ruby asked.

"Same thing. I was sitting in one of the reading chairs practicing."

"What do you mean, practicing?"

"I wanted to see if what had happened in the café was real, or if I'd imagined it. I wanted to see if I could do it again." She didn't say that she'd already wondered if the book would help her make sense of what had happened to her father. After all, if it had predicted her father's death, why not reveal more? "I wanted to find out if the Book Magic was a real thing."

"Got it. So when it dropped, was it open to a the page you'd been looking at?"

"It wasn't!" Daisy said. "You were reading, but then shut it hard, like you were mad or frustrated."

"I was," Pippin said. "It wasn't working."

"I think we're getting somewhere," Ruby said. "You dropped it, it fell open, and it did work?"

Slowly, Pippin nodded. "It did. Just like before. The words just floated off the page." She looked at the book, hope blooming in her chest. "I dropped the book both times, and it opened to a random page. Maybe that's it."

She picked up *The Odyssey*, held it three feet above the ground, spine facing down. And then she dropped it. It hit the hardwood with a thud, bounced, and landed on the front cover.

"Well that didn't work," Daisy said.

Dropping it from so high hadn't, but what about if she started closer to the ground. Pippin picked up the book, lifted it only a few inches, and dropped it again.

This time, it landed on the back cover.

Maybe it had been a fluke that the book had dropped and fallen open. Twice. Maybe she had to start with it on the ground. Ruby and Daisy watched her as she picked it up again, this time setting the spine on the hardwood. She held it by the front and back covers, the pages fanning out between them. She held her breath and let go.

The book flopped open. Ruby and Daisy leaned close, their eyes intent on the open pages. Pippin closed her eyes for a moment. She opened them—and gasped. In the center of the left side page, two lines floated above the rest. The letters were jumbled, but she managed to sort them out and read lines. She stumbled on the name, but otherwise got through it.

> *It carried him down to the depths of the*
> *endless and tossing main sea.*
> *So Aias died, when he had swallowed*
> *down the salt water.*

DAISY SPOKE FIRST. "Do you think it's about your dad again?"

Pippin hadn't spoken to anyone about what Lieutenant Jacobs had told her and Grey about the nick on her father's rib. Slowly, she shook her head. "But he didn't drown."

Ruby looked up sharply. "How did he die?"

"They think he was stabbed."

"Is it telling you to watch out so you don't drown?" Daisy said, breaking the moment of silence that had been warranted.

It was possible, but Pippin didn't think so. Maybe someone had been on the boat that sank so long ago. But no, divers had searched and no body had been found. She thought this bibliomancer thing depended a great deal on gut feelings, otherwise how was she supposed to figure out what an obscure passage from a book had to do with real life.

Or death.

"I think it's about someone else," she said. She considered the sunken boat again, but then her skin turned cold and she felt the color drain from her face.

"What?" Ruby and Daisy asked, echoing each other. In an instant, Ruby seemed to reach the same conclusion. Her jaw dropped.

Pippin looked up at them, her heart nearly pounding right out of her chest. "The man who drowned in the cove."

THE MINUTE RUBY and Daisy left, Pippin sat at her desk and searched the Internet for information about the man who'd drowned in the cove. Professor Maxwell Lawrence. His face was familiar, but she couldn't place it. She'd seen him before, though. It would come to her.

Quincy Ratherford had written about him for the Gazette, and now Pippin was scribbling notes on a sheet of paper. The professor had been a husband. A father. And according the article, soon to be a grandfather. She didn't know what the book was telling her about this man, but she knew what she had to do to figure it out.

Ten minutes later, she stood with Grey in the kitchen of Sea Captain's Inn. The steady popping sound of a nail gun was giving her a headache. "Are they almost done?"

"You wanted a ton of shiplap," Grey said.

"That didn't answer the question." She thought that his mood might improve after he'd revealed his business venture to her, but it hadn't. He was on the edge of surly.

"The last of it is going up right now. We need to do the bathroom tile upstairs, finish the widow's walk, then just the punch list."

She raised her brows. "Punch list?"

"All the little things that need to be finished up or fixed. The wrap up."

"Got it."

He grabbed a can of beer from the refrigerator and popped the tab, taking a healthy swig. "What'dya want to talk to me about?" He leaned against the island, one arm in his short's pocket, the other dangling the beer can.

"I'm going to go talk to Max Lawrence's wife."

He didn't blink. "Okay, I'll bite. Who's Max Lawrence and why are you going to talk to his wife?"

She took a breath before saying, "He's the man who drowned the other day."

"The guy in the cove? The kayak accident?"

"Yes."

He took another sip before speaking again, then all he said was, "Why?"

This was the tricky part. Being twins, at least for them, meant that their connection to one another was strung tight as a high wire. She already knew Grey would not agree with her plan. "I think his death has something to do with Dad's."

He stared at her like she'd brought home a unicorn for a new pet. "What?"

"I think his death is connected—"

"To Dad's. I got that. I guess I mean why? Peevie, they happened twenty years apart. How can one possibly have to do with the other?"

"The book—"

He held up a hand, stopping her. "Look. You're just learning this bibliomancy thing. So some words pop up off a page. You're the one assigning the meaning to those words. There's no way to know if you're right about that meaning."

"I know that, Grey." Despite the fact that she'd been prepared for his opposition, Pippin felt exasperated, and she was pretty sure her expression didn't belie that fact. "I know it doesn't make logical sense, but I know I'm right. That man didn't just drown."

Her brother set down his can of beer so he could focus fully on her. "Pippin. Think about it. Say it's true, which is a long shot. But say it is. That means there's a murderer on the loose. If you go digging around, you're putting yourself in danger."

Of course she'd considered this. "And I'll be careful, but Grey, I—"

"I know," he said, throwing his hand up again and finishing her sentence for her. "You have to do it."

Chapter 18

"The world will provide you with every imaginable obstacle, but the one most difficult to overcome will be the lack of faith in yourself."

~Callie Khouri

*P*ippin arranged for yet another meeting with Mr. McAdams. She felt a bit like he was the Great and Powerful Oz, and that he had all the answers she sought.

She left Travis, Jimmy, Kyron, and Grey at the house with their bathroom tile and headed to town. She took her old Land Rover. It wasn't the most fuel-efficient car, but it had style. She needed it today. From The Open Door, she was going straight to Professor Maxwell Lawrence's wife.

Parking was scarce in Devil's Cove—another reason it was usually better to take her bike to town—but she found a spot, walking the one block back to the bookshop. The shops sat shoulder to shoulder along the east side of the street, their backs to Roanoke Sound. Her fingertips fluttered over the cascading flowers just outside the door. She stopped just inside to take in the bookshop that the elder McAdams man and his grandson had created, this time noting details she hadn't before.

It was cozy. She hadn't registered that before. The wainscoting on the lower portion of the walls was painted a creamy white, the walls above a pale yellow. Warm and welcoming. Shelves ringed the room, skirting around the front windows facing the street and the counter, but otherwise filling nearly every space along the perimeter. Other shelves, like the one Jamie had found *The Odyssey* on, were lined up in the interior creating a maze. The rows and rows of books were divided by genre and organized alphabetically by the author's last name. The number of stories contained by the four walls of the bookshop was astounding, each shelf filled with accountings of people and places coming to life thanks to the imagination of the authors who wrote them.

Just past the checkout counter was a healthy supply of non-book items: notecards, book quotes printed on rustic pieces of wood, calendars, journals. It was a used bookstore that also featured knickknacks for the book lover and rare books for the collector. Those were housed in a shelving unit that had sliding glass doors that locked, and according to Daisy, the even rarer ones were in a back room under lock and key.

"Pippin."

Jamie, his arms heavy with a stack of hardcover books, strode toward her. "Hey," she said, offering a little wave with one hand.

"Here for a book?"

"Oh. No, actually."

"Ah. Another meeting with Grandad, then?"

"Yes."

"Well shucks," he said with an exaggerated frown. "And here I thought maybe you'd come to see me."

She felt her cheeks flush. She had to admit she didn't mind seeing Jamie again. He was easy to look at, if on the arrogant side...and married. "Aw well, maybe next time," she said, wishing she could pull the flirty words back into her mouth. She didn't *do* flirty. And she wasn't like Grey, who could have one-night-stands and short term relationships without attachment or a care in the world. Just like her, Grey didn't do long-term. Too much risk involved with that. People left. But unlike Grey, Pippin didn't do *any* type of relationship. What would happen if she got too attached? Felt too much? If the man, whoever he might be, left, it would prove her point that she should never have gotten involved. If he stayed, he risked facing his own emotions when the Lane family curse took her life. No, she'd already decided that her life would be spent solo. All the more reason she wanted to find that dog. She could be her companion.

He gave her a crooked grin. "Be still my heart."

Her heart gave a little flutter. Oh God. She needed to nip this in the bud right now. "Look, Jamie, I appreciate your help, but I just found out my father was murdered and—" She started to say that the death of the professor might be related but stopped herself. She didn't want to announce that in this public space.

"And?" he prompted.

"And I just have to stay focused on that."

If he was put off by her pronouncement, he didn't let on. His expression showed his puzzlement at what she'd said. "What are you staying focused on, exactly?"

"My dad. His murder."

"The sheriff is investigating?"

She sighed. "They are, but I'm not holding my breath. The lieutenant in charge doesn't seem optimistic."

"It has been twenty years. It's already a cold case, right?"

She was so tired of hearing those two words. Twenty years. Twenty years. Twenty years. Leo was still her dad, and he was still dead. "Which is why I'm involving myself. I need to figure out what happened to him."

"What do you plan on doing?" he asked as he shifted the books in his arms.

She glanced at the stack. He always seemed to be carrying a stack of books. "Don't you want to put those down?"

He shrugged, the ghost of a smile still on his lips. He didn't say anything else, waiting for her to answer his question.

But she didn't want to answer his question. Beyond talking to Mrs. Lawrence, which was truly a fishing expedition, she didn't have a plan.

"Good grief, Jamie. Escort the girl upstairs!!"

They both turned to see the elder Mr. McAdams standing in the doorway opening that led upstairs to his flat. "I'll do that, old man."

Pippin looked from one man to the other. They had an easy rapport. The elder Mr. McAdams flapped one hand at his grandson. "If you weren't so young and ill-mannered, I would not have to remind you of things like this."

"I don't need an escort," Pippin interjected, leaving Jamie and his books as she hurried toward Mr. McAdams.

But Jamie was quick. He dropped the stack on the checkout counter and strode to the doorway. His grandfather released his hold on the door. Jamie caught it, holding it open for her. "Noah, I'll be back in a little while," he called over his shoulder.

For the first time, Pippin caught sight of a gangly looking teenager who wheeled around a book cart, returning volumes to the shelves. White AirPods poked out of each ear, but he heard through whatever he was listening to and looked up, nodding his acknowledgement to Jamie.

The two McAdams men certainly knew what they wanted, and they seemed to be in cahoots. Jamie ushered her upstairs, following behind.

Mr. McAdams opened the door to his flat, standing back to let Pippin pass first. Jamie held the door for his grandfather, then passed through last, closing the door behind him.

"Something to drink, my dear?" Mr. McAdams moved to the small kitchen, one hand on a cabinet door, awaiting her reply.

"I'm good, thanks," she said. She sat on the couch having a déjà vu moment. Daisy's presence had been replaced with Jamie, but otherwise it was just as it had been the last time she'd been here, complete with Mr. McAdams's black attire and slicked back silver hair.

He looked at Jamie, asking the same question without the words. Jamie shook his head and waved one hand in reply, so Mr. McAdams abandoned the kitchen and came to sit across from Pippin. "What can I do for you, Ms. Hawthorne?"

She thought about telling him to call her Pippin, but changed her mind, realizing that it probably wouldn't do any good. The man was the old school type who would always address her with the polite respect of his generation.

She glanced at Jamie, a wave of self-consciousness flowing through her. Did he believe her as fully as his grandfather did, or would he simply conclude that she was crazy. As if he could read her mind, he sat down in the other side chair and crossed his legs, adjusting his wire-rimmed glasses, and said, "I'm a believer. Of the bibliomancy," he added when he registered the question mark on her face.

Like father, like grandson, she thought. "I've been practicing," she began.

Mr. McAdams gave a smile that seemed to say that he was pleased about it. "With Homer's *Odyssey*, I presume."

"Yes. Only with that."

"Good, good." He gave a satisfied nod. "And what can I help you with?"

She'd thought that her gut had a lot to do with the so-called magic, and now Grey's words came back to her. They'd created a sliver of doubt in her mind. Was the meaning she'd assigned the words that floated above the page the *right* meaning, or was she completely off track? "I guess I've come for reassurance," she finally said.

"About what, my dear?"

She told them what she'd seen when she and Daisy and Ruby had been in Leo's hidden room. "It was one sentence. It was as if the words tore themselves away from the rest of them, lifting so I could see them."

Mr. McAdams crossed one leg over the other. He stroked his neatly trimmed goatee. "Fascinating. Continue."

She'd managed to memorize the short passage and recited it to them now. "*It carried him down to the depths of the endless and tossing main sea. So Aias died, when he had swallowed down the salt water.*"

"It's not about your father," Mr. McAdams said. Pippin looked up sharply, and Mr. McAdams flapped one innocent hand. "I know Lieutenant Jacobs well. He mentioned in passing what the medical examiner said. Stabbed, not drowned."

Jamie just watched her with his almost translucent brown eyes. She shifted under his gaze, wishing his scrutiny wasn't so unnerving.

"Right."

"You think you know who it *is* about." A statement, not a question. Mr. McAdams understood without her having to say it.

"The man they found. The kayak accident—"

"Professor Lawrence," Jamie said, speaking for the first time.

The elder Mr. McAdams looked at him. "You knew him."

Jamie's expression turned grim. "We're both part of a... discussion group."

Mr. McAdams eyes showed understanding. "Ah, *the* discussion group."

Pippin looked from one man to the other. "What discussion group?"

Jamie answered. "It's a group that meets once a month to discuss a predetermined topic."

"Like what kind of topic?" she asked.

"Sometimes literature. Current events. Historical events. You name it."

"So kind of a men's book club?" This guy was super educated, and here she was without a college degree, a wanderer who inherited her parents' house, had nothing to show for herself at the age of twenty-nine, and still struggled with reading. Whatever flirting she thought he'd done downstairs, she had nothing to worry about. Even if he hadn't been married with children, once this guy knew all the down and dirty details about her, any interest he might have had in her would evaporate.

Mr. McAdams considered Pippin. "What makes you

believe the man drowned in the book passage is Professor Lawrence?"

This was why she needed the reassurance. "It's a feeling. When the bibliomancy thing happened, I just knew. And I think his death has something to do with my dad's."

At this, both McAdams men sat back, uncrossed their legs, then crossed them the opposite way. They were mirror images of each other, fifty years apart.

"And you plan to look into it," Mr. McAdams said.

Goosebumps rose on Pippin's skin. "You have an uncanny ability to predict what I'm thinking."

He smiled disarmingly. "A gift."

"Not for me when I was in my teens," Jamie muttered under his breath, but loud enough that both Pippin and his grandfather could hear.

"Exactly why your parents always sent you here for the summer," the elder man said drolly.

Jamie looked aghast. "You mean it wasn't for the beach and the surfing?"

Mr. McAdams waved away the words, not deigning to respond to Jamie's mock horror. He looked back at Pippin and the levity that had been on his face for a moment disappeared. "You must be careful, my dear."

So he wasn't going to try to discourage her. She hadn't expected that. "You believe me?"

"I have no reason not to. You're the bibliomancer, not I. You know what you saw. What you read. How you interpret it is part of your gift. I suspect that you must listen to the feelings you get when it happens."

In that instant, she felt her body relax. Felt the weight in her chest release and float away. Grey hadn't *not* supported her in this, but he also hadn't exactly given his blessing. And that's what she needed. Someone to tell her that she was on the right track. Doing the right thing. Chasing the right lead.

She clapped her hands against her thighs, the sound muffled because of her jeans. "Great. Okay." She smiled. "I'm off to see the widow. Wish me luck."

"Wait. You're going now? To see Mrs. Lawrence?" Jamie asked, standing.

"Right now," she said, more energized than she'd been in...well, since she could remember.

Jamie and his grandfather exchanged a glance that she couldn't read.

She looked at them. "What?"

"I would like my grandson to go with you, Ms. Hawthorne. If you are amenable to that."

The ease she'd been feeling dissipated. "I don't need a babysitter."

Mr. McAdams closed his eyes as he gave a single bow of his head. "Of course you don't. But you may need his past relationship with the professor in order to talk to the man's wife. She is grieving."

She hadn't thought that far ahead. In her mind, she imagined that she'd knock on the door, introduce herself— as what? A curious party? A bibliomancer?—and she'd be invited in for sweet tea and a chat. But of course, that was not how it would happen, was it? That was naïve.

Mr. McAdams didn't wait for her to acquiesce, or even just to reply. He looked at Jamie. "Young Noah can cover the bookshop, yes?"

"Yep," Jamie said. He'd pulled out his phone and quickly texted someone, presumably Noah.

"I will check on him," Mr. McAdams said.

"See you later, then," Jamie said, and before she could think, he was ushering her down the rickety outside stairway in the back of the building and to his car. "I'll drive."

That's when she put on the brakes. "No, thanks. *I'm* going to drive. My car is parked behind the yarn shop. If you insist on coming, you can drive with me, or you can follow me in this—" She broke off to look at the sporty silver Audi they stood beside.

"This...?" That infernal ghost of a smile was back. He was making fun of her.

"This *grownup* car," she finished, grasping for something to say. *Of course* he had a grownup car. He had a kid. He *was* a grownup.

He smirked. "And that's a bad thing to you?"

She shrugged, going for indifference. The fact was, she was impressed by the car. It was grownup in a good way. Newer than her Land Rover—by a lot. Shiny in a way hers would never be. Air conditioned. "It's fine. I just prefer mine."

He pressed the button on his key fob and started off. "Okay, let's go then. You drive us to this fishing expedition."

She had to scurry to keep up with him, then to overtake him so she was in the lead.

Jamie McAdams, she thought, was going to be a pain in the neck.

Chapter 19

"No two persons ever read the same book."
    ~Edmund Wilson

*T*he drive to the widow's house would take twenty minutes if there was no traffic. They had to cross the swing bridge connecting Devil's Cove to Sand Point, and they would be at the mercy of the intercostal waterway traffic. If there was a ship or yacht that needed to get through, the bridge would swing, allowing passage. That could slow traffic. Luckily the Sound was clear, which meant no traffic. She pushed away the memories that surfaced as she sped across the bridge, as well as the emotions that came with them. She swallowed, controlling her voice. She didn't want Jamie to start asking her questions, so she asked her own instead. "You're kind of a brainiac, huh?"

It wasn't the most eloquent icebreaker. Perhaps a defense mechanism since she felt woefully uneducated next to him.

He gave her an amused side-eye. "Depends how you define brainiac, I guess."

She gripped the steering wheel with her hands at eleven and two, keeping her focus on the road. "Lots of college. The doctorate. Reading lots of books."

"With your bibliomancer gift, I'm sure you read a lot of books, too."

Her head shook before she could stop it, a frown following. "No. Not really."

She felt his gaze on her. "Why not?"

She stared straight ahead. "I just learned about the bibliomancer thing," she said.

"Okay, but what about before that?"

She debated what to say. That her mom forbid books in their house? That her father had respected that wish even after Cassie died? That she'd struggled all through school and was labeled a reluctant reader by her teachers? The word dyslexic had been tossed around throughout the years, but no one had ever done anything about it. She finally settled on, "I've never liked reading that much."

"Hmmm," Jamie said. Just, "Hmmm."

"What does that mean?" It came out more snappish than she'd intended, like a prickly cactus, but she bristled at the judgement she read in his single, "Hmmm."

Jamie, though, didn't seem put out. He just shrugged. "It's a shame, that's all. There are so many great books in the world. You're missing out."

Didn't she know it. She'd loved the parts of the mysteries she'd tried to work her way through as a teenager, but reading was hard. It had only gotten harder over the years. It was like learning a language—so much easier when you were a kid and your brain was a sponge, and exponentially more challenging to make the connections as an adult. She tried to practice, but most of the time it was easier to give up than to push through.

She knew she was missing out. She wished she was a better reader. God did she wish it. But she didn't want to acknowledge that to Jamie McAdams, a man who was little more than a stranger to her. As she drove across the bridge, she asked, "Why Medieval Irish?"

Her effort to change the subject was clumsy and obvious, but to Jamie's credit, he went along with it. "My mom's Irish. From Ireland Irish. Erin O'Donnell. She used to tell me stories about her parents and grandparents in the old country, and I fell in love. I did my masters at the National University of Ireland in Galway and my doctorate studies at Maynooth."

"I have no idea what either of those are," she said.

"Galway is in the west of Ireland. Maynooth University is in County Kildare."

She immediately imagined the rolling hills and vales, painted in a hundred different shades of green. She'd never been, but her roots were planted there. She'd see it someday.

"So you spent a lot of years on the Emerald Isle," she said, glancing at him, before looking back at the GPS and taking the next left. "You didn't want to stay there?"

He turned back to face front. "I thought about it, but my mom got sick, and I didn't want to be so far away from her."

Pippin wasn't sure she should ask the next question, but her mouth seemed to have a mind of its own. "Is she okay?"

"Actually she is. It was breast cancer, but she went through chemo and radiation, and she's been in remission ever since."

Pippin's hands loosened their grip on the steering wheel. "That's great."

He glanced at her and nodded. "Yeah, it is."

"And your grandfather—"

"Cyrus McAdams," he said. "They broke the mold after making him."

Cyrus. The name fit him. "He's an interesting man. Your father's father?"

At this, Jamie's face turned grim. "Right. My granddad is the only real father I've known. My dad left when I was three years old."

Pippin's eyes darted sideways, stealing a quick look at him. They had more in common than she'd thought. "My dad left us when we were nine. Except..."

"Except that he didn't really leave you," Jamie said softly. He'd known where she'd been going and finished the thought for her. "Right."

They drove in silence, Pippin following the directions on the GPS. After a few minutes, she brought up the subject that had been burning a hole in her mind. "And your daughter?"

"Daughters," he corrected.

"Two?" But even as she asked, she had a flash of him whispering something to the young girl behind the counter at the bookshop during her first visit.

"Mmm hmm. Seven and eleven."

She thought about asking about their mother but decided against it. She didn't need to get too friendly with Jamie McAdams and learning about his entire family was definitely too friendly.

"You really think Professor Lawrence's death has something to do with your father's?" Jamie asked after a minute of silence. Apparently, he'd also decided to steer clear of the personal stuff.

Pippin slowed, taking the final turn into a residential

area. "I don't know, but if I trust the message from the book, then yes."

A minute later, they pulled up to a quaint white clap-board house and walked side by side up the brick walkway. Jamie lifted the brass door knocker and rapped three times.

A thin woman with a sharp angular face answered the door. Her brown hair was parted in the middle, her gray roots growing out. Pippin had imagined her differently, though she'd had no frame of reference. In her mind, a grieving widow would have red-rimmed eyes, would be clutching a tissue, and would be pale and distraught. The woman was the opposite. Her eyes were bright. She was tissue and tear free. And her cheeks were lightly pinked. Only the stripe of gray bisecting her head gave any indication that things were maybe not quite normal. She stared at them, not speaking, but with her eyebrows raised expectantly.

Jamie spoke before Pippin could. "Mrs. Lawrence. I'm Jamie McAdams and this is Pippin Hawthorne." Her eyes snapped to Pippin when she heard the name, but Jamie went on. "I knew your husband from the *Synkéntrosi*."

The word sounded Greek. The name of their discussion group, Pippin thought. Leave it to a bunch of brainiacs to pick some obscure word for their moniker.

"Of course. I think he's mentioned you," she said. The explanation had done the trick. Mrs. Lawrence stepped back and opened the door wider. "Please. Come in." She led Pippin, followed by Jamie, into a small study on the right side of the house. "This was his room," she said, trailing her fingertips over the back of the chair pushed under the desk.

"We don't want to disturb you, ma'am—" Jamie started, but the woman cut him off.

"Don't call me ma'am."

This caught Jamie off-guard and he blinked, regrouping. "Of course. Mrs. Lawrence, then?"

"Lorraine is fine." She gestured to the chairs. "Have a seat."

The woman had invited them in, despite not knowing a thing about them, but her hospitality ended there. She didn't offer them a drink, or even water. Not that she had to, but the lack of it belied the typical Southern hospitality of North Carolinians.

Pippin and Jamie sat in the two leather recliners, backs to the bay window. Lorraine looked around as if she just realized she had nowhere to sit other than her husband's desk chair. She hesitated before pulling it out and perching on the edge of it. "What about *Synkéntrosi*?" she asked.

Pippin tried to puzzle out the woman's feelings. She didn't wear her grief in the typical ways, yet it emanated from her nonetheless.

"Max was so...animated...at the last meeting," Jamie said, beginning the fishing expedition. "It's hard to believe he's gone. I guess I...I'm looking for closure."

He'd gone for the psychology buzz term for acceptance. Good tactic.

"I appreciate that," Lorraine said, "but I don't see how *I* can give *you* closure." Her tone wasn't snappy exactly, but it also wasn't exuding geniality, either.

Pippin began to wonder if Lorraine would be able to help them at all. "Mrs. Lawrence—"

"Lorraine," she corrected.

Jamie sat back and crossed his legs, his left arm resting on the armrest of the chair, his fingers tapping. "Lorraine. I don't want you to give me closure. I'm hoping to help *you* find it."

She raised one brow, looking skeptically at him. "And how will you do that?"

"By figuring out what happened to Max out in the cove."

She scoffed. Not the response Pippin had expected. The woman was cynical. She'd lost her husband, and for her there was no rhyme or reason for it. Jamie forged on, though, ignoring her scoffing. "The police are saying it was an accid—"

Lorraine sat up suddenly. "It was not an accident. My husband was very skilled on the water. No, it was not an accident. It was not at his hand, like some people have said. No, Max's life was taken from him," she snapped, "and the police are not doing anything about it."

Pippin shot a glance at Jamie. She hadn't known why the book had led her to Max, but maybe this was the reason. If the police weren't investigating his death as a murder, maybe Pippin needed to.

Jamie nodded thoughtfully, pausing for a moment out of respect. "What do you think happened, Lorraine?" he asked after a few seconds.

Pippin noticed how often Jamie used the woman's name, as if he were building a level of intimacy with her so she'd open up. Another good tactic.

Lorraine leaned forward, her voice dropping to a harsh whisper. "Someone got to him out in Devil's Cove."

"But why? Who would have wanted to kill him?" Pippin asked, scooting to the edge of her chair to close the distance between them.

She shrugged. "That I don't know. He was a boring professor. A rule-follower." She placed a shaky hand against her chest. "But he was *my* boring professor, and he was *my* rule-follower. And now..." She trailed off, her composure cracking.

"He was an experienced kayaker, wasn't he?" Jamie asked. "One of our discussion topics a while back was the conservation efforts down in Florida. It prompted him to tell the group about his experiences in the Everglades."

Lorraine nodded. "He used to lead swamp tours down there while he was in grad school." She swung the chair to the left slightly, extending one arm to hold onto the edge of the desk as if to steady herself. "He went back over the summer to do it again. He practically grew up on his family's boat."

"Which is why you don't believe it was an accident," Jamie said.

Lorraine tilted her head back and stared at the ceiling for a moment before looking back at them. "Exactly. He always wore a lifejacket—"

"The newspaper didn't say anything about a lifejacket," Jamie said.

"He didn't have one on when he was found." Lorraine's voice started to tremble, the chasm between her stoicism and her emotions widening. "But I know Max. He was a stickler for safety. Like I said, he was a rule-follower. He wouldn't have gone out without one. And he was an expert swimmer, for another. Team captain in high school. Water polo all four years and in college, too. The cove is protected. There's no rough water. It was not an accident." Her voice finally broke, her emotions suddenly cascaded through her. "People say you aren't given any more than you can handle, but I don't know. I feel like I'm barely hanging on."

She reached for a clear crystal tumbler a quarter of the way filled with an amber liquid. So this was how she was controlling her grief. Paper and folders sat in a haphazard stack on the left side of the desk. A collection of framed photos were in the back right corner. One was of a young man and a pregnant woman. Probably their daughter. Another was of Lorraine and a man Pippin knew was Max. That spark of familiarity struck her again, but the answer was just out of reach. The couple stood in front of a sailboat, crystal clear water in the distance, cotton ball clouds dotting the sky. The neck of a discarded bottle laying sideways on the desk stuck out from behind the photo frames...more evidence of Lorraine's coping mechanism. The third photo was of Max in a black robe, hood, and doctoral tam with a tassel. His PhD graduation photo.

A niggling feeling swept through Pippin. He looked so familiar, but she couldn't place him.

"First the break-in. Then Max dying. What next?" Lorraine moaned. "What next?"

Pippin and Jamie looked at each other. "What break-in?" Pippin asked aloud.

Lorraine swallowed the liquid in her glass, abruptly reaching for a decanter on a small liquor cart next to the desk and pouring herself four fingers of the scotch. She took a healthy swig before spinning her chair around to face them again. Pippin's eyes locked on a family photograph on the corner of the desk. Lorraine and a young woman Pippin presumed was her daughter during her teen years perched on a railing at the beach. Two men—most likely Max and their teenage son—stood on either side of the women. The twilight sky over the Atlantic was the background. It was a snapshot of happier times. Times this family would never recapture, Pippin thought, and her heart ached a little more for Lorraine, and for her children.

"It happened a few nights before Max's death. Thankfully we'd gone out to dinner, so we weren't here, but we came home to find the place had been ransacked."

"Was anything taken?" Pippin asked.

Lorraine blew out a heavy breath. "An old locket of mine. Not worth anything, so the thieves struck out there. Max's laptop. That's all."

"But you said the place was ransacked?" Pippin asked.

Lorraine took another swallow of her drink. "Things tossed out of the drawers, off the closet shelves. Even the clock and the paintings were ripped down."

Jamie shifted in his seat, looking puzzled. "What were they after?"

Lorraine's jaw pulsed. "I think Max knew, but he never said."

They followed her gaze to the clock hanging crooked on the wall next to the door. Had they overstayed their welcome?

Once again, Pippin and Jamie looked at each other. "Why do you think he knew what they were after?" Jamie asked.

Suddenly, like a curtain coming down, Lorraine's expression turned stony, the emotions she'd let through buried again. "How do I know you are who you say you are?" she demanded.

This was a question she should have asked before she'd let them through the door, Pippin thought.

Jamie shifted forward enough to remove his wallet from his back pocket. He fished out his driver's license and handed it over to her, followed by a business card shaped like a stack of books.

"Jamie McAdams," Lorraine read aloud. "You work at The Open Door?"

"That's right," he said, not bothering to say that he was co-owner of the shop.

"Where the *Synkéntrosi* group meets?"

He nodded and her gaze turned to Pippin. "And you?"

Pippin had a decision to make, one she'd wrestled with since she'd decided to barge in on this woman. Did she tell her the truth—or some semblance of it—or did she not? She went with a hybrid. "I heard about your husband's death, and something about it just didn't sound right."

Lorraine stared at her hard. If her eyes were lasers, they would have burned holes right through Pippin. She tried to stop herself from squirming under the scrutiny. A moment later, she shifted her steely gaze to Jamie, and then, quick as a flash, she stood. The chair she'd been sitting on was on casters. It shot backwards from the force of her sudden movement.

Pippin and Jamie watched her as she strode to the bookshelf, returning to her chair with a book in her one hand. "I found this yesterday." She flipped the book open and pulled out a single sheet of paper.

Lorraine finished what was left of her scotch. She set the glass down with a *thunk* as she held the paper out to them. Two sentences, written in neat, tight print, were in the center. Jamie reached for it and read it, his voice low.

It belongs to me. I want what he gave you.

Chapter 20

"Every book is a quotation; and every house is a quotation out of all forests, and mines, and stone quarries; and every man is a quotation from all his ancestors."

~Ralph Waldo Emerson

*P*ippin fisted the steering wheel, replaying the last few minutes she and Jamie had spent in Max Lawrence's office. "It was murder, plain and simple," Lorraine had said.

"Did you tell the police about the note?" Jamie asked her.

Lorraine had poured herself another finger of scotch. Pippin was surprised the woman could still sit upright. "Not yet," she said, her words starting to slur together.

Pippin had reread the short message.

It belongs to me. I want what he gave you.

LORRAINE HADN'T BEEN able to give them any other information. She didn't know if anything from Max's study was missing. "It's possible," she'd said, "but this was his domain. Sometimes I sat in here to read while he worked, but mostly I stayed out. It's a man's room."

That was true. The rich leather of the chairs and the dark wood was the typical decor taken straight from a men's club. Much like her father's study, she thought. Before they left, Pippin asked one last question, a hopeful lilt in her voice. "Lorraine, did your husband know my father? Leo Hawthorne?"

"Of course. The body they just—"

She broke off, as if she realized that the body she casually referred to was actually the twenty year old remains of Pippin's father. Mrs. Lawrence blinked, and her eyes clouded. "I'm so sorry."

Pippin's head wagged between a nod and a shake. "It's okay."

"I remember the day he disappeared," she said. Her gaze travelled up, and she seemed to speak to the empty space in the room rather than to Pippin specifically. "Max was shaken when the news came out. He told me that Leo Hawthorne was an upstanding man. That he wouldn't leave his kids behind. After your father disappeared, Max thought that something had happened to him. He never bought the disappearing act theory. He even talked to the sheriff, but everyone was convinced that the man had just run off."

Pippin's skin pricked, like a million thorns from a rosebush pressed down on her, as she listened to Lorraine's memory. Would her father still be alive if the sheriff had listened? "Do you remember anything else?"

The woman's eyes were dark. Clouded. She took a swig of her drink and thought. She started to move her head but stopped and sat up. Still holding her glass, she pointed at Pippin. "Your father gave something to Max to hold onto. God, I'd forgotten that." She dipped her head and spread her hand across her forehead, rubbing her temples with her thumb and middle finger. "What was it?"

Pippin's breath caught, the words of the note left at her front door returning.

LEO ENTRUSTED ME WITH SOMETHING. *It belongs to you. Please meet me tomorrow at noon at the fishing pier near the cove.*

MAX LAWRENCE MUST HAVE WRITTEN the letter. She held her breath as Lorraine glanced around the room, looking at the shelves, at the desk, even at the floor, as if something would jog her memory.

"It was so long ago," she finally said with a shake of her head. "I don't remember."

"Can I...do you have something your husband wrote? His handwriting?" Her voice trembled. Jamie stared at her, looking baffled.

It took Lorraine a minute and a scouring of the desk drawers before she produced a black and white composition book. "He preferred these to leather or moleskin," she said.

A composition book with paper just like the one the mysterious note had been written on. Pippin opened it up to a random page and her suspicion was confirmed. She looked at Jamie, wishing she could tell him right this second about the discovery. Leo had given Max something. Max had written to her and Grey, wanting to give it back, but he'd died before he'd been able to do that.

At least she had the answer to why he hadn't shown up that day on the fishing pier. He'd already been dead.

So many questions flashed in her mind. *Who had ransacked the Lawrence house? Were they looking for whatever Leo had given Max? Had Max changed his mind? Had he made an arrangement to give it to someone else? Had it been a rendezvous at the cove, or had he been ambushed? Why, oh why had Max been killed?*

The Odyssey had pointed Pippin to Max. Now she had a gossamer thread connecting Max to Leo. The rest was up to her, but she was drawing a blank. In that moment, she wasn't sure what compelled her to tell Jamie about her father's secret room, just as they reached the intersection where she could either turn to go to The Open Door or take another street to get to Sea Captain's Inn, she told him how she'd discovered it.

"Do you mind...could I..."

She glanced at him. "You want to see it?"

He didn't bother trying to fight the smile that played on his lips. "Thought you'd never ask."

Instead of heading to the bookstore, she turned left on Rum Runner's Lane and parked right in front rather than on the narrow paved driveway. She automatically scanned the pampas grass.

"What are you looking for?" Jamie asked.

"There's a dog that hangs out around here. I've been trying to catch her."

"What are you going to do with her when you do?"

Pippin hadn't thought that far ahead. "I guess I'll decide that if I'm able to win her over."

She led him across the yard, up the porch. A collection

of pots stood off to one side, several bags of soil propped up next to them. Soon they'd be lush with flowers. Next, she'd plant the borders of the front walkway. Digging her hands into the soil was almost better than caffeine.

She waved at Jimmy, but he was focused on the wood he was cutting with the table saw. A thick orange extension cord was plugged into an outlet on the porch and strung through the railing. It draped over the flower garden and connected to the power cord for the saw. Jimmy was in his own world, so they passed him by.

Jamie stopped just inside the door, taking in the great room, the kitchen, the staircase leading to the second floor, the live edge of the wood mantle. Pippin tried to see it through his eyes. Did it look as wonderful as she thought it did, or was her perspective biased because of her memories, along with the blood, sweat, and tears that had gone into the renovation?

"Wow," he said looking from one side of the room to the other. "This place is spectacular."

Her chest swelled, all of their work validated. Every bit of it *was* spectacular, down to the very last nail.

She led him through the great room, crossing paths with Travis carrying a piece of shiplap up the stairs. "Almost done with the master," he said, giving Jamie a guarded once over. His eyebrows pinched together, and he looked suspicious, as if he wasn't sure Jamie had good intentions.

"I'll be up in a little while to check it out," she said, resisting the temptation to scold him...or laugh. She listened to her gut. She hardly knew either man, but between the two, she trusted Jamie McAdams.

Travis lifted his chin in silent acknowledgement to Jamie before continuing up the stairs. Pippin felt his eyes watching them as they passed him by. She caught a glimpse of Kryon in the kitchen downing a bottle of water. His back was to them, so they scooted past.

"This way," she said, leading Jamie to Leo's study, quietly closing the study door behind him. She walked right up to the shelf along the far wall. She took hold of the right edge and gave a gentle pull. The secret door was heavy but opened easily on the invisible hinges.

Jamie stared.

Pippin smiled to herself. She figured there wouldn't be many things she could do that could surprise Jamie McAdams, so she relished the moment as he gave a low whistle followed by an awed, "Whoa."

She led him up the stairs, around the tight corner of the landing, and into the hidden room.

"Was this here, or did your dad create it?" he asked after he'd taken it all in.

"Honestly, I don't know. He had his study below with some of his books. My mom wouldn't have any of them—"

"Because of the bibliomancy thing."

The way he said it felt dismissive. "Right."

"So either your dad created the room to keep the rest of his books, or it was here and he turned it into his secret study."

"I don't think he could have had it built or my mom would know. My guess is that he discovered it somehow, moved some of his books and things up there, and didn't tell her."

"Or maybe she knew about it and just didn't come in," Jamie suggested.

Just like she had the first time she'd been in this room, Jamie stood in front of the shelves and tracked the pads of his fingers along the spines of the books. "No clues about his death in here?" he asked.

That wasn't dismissive. That was him acknowledging that she had this ability and that the books told her something. "None." She pointed to the bulletin board. "He was trying to trace my mother's family back to...to...I don't know, the beginning? Your granddad was helping him. Them."

He turned and took a moment to look at the rest of the room. "I wonder..."

"What?" she asked.

"I was thinking about the note Lorraine Lawrence pulled out of that book." He gestured to the volumes lining the shelves. "Could your father have hidden something in one of his?"

"I thought of that," she said. "He had his favorites."

"Tolkien," Jamie interjected.

She smiled. "Right. And a few others." She pointed to the top shelf on the far left, thinking of the late nights she'd spent in here since discovering the room. "I pulled out each one and shook them. Nothing."

Jamie turned, his eyes narrowing as he studied the room. Pippin knew what he was thinking—that maybe Leo had hidden something elsewhere in the room—something that could help them figure out the truth.

But where? Since discovering the secret study, she'd spent hours up here, some of them with Grey, a few with Daisy and Ruby, but most of them alone. She'd looked in every nook and cranny, in nearly every book, but hadn't found a thing.

She wasn't ready to give up, though. She stood next to Jamie and looked for anything she might have missed. She had an idea suddenly. A place she hadn't looked. She took the three steps to the bulletin board. Glancing over her shoulder at Jamie, she said, "Help me?"

He understood what she was doing and a second later,

they'd lifted the board off of the picture hanging hooks and set it on the floor, leaning it against the wall. A part of Pippin thought maybe there'd be a built-in safe behind the big board. Filled with what? Her father hadn't had anything worth a lot of money. Nothing he needed a safe for.

The wall was just a wall.

She sighed.

"It was a good thought," Jamie said.

They hung the board's wire back on the hooks and turned back to the room. Jamie was the next to move. He went to the chairs, crouched down to grab ahold of the front legs, and tilted the first one back. He peered at the underside of it. As he set it back down, he looked at her and shook his head.

"Try the other one," she said.

He moved to the other chair and repeated the process of lifting and looking, once again finding nothing attached to the bottom.

There were no other hiding places that Pippin could think of. She'd checked every bit of the bookshelves thinking that maybe Leo had created some sort of false wall or compartment. After all, he had an entire secret room.

But she'd found nothing.

Dark clouds had crept into the March sky. The coziness of the room made her feel closer to her father. She could picture him up here, holed away with his books, exhausting every possibility when it came to solving the mystery of her mother's family. She glanced at the clock. Nearly five. How had it gotten so late?

Her gaze slipped away, but something lurked in the back of her mind. The clock and the artwork in Max's study askew on the wall. She looked back at her father's clock. The face itself, which was about five inches in diameter, was mounted in a much wider rectangular frame made of what looked to be reclaimed wood case.

Jamie followed her gaze. They moved at the same time, but Pippin got to the clock first. She lifted it from its hook and turned it over. The back was covered with a thin plastic panel. At the top was a release mechanism. She crossed the room and sat in one of the chairs, knees together, feet apart, the clock face down on her lap. Jamie sat in the other chair, his body angled her way. He watched her intently as she depressed the little clip holding the cover onto the frame, pulling it away to reveal the inner workings of the clock itself. Beneath that was a space large enough to hide something...and in that space was a folded small goldenrod envelope.

She flattened it then flipped the envelope over to look at both sides. There was nothing written on either side. She undid the clasp and slid the contents out. It was a small plastic sleeve with a worn, thick piece of something inside. Leather? There was writing on it, but she had no idea what it said...or what language it was written in for that matter.

She held it out. Jamie took it. His face instantly paled. His chest rose and fell, his breathing audible and shaky.

She grew instantly alarmed. "What's wrong?"

He looked at her, his expression nothing short of incredulous. "Pippin. This is an ancient text. Old Irish. It's written on papyrus. It's an historic document. A primary source from, I don't know, maybe the first century?"

Her head started pounding, as if all the blood in her body had surged upward, pushing like crashing waves against her skull. From the window, she could see the dark clouds turning inky. A spring storm was coming. Ominous. It was as if the world around her reflected the discovery they'd made.

The air in the room turned stale and heavy. How was this ancient piece of papyrus covered in Old Irish, if Jamie was correct, connected to her parents? Why had her father hidden it? "Can you read it?" Pippin asked him. He was a scholar of Medieval Irish, after all.

He gave a sardonic laugh. "No."

"But—"

She broke off as he continued. "It looks like Old Irish, which is incredibly complicated. It derives from...actually is one of the oldest of the Goidelic languages. The morphology and allomorphy of Old Irish, or sometimes Old Gaelic, are incredibly complex—"

Pippin held up her hand to stop him. "You lost me at complicated."

One side of his mouth rose in a half smile. "Let me back up. Old Irish is one of the Insular Celtic languages. One of the oldest languages in Ireland," he clarified when she raised her eyebrows.

"And morphology—" she asked. "And the other thing. Allmalogy?"

"Allomorphy," Jamie corrected. "It has to do with the unpredictability of the stems and suffixes. Also the consonant mutations, which create a particularly complex sound system. Like the words 'hunted' and 'fished'. Both have the -ed ending, but those letters produce a different sound in each word. Morphology is basically the study of words. How they're formed. Their relationship to other words within the same language. It looks at structure, parts of speech, intonation. Context can change a word's pronunciation and meaning, for example—"

Pippin waved her hands to stop him. "I get the gist," she said. "Can you translate it? Eventually?"

"Old Irish is not my area of expertise." He sounded so disappointed.

"But you can do it?" she pressed.

He dropped his gaze to his lap for a moment before looking back at her. "It'll take some time, but yes. I think so." He took another minute, examining the papyrus through the plastic. As he went to slide it back into the goldenrod envelope, he stopped. "Look," he said.

He held open the flap of the paper envelope and pointed to some words written there. Pippin leaned over the table to look. Her heart caught in her throat. It was her father's writing. Of that, she was one hundred percent certain. Three words were written on the inside flap. William Butler Yeats.

It was a message, she thought. Her father, from beyond the grave, was sending her a message. She jumped up and went to stand in front of the bookshelf that housed a few volumes of poetry. She scanned the titles until she came across an old hardback copy of poetry by Yeats.

Her father had believed in the Lane women and their gift of bibliomancy. Once again, her blood pulsed in her head. She felt as if she was uncovering information bit by bit—a trail of clues that would give her the answers she sought.

PIPPIN SAT ON THE FLOOR, cross legged, only this time, instead of Ruby and Daisy across from her, Jamie sat there watching her, his eyes curious behind his horn-rimmed glasses.

"I don't really understand it all," she said, giving him this information up front in case it didn't work.

Jamie gave her a reassuring smile. "I'm just here for the ride."

Great. Instead of alleviating her anxiety, that comment ratcheted it up. A ride assumed something interesting or exciting would happen, neither of which might be true in this situation.

A feeling of self-consciousness settled inside her, but she pushed ahead, going with what had worked before based on what she, Ruth, and Daisy had surmised.

Jamie watched her intently as she held the book aloft, looked at it, and said, "What can you tell me?" She placed it on the floor, on its well-worn spine, riffled the pages with her fingertips to loosen them up, and let go. The book fell open to a poem. She stared at it, waiting for words to float off the page. None did. She started to read the first line, but stopped, picked up the book, and handed it to Jamie. If he hadn't been here to witness the discovery of the ancient papyrus, she never would have let him be a witness to her efforts at bibliomancy. Her struggle as she tried to make sense of the words on the page was not something she was willing to share him, however.

He took the book without question, cleared his throat, and read.

My Descendants

Having inherited a vigorous mind
From my old fathers I must nourish dreams
And leave a woman and a man behind
As vigorous of mind, and yet it seems
Life scarce can cast a fragrance on the wind,
Scarce spread a glory to the morning beams,

> *But the torn petals strew the garden plot;*
> *And there's but common greenness after that.*
> *And what if my descendants lose the flower*
> *Through natural declension of the soul,*
> *Through too much business with the passing hour,*
> *Through too much play, or marriage with a fool?*
> *May this laborious stair and this stark tower*
> *Become a roofless ruin that the owl*
> *May build in the cracked masonry and cry*
> *Her desolation to the desolate sky.*
> *The Primum Mobile that fashioned us*
> *Has made the very owls in circles move;*
> *And I, that count myself most prosperous*
> *Seeing that love and friendship are enough,*
> *For an old neighbour's friendship chose the house*
> *And decked and altered it for a girl's love,*
> *And know whatever flourish and decline*
> *These stones remain their monument and mine.*

"WHAT DO YOU THINK IT MEANS?" he asked.

She didn't answer because she needed a few minutes to try to puzzle through it. In school, like it would be for any reluctant reader—or in her case, a forbidden reader—poetry had been a challenge and a frustration. She asked him to read it again, which he did. When he finished, she gave a frustrated sigh and said, "I don't know."

If the poem held hidden meaning, she couldn't decipher it. She took the book back from Jamie, closing it. For the second time, she asked the question, "What can you tell me?", then placed the book on its spine.

She let go.

"Same page," Jamie said.

But still, no words pulled away from the page. No lines

stood out to her. "What message do you have?" she muttered.

"What's supposed to happen?" Jamie asked.

She looked up at him. "The words turn a little darker and float right off the page."

"And that's not happening right now," he said. Statement, not question.

"And that's not happening right now," she confirmed.

She picked up the book and read the poem for herself— slowly—to see if she could glean anything from the words. She drew in a sharp breath. For a moment, she thought the words grew lighter, turning to a faded black on the page. But no...

"Oh!" It wasn't the words of the poem that had grown lighter, but the title that had grown darker.

"What is it?" Jamie asked.

Instead of answering, Pippin placed the book on the floor between them. She closed her eyes to the count of ten, then opened them, staring right at the open pages. Once again, the poem itself seemed to fade in comparison to the title.

She flipped the book around. "What do you see?" she asked Jamie.

He placed his hands on either side of the book, studying it. After a moment, he gave a small shrug and let go. "Nothing. Just the poem."

Of course, because he wasn't the bibliomancer. In that moment, Pippin realized that she didn't need validation for what she was experiencing. She had to start trusting herself.

She put her forefinger on top of the poem's title. "This looks bolder for me. Darker."

Jamie's brows pulled together. Pippin could see that he was trying to understand. "And that means..."

Good question. *She* assigned the meaning. She had to decipher the text, but she couldn't force it. "Something about the people who came before me."

"Or the people that come after," he said.

Right. It could go either way. She thought of the family tree Mr. McAdams had been helping her parents with. The family tree that her father had pinned to the bulletin board in his secret room.

"My descendants," she said quietly. "What about them?"

THE OLD PIECE of papyrus was too valuable to be taken out of the hidden room. "It's been safe all these years," Pippin said. "It should stay here."

"Agreed," Jamie said. "I'll take a few pictures of it so I can work on translating it."

"The plastic must be archival safe, right?" Pippin asked. Surely her father would have made sure it was to protect this artifact.

"I would think so. It won't photograph well through the sleeve, though."

"There are gloves in the desk!" Pippin jumped up and retrieved a pair of cotton gloves she'd seen in her father's desk when she'd first searched the room. He must have had them for this reason. She donned them and carefully slid the papyrus out of its protected covering and laid it on top. After Jamie took a set of pictures from above, she slid the old paper back into the protective sheath.

Pippin offered to drive him back to The Open Door, but he declined. "Thanks, but it's okay. I'll walk."

Pippin slipped the papyrus back into the goldenrod envelope and tucked the envelope back into the space in the back of the clock. She replaced the covering and hung it back on the wall. "Keep me posted on the translation?" she asked.

"Of course," he said. He was lost in thought as they walked down the stairs and back into the Leo's old study. Pippin closed the secret bookshelf door behind her and led him back through the great room.

He turned to her before descending the porch steps. "Be careful, Pippin. If Max Lawrence's death *is* connected to your father, and his wife is right about it not being an accident, that means there's a murderer out there."

His words stuck in her head as she made herself a sandwich for dinner. She had two distinct things to think about. Her father's work, which had to do with the Lane family, and the object over which Max—and possibly Leo—were killed.

Chapter 21

"You never really understand a person until you consider things from his point of view... Until you climb inside of his skin and walk around in it."

~Harper Lee, from *To Kill a Mockingbird*

"*Y*ou have to give me some time, Pippin. Rome wasn't built in a day," Jamie said the third time Pippin called.

"That's a little cliché for a professor," Pippin said with a roll of her eyes.

"I'm not a professor and clichés are clichés for a reason. If the shoe fits," he said, not missing a beat.

"With all those degrees, you could be a professor," she grumbled.

He chuckled. "I'm gathering that patience is not one of your strengths."

She sighed. "I'm working on it."

"And I'm working on the translation."

She could hear the smile in his voice. At least he wasn't irritated by her incessant phone calls. She had to remember that he had a bookshop to run. "I know. Please keep me posted," she said for what felt like the tenth time.

"You'll be the first...and only person I call."

She knew he would, and she knew she had to let go. At some point, she had to learn to trust someone. It might as well be him.

Another several hours passed and she itched to call him again, but she resisted. Instead, she finalized the advertisement she was running in *The Devil's Cove Gazette* announcing Sea Captain's Inn and the open house. She'd have photos taken of the rooms once they were furnished. She'd had Grey convert part of the walk-in pantry to a scullery, complete with a sink and dishwasher. It felt old-fashioned, but when she hosted dinners or weddings or other events, she wanted to keep things clean and the messes out of sight. All the while, she thought about the connection between Max Lawrence and Leo Hawthorne. What could Leo have given Max that was worth their lives?

She thought about the men's discussion group Max had been a part of. *Synkéntrosi.* Leo had died long before it had begun as a formal group, but what if it had existed informally before that? She could ask Jamie, but she feared he might not answer his cell phone if she called him again. So she texted instead. *How long has your Synkéntrosi group been going on?*

Not a second later, the status of her text showed that he'd read it. She drummed her fingertips on her desk as she waited for his reply. Three blinking dots appeared, followed by his response. *About fifteen years. I joined them about five years ago.*

Do you think any of them met informally before that? she texted.

Jamie was an attentive texter. He replied right away. *Not all the same guys, but yeah, they met for a couple of years before they became formal.*

Her fingers flew across her phone's screen. *Who's in the old guard that's still part of it now?*

This time the response didn't come immediately. Pippin tapped her fingers again as she waited. Finally, her phone beeped with an incoming text. Instead of him listing all the people in the group, he'd sent a photo of a membership roster. On the far left was a column with the members' names. Next to that were the addresses, and on the right was a column for Year Joined.

Handy.

Jamie's name was at the very top, followed by his grandfather, Cyrus McAdams. Pippin skipped over them, stopping when she saw Mick Barclay's name. The marina owner was part of the group? He hadn't struck her as the intellectual type. Then again, she knew better than to judge a book by its cover.

She made a mental note of Mick's name as she kept going, coming to halt at another familiar name. Harold Manatee, Daisy's assistant librarian, was a member. He was far too young to be part of the old guard, so she dismissed him. Pippin didn't recognize any other names until she got to Quincy Ratherford, the local newspaper reporter. She could see him participating in what was, essentially, a men's book club. She'd have to ask him about it. Jed Riordin, the man who'd come by the house saying he'd known Leo, was listed right after Quincy. Matthew Sacks and James Salisbury came next, followed by Roger Terranty, George Underwood, and Aaron Wallace. None of the names meant a thing to her.

Thanks, she texted to Jamie, who sent her a thumbs up emoji.

Pippin resisted mentioning his translation task, instead reviewing the names on the list again. She discounted the McAdams men. She knew the connection between Leo and them, and between Max Lawrence and Jamie.

She paused at Mick's name. The theory about her father leading the charge against the marina expansion was a theory, but she was operating under the assumption that what had happened to Max had something to do with her father, and some mysterious object. Max was a seaman, but did he have a connection to Mick?

She thought about Quincy Ratherford next. He'd known her father, at least peripherally. He'd written about the sunken boat at the marina. He'd done a write up about her father's disappearance., and again about the discovery of his body. Now she knew that, like Mick, he'd known Max through the *Synkéntrosi* group—something he hadn't mentioned.

The last name she recognized from the list was Jed Riordin. She'd never heard the man's name before he'd shown up at her house unannounced. That was suspicious enough. He'd claimed to have come to offer her his condolences, but could he have had a different motive? He'd been interested in her father's study. In his old books. He'd mentioned her father's collection of ships.

She pictured the shelves in her father's secret room. The books. The miniature carved ship sitting on a stand on one shelf, a ship in a bottle on another.

A message in a bottle. Her mind slammed to a stop.

Jed had asked about her father's collection. He'd asked about the ships in the bottles.

She raced from her office in the front of the house to her father's study in the back. Through the back windows, the expanse of the water was dotted with whitecaps, the churning of the water a reflection of her roiling insides. She yanked open the bookshelf. Careened up the stairs. She rounded the narrow landing, scooting along the railing, then went straight to the bottle with the model ship. A memory flashed in her mind. She'd asked her father how the ship got into the bottle.

"Magic," he'd said, and as a little girl, she'd believed him.

Now she picked it up. Turned it over and around, looking through the glass to see if something else was inside. She pried the cork out of the opening and turned the bottle so she could look down the neck, but all she saw was the intricately carved ship with its cloth sails. Her shoulders sagged. It was just a miniature ship.

As she replaced the cork, though, her mind shot back to the visit she and Jamie had paid to Lorraine Lawrence. She pictured Max Lawrence in her mind. That familiarity that had sparked when she'd seen the photographs on his desk. And then, like a tidal wave crashing down, it hit her. Max Lawrence had been the man she'd seen at Devil's Brew Café. When she'd asked Jamie how long Odysseus had been gone from home, he'd been the one to answer the question. If he'd put two and two together, he'd known who she was, and that she and Grey were back in Devil's Cove.

He could have come up to her that day and told her he had something of her father's that needed to be returned. But he hadn't. He'd written the note and left it under her mat rather than speak to her in public.

Why?

Something else tugged at her thoughts. She closed her eyes, letting the image float into her head. Suddenly she jolted, nearly dropping the bottle she held. She clutched it tightly, as if letting go of it would make her thoughts evaporate. She dug her phone from her pocket, dialing Jamie.

"I don't have it done yet, Pip—" he started, but she interrupted him, blurting, "We have to go back to Mrs. Lawrence's house."

Chapter 22

"Good neighbors always spy on you to make sure you are doing well."

~Pawan Mishra

*J*amie didn't ask any questions over the phone. "I'll drive," he said, and then he hung up before Pippin could argue. She waited for him outside, pacing impatiently. She thought she saw the curtains across the street flutter, but she forgot about it when Jamie's silver Audi appeared.

As she climbed into the passenger seat, she had to acknowledge that his *grownup* car had pretty nice features. Leather seats. A nice sound system. A/C. She could appreciate the luxuries, but most of all, at the moment, she was glad she wasn't driving.

Ten minutes later, they sped across the bridge to the mainland.

Pippin held her phone in her hand, Lorraine Lawrence's

address plugged into the map app, but Jamie didn't need it. He remembered the route, and each time she was about to say turn right here, or go straight, he beat her to it. Another ten minutes passed, and they rolled up in front of the Lawrence house.

She'd told Jamie her theory on the way over, but now that they stood on Mrs. Lawrence's front porch poised to knock, the idea sounded ridiculous. First of all, why would her father put a message in a bottle with a miniature replica of an old sailing ship? And second, assuming he did do that, why give it to Max Lawrence? Why hadn't he just left it in his secret study? The only reason she could think of was that Leo feared his room would be found out...or that she and Grey would never discover it. By giving it to Max, he'd tried to ensure it—whatever *it* was—would eventually get back to his children.

"Don't overthink it," Jamie said, as if he could read her mind. Any doubt he'd had about her ability as a bibliomancer was long gone. She felt as if she could add him to the list of friends she was collecting in Devil's Cove.

She knocked, then knocked again. Finally, after a solid two minutes, Mrs. Lawrence threw open the door. Pippin's gaze dropped to the woman's hand, hanging by her side, a crystal glass dangling in a loose grip, clear liquid on the verge of sloshing onto the floor. "Back again?" she slurred, all semblance of her stoicism gone.

Pippin launched into the spiel she'd mentally prepared. "Mrs. Lawrence—" The woman scowled and Pippin quickly amended to, "Lorraine. You mentioned yesterday that you thought my father gave your husband something."

Lorraine's body swayed slightly. She held onto the edge of the door with one hand, keeping herself steady, her glass still precarious in her other. She didn't respond, so Pippin produced the ship in the bottle she'd brought with her.

Lorraine's eyes went as wide as they could, given her alcohol-induced state and she pointed, her arm rotating in the air. "Maxy haz one a' those."

"Could it be the thing my father gave him?" Pippin asked, barely controlling the urgency in her voice.

Lorraine's brow furrowed as she thought, then looked at Pippin and Jamie with glassy, unseeing eyes. "Could be."

Pippin felt a rush of excitement. "Is it okay...could we take a look at it?"

Lorraine's eyelids had grown heavier, sinking over her bloodshot eyes, but she nodded and stepped back. The liquid in her glass finally made it over the edge. Jamie lunged forward, grabbing the glass from Lorraine before it fell.

She jerked back as she tried to grab it back from him. "What are you—" she started, but broke off when she saw the puddle the stream of liquid had left on the floor. She let out a moan as her shoulders hunched. Her chin dropped against her chest.

Jamie wrapped a supportive arm around her and ushered her into the study they'd been in last time. As he got Lorraine situated in one of the chairs, Pippin beelined for the desk. It looked like nothing had changed since the day before. The bottle. An empty glass. The photographs. The neck of a bottle poking out from behind a frame.

She'd thought it had been a discarded bottle of liquor, but she was pretty sure she'd been wrong. She could see that the bottle on Max's desk had the same cork as her father's. Still, she held her breath as she reached out to move one of the photographs revealing the entire thing. Just like her father's, it contained a miniature old-fashioned sailing ship.

Pippin grabbed it and gave it a quick examination, but nothing suspect jumped out at her. No secret message was written on the ship's sails. There wasn't a spot in the ship where something could be hidden. She spun around just as Jamie left Lorraine and came over to her. She gave him the bottle. He examined it from every which direction just like she had. "If there's something hidden in here, I'm not seeing it."

Could the ship itself be the important thing? Pippin studied it again, but it looked just like any other tourist version, albeit much nicer than any that could be bought in a souvenir shop on the pier.

She'd put her father's ship in a bottle down when she'd picked up Max's. She retrieved it now from the desk and held it out next to the one in Jamie's hand. Bit by bit, she catalogued them, looking for differences. They had the same cork. The same bottle shape. The same thick, distorted glass and soft tint. Each sat on a stand, though she'd left her father's on the bookshelf in the secret room.

One of the ships secured inside had three masts and square sails. A square-rigged clipper. The other had two masts, the first shorter than the mainmast, and it had a square topsail. A topsail schooner. Some of his miniatures he'd bought, but she had a vague recollection of him sitting at his desk with a mounted magnifying glass, painstakingly building a ship piece by piece inside a bottle. Maritime art was a thing of the past, except to people like her father whose passion kept it alive. How the mass-produced ones were made, she had no idea, but these, she knew, were Leo's creations.

She gave a frustrated sigh. She'd been so sure there was

a clue in the bottle, or even that it was the thing he—and Max Lawrence—had been killed over.

"We could break it," Jamie suggested, but she could see from his pained expression that this wasn't something he wanted to do.

"Take it," Lorraine said from behind them, her words still slurred. "Max kep' it on hish desk, but he didn't...he didn't care 'bout it. It's been shtuck it b'hind the family photosh forever. Jus' take it."

Pippin didn't want to give Lorraine time to change her mind. She grabbed the stand that went with it, thanked her, and a minute later, she and Jamie were heading back to the island. They got to the bridge, stopping to wait as the middle section, which had turned to let a personal yacht through, slowly spun back into place. "They're replacing it with a high-rise," Jamie said, his voice a little melancholy.

Pippin's hands tightened on the bottles in her lap. She wasn't sure how she felt about losing the old swing bridge. On the one hand, it might keep her unwelcome emotions at bay. That Pavlovian response she got every time she crossed it. But on the other hand, it was a landmark. It said *hello* and *goodbye*. It was the backdrop for photographs that had been made into postcards sold at the island's tourist shops. It had been around for more than fifty years.

"It's an old relic," Jamie was saying. He'd rolled down the driver's side window and had his left arm resting on the frame. "It's time, but my girls'll miss it."

Pippin looked at him. He wore a sad smile, as if he could imagine his daughters watching the old swing bridge coming down.

The bridge creaked back into place, reestablishing the crossing over the Sound. Jamie drove slowly, following the pace of the cars ahead of him. The cool breeze blowing through the window fluttered Pippin's hair. Jamie bent his arm at his elbow, grasping the top of the window frame, his other hand holding the top of the steering wheel. "It was a good idea," he said after a minute.

"What was?" she asked.

"The ship in the bottle," he said.

Jamie dropped her off. He hadn't said it, but she knew he needed to get back to the bookshop...and to his family. She stood on the steps leading to the porch watching him drive away, hearing his words in her head. He'd thought the same thing she had. She looked at the bottles, one in each hand. She was careful to keep them horizontal so the ships wouldn't become dislodged. She'd already tempted fate with that by turning them this way and that.

Up on the porch, she set the bottles down on the table between the rockers to open the door, nearly dropping the stand she still held when someone behind her said, "Hey sweetie."

Pippin jumped, the high-pitched voice startling. It was a good thing she hadn't been holding the bottles or she'd have dropped them. She turned to see a woman standing at the bottom of the steps. She was elderly. But that word didn't quite fit. Old, yes, but at the same time, bursting with youth. Truthfully, Pippin couldn't say what decade the woman's age fell in. She had snowy white shoulder-length hair, but most of it was dyed a bright blue. She wore a whimsical three-quarter sleeve ribbed top, the horizontal stripes in bright pink, lavender, turquoise, azure, and sunflower yellow, each stripe a different width. The particular color of blue in her hair matched the turquoise stripes of her shirt. She wore a hot pink skirt with a silver zipper up the front and two front pockets featuring appliquéd flowers, and yellow flowered clogs that, oddly, seemed to bring the whole outfit together.

A small box purse hung on a bead chain at the woman's hip. Pink fingernail polish. A pair of chunky black-framed glasses. Pink eyeshadow smudged across her eyelids. And pink lipstick. This woman was one of a kind.

"Hi," Pippin said. She moved to the top step, waiting for the woman to say more.

"You don't remember me, do you? Of course, you don't. What has it been, twenty years?" The woman nodded to herself, confirming what she'd said. "Yes, twenty years, nearly on the dot, if I'm not mistaken." She gestured across the street with one hand, an unlit cigarette between her fingers. "I live there. The one with the white pots."

Pippin held in a laugh. The house was a very colorful lavender and teal, but the descriptor she used was the very plain white pots. Of course, they *were* planted with an array of bright and colorful flowers, so there was that.

Most importantly, though, was the fact that this woman's house was the one with the fluttering curtains. This was the person who'd been watching her. "You lived here when my parents were alive?"

The woman's smile seemed permanently carved onto her face, lipstick-smudged teeth and all. "I grew up in that house. Even my husband and I—husband number one, I mean—lived there. He was also husband number three, so actually we lived there twice. Husband number two had his own place, so I tried that on for size. Not for me, so I came back to my bungalow. So, to answer your question, I did live here when your mama and daddy were in this house." She pointed her wrinkled cigarette at Pippin and said, "And when you and your brother were littles."

Another person who'd known her parents. The ships in the bottles could wait. "Would you like some iced tea?" she asked.

The woman was halfway up the steps before Pippin had finished the question. "Don't you want to know my name? It's Hattie Juniper Pickle. And you're Pippin."

"I am," Pippin said, a little taken aback. Hattie Juniper Pickle was a mouthful of a name, but it fit her. "Nice to meet you." She hesitated, not sure if she should call her Hattie, Hattie Juniper, Mrs. Pickle, or something else entirely.

"Hattie's fine," the woman said, seeming to sense Pippin's indecision. "Sweet tea, if you have it."

Pippin opened the door and Hattie scurried past her. Pippin grabbed the ship bottles and followed her neighbor inside, kicking the door closed with her foot. She detoured to her office, deposited the bottles and stand on her desk, and hurried back out to the great room.

Hattie Juniper Pickle wasn't there.

"Hattie?" Pippin called.

"Over here!" She appeared from behind the fireplace waving at her. She was a spry old thing. "Where do you keep the cups?" she asked.

Pippin opened a kitchen cupboard and pulled out two clear glasses. "They're brand new," she said.

"You got yourself a beau?" Hattie asked.

Pippin felt sure that Hattie knew the answer to that, but she answered anyway. "No. No beau. My brother and I inherited the house when our grandparents died."

"Hmm," she said, then, for the first time, her lipstick-smeared smile faded. "Tsk, tsk. Your grandparents. They're gone now, then?"

"Did you know them?"

"Only from way back when. They didn't come around much, now, did they? When you were young, I mean. Where's the sugar, honey?"

"It's already sweet," Pippin said.

"Can't be too sweet for me," Hattie said, so Pippin opened a drawer and took out several packets of sugar. One by one, Hattie tore them open and dumped the sweetener into her tea. Pippin started to hand her a spoon, but she held up a hand, stopping her. Instead, she swished the glass around to mix the sugar in, but a good amount of the white granule sank to the bottom of the glass.

"Where was I? Oh yes. Your grandparents, they came only once or twice as I remember, and I know everything that happens on this street. Saw them after your mama was gone. Arguing with your daddy right out here in front, but your daddy wasn't having it. He shooed them off, hollering that he'd figure things out and show them, once and for all. He could take care of his children, thank you very much. Then, of course, they came back to clear out the house. I was sure they were gonna sell it. Now, I'm not normally wrong, but I admit I was off about that."

Hattie spoke in speed sentences and Pippin tried to keep up. One thing Hattie said struck her. It sounded to her like her grandparents tried to convince Leo to leave Devil's Cove and move to Greenville, but he'd stood his ground. She wished he'd have gone with them. Things might have turned out differently.

"Tell me what my dad said again," Pippin requested.

Hattie sipped her tea, unlit cigarette still in hand. She was talented with that thing. "I remember it clear as day. It was a heated argument. See, your grandparents, they didn't much care for your mama. Now I never could figure out why. She seemed like a nice enough woman. Doted on you and your brother. But then we all heard the rumors and it made more sense. They were spooked, and I bet they didn't want your daddy filling your heads with magic talk."

"Magic talk," Pippin repeated.

"Sure. Folks 'round here thought she had some magic in her. Even after she died, when your daddy, poof!, vanished, some people thought the magic got him. Now, 'course, we know different. Murder. I knew it."

Pippin choked on the liquid sliding down her throat. "What do you mean?"

Hattie set her box purse on the counter, flipped the latch, and opened it. It was like a mini pink lunchbox. She shoved aside a personal pack of tissue, two tubes of lipstick, and a pair of sunglasses—the frames thick and pink. Then somehow, she released a false bottom revealing another space. She dropped her cigarette in and closed it all up again. "Quit these damn things years ago, but I still like to hold 'em." Hattie leaned one hip against the island. "People came around here looking in the house after your daddy disappeared. They rifled through things. People got no boundaries." Her pink eyelids gave a slow blink. "Your daddy, he woulda died protecting your mama. I think he did."

Pippin's blood ran cold. "Wait, are you saying he died protecting her?"

"I'm saying that your daddy wasn't the only one who loved Cassandra. Unrequited, you understand."

Pippin ran her hand over her head, wrapping her hair up in her fist. Daisy had told her the entire story of Odysseus, including the suitors who camped out in hopes of winning his wife Penelope. It was as if her parents had lived some alternate versions of Homer's story. "So you're saying that whoever loved my mother may have killed my father? But she was already dead."

"Jealousy is an ugly beast."

Her first thought was of Max Lawrence. Could Max have been in love with Cassie? But that didn't explain why Leo would have given him anything, or his commitment to give it—whatever *it* was—back to her and Grey.

"That person's been here."

"Who's been here?"

"Your daddy's murderer, of course."

Pippin's blood whooshed in her ears. She met Hattie's gaze head on. "Do you know who killed my father?"

Hattie took a healthy swig of her sweet tea. She smacked her pink stained lips and stared at Pippin. "Don't you?"

"No!"

"Awe, simmer down, honey. All I'm sayin' is that you've had some people comin' around lately, and I've seen 'em before. People your daddy had dealings with. Take a look at those people, 'cause I'd bet my lunch one of 'em did it."

The blood that had surged to Pippin's head receded. Hattie didn't know anything specific, but her words stuck with her as she lay in bed that night. She ran through the people she'd seen around here lately, excluding Lieutenant Jacobs.

Jimmy, Kyron, and Travis, of course, were ever-present, but right alongside Grey. She remembered Travis looking strangely at her from the stairs. The hairs on the back of her neck went up. He'd looked suspicious, now that she thought about it. She'd ask Grey what he knew about any of the three men he'd hired.

Another thought struck her. Grey said Kyron was going to help him build his new business. From the interactions Pippin had had with Kyron, she thought he was a nice guy, but what did Grey really know about him? What if his reasons for getting close to Grey were nefarious?

She pushed the idea aside. Kyron and Daisy had been talking during his trips to the library. Certainly, she was a good judge of character and wouldn't be almost dating someone who could kill a man. Right? And anyway, Kyron couldn't be involved. He was somewhere in his late twenties, far too young to have known her father. That wasn't necessarily true with Jimmy and Travis. They were on the tail end of their thirties, maybe even into the early forties.

She moved on with her thoughts. Quincy Ratherford from the *Devil's Cove Gazette* said he'd come by the house to check the progress of the remodel at least ten times. He was in the men's club group with Max.

Mick, from the marina, had said he'd been by for the same reason. And he was also in the discussion group.

Max Lawrence wrote the note to her and Grey. Presumably, he'd also been the one to slip it under the mat, so he'd been here. Of course, now he was dead.

Servicemen had been around. People to check the heating system, to deliver things they'd ordered, someone to install the new stove. Pippin couldn't recall anyone else— and then her breath hitched.

Jamie.

Jamie McAdams had been here. He'd seen her father's secret room. He had a photograph of the papyrus with the Old Irish. She rubbed her forehead. Oh God, had she been wrong to trust him?

HATTIE'S PROCLAMATION that Leo's killer had been here at the house recently stuck with Pippin. She lay in bed, trying to push away the idea, but she tossed and turned, Jamie's face floating into her mind's eye, drifting away again, then slamming right back. She flung herself onto her side, smashing her pillow under her head. "It can't be him," she said into the empty room.

Could it? But no, surely Hattie couldn't have meant him. Wouldn't she know him as one of the owners of the bookshop?

Maybe she wouldn't. Jamie had said he'd grown up in Wilmington, then he'd done all his millions of years of schooling. Pippin had no idea how long he'd been living on the island.

After another restless thirty minutes with no sign of sleep coming, she slipped out of bed. She went down the stairs, and straight to her father's study. Through the secret door. She climbed the stairs to the secret study.

Jamie had been here with her in this room. He'd watched her as she used the book to receive a message. He'd believed her. She sat in one of her father's chairs, thinking. Then shook her head and stomped one foot. "No," she said. Jamie was not involved.

He knew Max, but he didn't have any connection to her father, aside from the elder Mr. McAdams. She briefly considered Cyrus McAdams, but he'd been friends with her parents. Or if not exactly friends, at least a trusted confidant. She had to believe her parents had been good judges of character, so she dismissed him, too. Lieutenant Jacobs had been right when he'd said it was a cold case and that clues would be hard to come by.

It felt impossible, but then she looked at the bottles, one with a schooner, the other with a clipper. The way to the truth about her father was through Max Lawrence. Her idea about the ship in the bottle her father had presumably given Max had been a dead end. She was grasping for meaning in every little thing.

She set the bottle that had been her father's on the stand she'd left on the bookshelf, placing the stand and Max's ship in a bottle next to it. Max's sat higher. The stands were different. Leo's was a cradle that sat on four legs. The frame that held Max's was a solid curved piece of wood that sat on a base. A solid base.

Pippin's mind whirled with the possibility. Maybe it wasn't the ship in the bottle that was important. Maybe it was the stand. There was a hidden door that led her up to this private room of her fathers. Similarly, could Leo have created a base with a secret compartment? She moved the bottle again and picked up the base, turning it over in her hand. She moved the pads of her fingers over the wood, feeling for any imperfection, and then realized that her father wouldn't have created it as an imperfection. If there was a secret compartment, it would be imperceptible.

In her gut, she knew it was there, and she would find it. She sat at Leo's desk peering at the base. Her father had a magnifying glass mounted to his desk. He'd used it for the marine art. For the ships in the bottles. She held the stand behind it and angled the glass until she was able to see clearly through it. She looked at every corner. Every angle. Every line.

Nothing.

She was just about to put the thing down again when she noticed a slight, almost imperceptible change in the grain of the wood on the bottom of the stand. She ran her thumb across it. It was smooth. No break that she could discern, but she kept searching, her determination renewed. Her father had been clever. If not for the photo Daisy had in her mother's album, she and Grey would never have known about this hidden room. The ship in the bottle may well have been a gift to Max Lawrence, but the base...the base held whatever Leo wanted to protect.

She pressed her thumb against the part of the wood she'd been examining.

Nothing.

Then she saw noticed something else. The smallest nick where the curved wood met the base itself. Pippin tried to run her finger over it, but it was recessed—tucked between the two parts of the stand. She used her fingernail instead, poking it into the crack. She pressed a little harder and felt the base shift in her hand. Separate from the cradle. Just like that, it came apart. In one hand she held the top of the stand where the ship in the bottle would rest. In her other hand was a flat, thin piece of wood, a hole in its center. The hole that fitted together with the part of the wood she'd thought was marred.

There was something there. She reached her fingers inside and pulled out a silver chain.

Her breath caught. The pendant attached to the chain was silver—or was it white gold? A faintly embossed Fleur de Lis decorated the front. The back had two trees on either side of something Pippin couldn't quite define. It was beautiful. Unique. The shape was an uneven circle. Her heart practically beat out of her chest. This was her mother's necklace. The one Pippin thought had been buried with her.

Her hands trembled. Her father had saved it. He'd made sure she and Grey would get it. She opened the clasp and slipped it around her neck, fastening it tight. The pendant lay against her skin, a weight against her heart.

Chapter 23

"There are many little ways to enlarge your child's world. Love of books is the best of all."
    ~Jacquline Kennedy Onassis

*P*ippin burst into The Open Door, purse slung over her shoulder, her copy of *The Odyssey* in her hand. The scent of the bookshop washed over her. Each time she came, the smell emanating from the rows and rows of books grew more acute. More soothing. She'd never known books could make her feel this way—comforted by merely being in their presence. It hadn't been that way in her grandparents' library. It wasn't that way in Daisy's library, either, come to think of it.

No, it was something about this place. The antiquarian books, maybe. The old and rare books the McAdamses had collected over the years had long histories, both within the pages, and through their owners. She'd come to see Jamie but was sidetracked by the locked case near the register, the books visible only through the glass.

The cat was sprawled out on top of the case, its tail wagging back and forth. It lifted its head, its pale eyes watching her. The cat's long light-gray hair looked soft. Five squiggly stripes marked the space between the cat's eyes, marking her like a tiger.

"You can pet her. She's sweet."

Pippin turned to see the girl who'd spoken. The same pre-teen girl who'd been behind the counter on Pippin's first visit to the shop. The girl she now knew was one of Jamie's daughters. "And beautiful," Pippin said. "What's her name?"

"Ms. Havisham." Pippin gave a little shrug and the girl added, "From *Great Expectations*. Dickens?"

"Of course," Pippin said. "I've heard of it, but I haven't read it."

The girl drew her brows together, as if she was trying to work out how that was possible, and if it was true, why was she standing in a bookshop? "You've never read Dickens?"

Pippin shook her head. "I have to confess, I haven't."

The girl folded her arms and kicked one leg out. Sassy. "What about *Jane Eyre*?"

"No, but I did see the movie," Pippin said.

The girl scoffed. "The movie! That's not the same thing. Okay, how about *Little Women*?"

Pippin pressed her lips together before saying, "The movie, but not the book."

The girl's eyes went wide. "Just say yes or no—to the book, not the movie. *Rebecca*."

"No."

"*Siddhartha*."

"No."

"*The Great Gatsby*."

"No."

"You've read *To Kill a Mockingbird*, though, right?"

Pippin sighed. "No, but I loved Gregory Peck in the—"

The girl squealed. "Don't say it!"

Pippin thought it instead. *Movie.*

"Don't you *like* books?" the girl asked.

"Heidi!" Jamie's voice boomed.

The girl turned, spreading her arms. "I was just asking."

Pippin met his apologetic gaze. "It's okay. I'm not well-read, that's all."

Heidi stared up at Jamie. "She hasn't read *To Kill a Mockingbird*, Dad. That's crazy, right? *I'm* only *eleven* and I've read it."

Jamie's face darkened. "Heidi, you're being rude."

Heidi gulped and looked back at Pippin. "I didn't mean anything by it. Promise."

Pippin knew she hadn't meant to offend. "It's fine," she said. "You're right. It's a classic, and that's going to be next on my list." A list she didn't actually have. Maybe she should start one, though. She loved the bookshop and the library, but if she didn't start reading, she'd have no reason to visit either one.

"I have something for you," Jamie said to Pippin.

Anticipation bloomed inside of her. "The translation?"

He flicked his eyebrows up and gave a satisfied smile. "Mmm hmm."

She absently touched her mother's necklace. "I have something, too."

Jamie pulled Heidi in for a side hug. "I'll be in my office. Let me know when Mom gets here."

Heidi nodded and scurried off to the front counter.

"She's eleven going on twenty-five," he said with a grimace. "A little too bold for her britches"

Pippin laughed. "I can see that."

"But smart as a whip. She'll make a great lawyer one day."

Pippin followed Jamie as he led her down a hallway lined haphazardly with book boxes. "It isn't always like this," he said, gesturing to the wobbly stacks. "I painted my office last weekend and put up new shelves. Haven't had a chance to reorganize."

"It's fine. I'm used to messes. Sometimes I think the renovations on the house will never be done."

"It looked like it was in good shape to me," he said as he opened a door and ushered her into a decently sized room. The walls were a pale green and white built-in shelving lined one entire wall. A standing desk was positioned in front of the window, which faced the parking lot, the Sound beyond it.

"No place to sit. Sorry about that."

She waved the apology away. A chair was the least of her worries. "You finished the translation?"

His boyish grin was contagious. She couldn't help but smile, even though she didn't know what they were smiling about. "I did."

"And?" she prompted.

"It's part of a scroll. A letter."

"A letter," she repeated.

He nodded. "The woman, Morgan Dubhshláine, wrote to a man. Titus. Or she had someone write it for her. A scribe."

She racked her brain, searching for any reference to either of those names, but came up blank. "Titus isn't an Irish name, is it?"

He shrugged. "Roman, probably."

That didn't make sense. "Why would an Irishman have a Roman name?"

He leaned against the doorjamb; arms folded over his chest. "See I don't think he would. It's been thought that the Roman Empire never landed on Hibernia—the Roman name for Ireland. Agricola, and those who came after, never conquered it. But there are more recent archaeological discoveries that have led historians to believe that the Romans *did* have a presence there between the first and fifth centuries. Artifacts have been discovered in Leinstar, close to Dublin, and they've unearthed burials on the island of Lambay."

Pippin stared. What did any of that mean? "If the letter was written in Old Irish, would Titus have been able to read it?"

Jamie angled his head to the side, considering. "Good question. Probably not."

"What does it say?"

"Morgan tells Titus that she will wait for him." His voice turned lofty. "That their love transcends the obstacles they face."

Pippin exhaled. Her father had been researching her mother's family history. He'd been trying to trace the origin of the curse. She wrapped her hand around the pendant at her neck. Had he traced them all way back to the time of Jesus?

"What did you find?" he asked her, pulling her out of her thoughts.

She released her hold on the necklace and held the pendant out to show him. "It was in the stand for the ship in the bottle! The stand, not the bottle. It was my mother's."

Jamie looked at it. "A touchstone to her."

She told him about meeting Hattie Juniper Pickle and

her theory that someone who'd loved Cassie had been to the house. She rubbed her temples. "I just don't know what it means. Who cares if Leo kept her necklace? Why would anyone kill him or Max over it?"

"Dad!" Heidi's voice bellowed down the hallway. "Mom's here!"

Pippin's stomach roiled. She didn't want to meet Jamie's wife, but she had no choice but to follow him out of the office and back to the bookshop floor. She saw the younger daughter first, this time from the front. Her brown hair and amber eyes were the same as her dad's. She wore a colorful cotton dress, mismatched but equally colorful tights, and black Mary Janes. She was a bit like a younger version of Hattie. The second she saw Jamie, she screeched, "Daddy!" and raced to him, leaping into the air, arms outstretched. He crouched, nimbly caught her, then stood, holding her against his side. Clearly this was a gymnastics routine they'd done before.

"Mathilda! How many times do I have to tell you not to run inside?"

Pippin cringed at the sharpness of the woman's voice. Their mother. Pippin looked at her, and her cringe deepened. This was Jamie's wife? She was severe looking, with her hair pulled into a tight ballerina bun. It would have given Pippin a headache to have her hair tugging on her temples that way. She had a long neck and the poise of a professional dancer, and, apparently, the temperament that dancers were so often associated with.

"She's fine, Miranda," Jamie said. His voice had lost the light excitement she'd heard in it when they'd been talking about the ancient text on the papyrus and the history of the Roman Empire and Ireland. Now it was sharp and tinged with what she could only describe as disdain. "It's my store."

Heidi's outfit was far more subdued than her sister's. She wore jeans, a button up shirt, and her brown hair was pulled back into a ponytail. The girls looked like opposites, but Mathilda slid down her father's body, Heidi grabbed her hand and pulled her close. They stood side by side holding hands, eyes wide, watching their parents. Sisters.

Miranda dropped the small purple duffle bag she'd been holding on the floor at her feet. "You'll have to do her laundry."

Jamie spoke evenly. "No problem."

"And she refused to read—"

"I don't like that book!" Mathilda wailed.

"It doesn't matter if you like it," her mother snapped. "You have to read it."

"Forcing her to read a book she doesn't like, at her age, is going to turn her off of reading all together," Jamie said through clenched teeth. It sounded to Pippin like they'd had this discussion before.

Miranda threw up her hands. "Of course! You know best, Jamie."

"Miranda," he ground out, an unspoken warning in his tone.

"I'll pick them up next Saturday," she said with a huff, and with that, she swung around, without a glance at her daughters—or at Pippin—and strode out the door.

Mathilda's eyes were wide and scared. Her lower lip was pushed out and over her upper lip like she was pouting, but Pippin knew she was scared. She remembered that feeling as a child of nothing being in your control. Their mother hadn't given them a hug or kiss. Hadn't even looked their way before she left. It was no wonder tears pooled in the bottom of the little girl's eyes. Heidi was more stoic. She held tight to her sister's hand, but she held her chin up, her shoulders down, and looked at her father. Something passed between them and Pippin knew they'd been through this scenario before.

Jamie turned away from his girls for a split second. His nostrils flared as he exhaled, but he brought his face back into calm control before he looked back at them. He clapped his hands. "Let's get these books put up."

He directed them to the stack of titles on the end of the counter. "All misplaced?" Heidi asked. When Jamie nodded, she grumbled to herself. "Really, people. Put things back where they belong."

"You help me, squirt," Jamie said to Mathilda. She took three books from the top of the stack. "Travel!" she announced, looking at the cover.

"Good job." Jamie ushered her off.

"Mind if I help you?" Pippin asked Heidi.

Heidi shrugged and headed to the mystery section. Pippin took that as a yes. She ditched her purse and *The Odyssey* on a shelf behind the counter and followed. The shelves were organized alphabetically by the author's last name. Heidi stuck a copy of a knitting-themed mystery on the top shelf, standing on her tiptoes to reach. She handed Pippin a sci-fi novel next, then pointed to the shelves behind them. Pippin slipped it onto the shelf in the correct spot. Heidi had already moved on.

"I take it you think I should read *To Kill a Mockingbird*," Pippin said when she caught up.

"It's a must," Heidi said. No ifs, ands, or buts.

"Do you have a copy?"

Heidi turned and stared up at Pippin. She placed one hand on her chest. "It's only the greatest book ever written," she said. "Of course I have a copy."

Pippin bit her lip to stop from smiling. This girl was a

ball of seriousness wrapped up in a tween body. "I meant, does the bookshop have a copy? One I can buy?"

A lightbulb turned on over Heidi's head. "Oh. New or used?"

"Either," she said.

Heidi gave a single nod. "Right this way."

Pippin followed Heidi to the Classic Literature used book section. The girl scanned the titles, then pulled out a copy of Harper Lee's book. "After I read it, do you want to talk about it with me?" Pippin asked

Heidi's sour face melted, and her eyes lit up. "Over ice cream?"

This time Pippin did laugh. "Sure. Over ice cream."

They chatted, with Pippin asking Heidi questions about her school, her favorite books, and her sister. She avoided anything about her mom and dad. Before long, they were back at the front of the store, rendezvousing with Jamie and Mathilda. "It was very nice meeting you both," Pippin said after she paid for the novel.

"It was *very* nice meeting you," Mathilda said in her sweet voice. "Will you come again tomorrow?"

"Tilly," Jamie said. "Pippin's very busy. She's renovating an old house. It's going to be an inn."

Mathilda's eyes furrowed. "In what?"

Heidi rolled her eyes and Jamie and Pippin laughed.

"It's like a hotel, dummy," Heidi said.

Instantly, Jamie touched Heidi's shoulder, giving it a little squeeze. "Hey."

Heidi dropped her chin. "Sorry."

Mathilda's lip had been quivering, but it stopped the moment the apology came.

"I like your name," Heidi said. "I thought we were the only ones with names from books."

Of course. Heidi was a classic, and Mathilda had to be from Roald Dahl. Pippin smiled to herself. She wouldn't mention it, but she'd seen both of the movies.

"But Daddy put an H in my name because he said he likes it better that way," Mathilda said. "What do *you* think?"

Pippin scrunched her lips to one side in a thinking way. "I think I like the H, too. It's a pretty letter."

Mathilda grinned up at Jamie. "I like the H, too, Daddy."

Jamie ruffled her hair. "I'm glad, squirt."

Pippin left The Open Door feeling lighter on her feet. Jamie's girls were sweet. She'd have to read *To Kill a Mockingbird* now. No way would she let Heidi down. She just hoped it wouldn't take her forever to sludge her way through it.

Back at home, she dropped her purse on her desk, plunging her hand in to grab some lip balm. Her hand skimmed the framed photo Chavi Santiago had given her. She'd completely forgotten about it. She took it out and saw, not surprisingly, that the glass had cracked. She'd have to get a new frame. She sat down, looking at the photo. Her father had been so young. So handsome, but in the picture, he looked worried. She laid the frame face down and undid the clasps. She removed the piece of black cardboard, then the photo underneath it. Only it wasn't a single photo in the frame. There were two. The one with Daisy, Chavi Santiago, and Leo had been the one visible. She pulled them apart to look at the one underneath, starting. It was one of the photos she'd seen at the marina, the one with Daisy in a life jacket next to three men, all holding onto a massive blue fin tuna. She laid the photos side by side. It was clear they were taken on the same day. The water behind them. The same fish. Their position on the marina—in front of two boats. In front of the *Cassandra*.

Her father must have taken the picture of the three men

with their catch, then one of the other men—she couldn't remember their names—must have taken the other. She'd wondered what her father had been staring at. Not the camera, so not the cameraman. No, he was looking off to the side, over the shoulder of the picture taker. At the other man?

She went back to the first photo, studying their faces. Chavi Santiago had aged well, despite his years in the sun. True, he looked older, but his skin was mostly unlined, just as it had been twenty years ago. She looked at the other two men more closely. The one on the right looked familiar. She flipped the photo over. There, written in faded pencil, were a list of initials. J.R. C.S. The third set of initials was faded too much to make them out. She thought there was a G. Maybe an S. She couldn't be sure.

She flipped back to the photo, staring at the familiar looking man until something clicked. It was Jed Riordin! She studied the face, nodding. Yes, the man on the right was definitely the same man who'd stopped by the inn claiming to be an old friend of her father. Chavi Santiago she recognized. She moved on to the third man. Something tugged at her memory. She catalogued his features. His skin was lined, and Pippin placed him at five or ten years older than the other two men. He wore sunglasses propped on a round nose, but they didn't hide his sneer. Despite the dark lenses, she knew he was staring at her father behind the camera. Stubble marked the man's jawline and upper lip, but it wasn't until she looked at his arms that she knew. He wasn't as tattooed back then, but there was no mistaking the girl in the grass skirt.

The man was a young Salty Shannon.

Chapter 24

"And above all, watch with glittering eyes the whole world around you because the greatest secrets are always hidden in the most unlikely places. Those who don't believe in magic will never find it."
~Roald Dahl

There was only one thing Pippin could think to do. She grabbed her copy of *The Odyssey* and set the spine of it on her desk. "Tell me," she said. She released the covers and the book fell open. Instantly, a line darkened, lifting off the page. She peered at the words, willing the letters to stay where they belonged long enough for her to read what they said.

Few sons are like their fathers--most are worse, few better.

SHE TOOK the book up again, said, "Tell me," and let it fall open. This time different words darkened. Lifted. Slowly, she pieced the sentence together.

Iron has powers to draw a man to ruin.

SHE DID IT A THIRD TIME, holding her breath as she let the covers fall.

Take courage, my heart: you have been through worse than this.

TEARS WELLED IN HER EYES. She felt as if the last message was from her parents. "I will," she said aloud after she'd deciphered the eleven words.

She repeated the other two lines the book magic had revealed. Several things hit Pippin at once. Her mind raced through them, landing on an image. An image she'd seen more than once. She looked at the first line the book had shared.

Few sons are like their fathers--most are worse, few better.

SHE THOUGHT of Jimmy's tattoos. She'd only caught a glimpse of the one under his tank, but the more she thought about it, the more certain she was that it was the same circle in a V that Salty had on his forearm. She didn't know what it meant, but it connected the two men.

They'd both been regulars at Devil's Cove Landing when her dad had his boat there, and they'd both been there the day before her father disappeared. Bev had said her son and Jimmy had gotten into trouble at the Cove—where Max Lawrence had died.

"Oh my God," she whispered. Only the plant—devil's ivy, which she'd potted and set on her desk, heard her. She knew Max had been the man she'd seen at Devil's Brew. She'd been trying to figure out why he hadn't simply spoken to her. He hadn't wanted to be overheard—by Travis, Jimmy, and Kyron. They'd been sitting at the table in front of Max.

Her hand went to her necklace. The thing her father had hidden away. Pippin remembered Jimmy sneaking onto Leo's boat before it was hauled away. She'd wondered at the time why he'd done that. Was the pendant what he'd been after?

Something else came to mind. That day Jimmy's wife had shown up with his kids. The kids had looked at Salty and he'd been silly with them. They'd giggled—like they knew him.

She went back to the quote. Fathers. Sons.

She said Salty's name over and over. Something about it. Bev had said the man's boat was called the Old Salty G. Salty Shannon, Bev had said.

Her mind caught on something. Bev had stacked the two names when she'd written them out.

Salty
Shannon

RATHER than

Salty Shannon

WHAT IF SHANNON wasn't Salty's last name. What if it was his *first* name?

The Old Salty G. G as in... "Gallagher," she whispered. "Shannon Gallagher." That had to be it. Shannon Gallagher. Jimmy Gallagher. They were father and son.

Bev had said the police had barreled by her, Mick, the boys, and Leo. One of those boys could have been Jimmy. Could *he* have pulled the plugs on the boat that sank?

Was Jimmy worse or better than his father?

She tried to concentrate on the why. *Why* would Jimmy have sunk a houseboat? *Why* would Salty have killed her father? *Why* was Max Lawrence killed?

Her hand strayed to the necklace again. She remembered Bev and Mick's comment about treasure hunters, then she recalled the legend about Devil's Cove's origins. Those rum runners had managed to take some treasure from their ship before it sank into the Atlantic.

Pippin's hand tightened around the pendant. Could her mother's necklace have come from that sunken ship?

Pippin grabbed the two photos and ran from her office, bumping smack into Jimmy as she barreled out the front door. He dropped the device he'd been holding—a stud finder, she thought—and a set of batteries. The photos slipped from her hand. "Whoa! Where's the fire?"

Her heart hammered. Her mother's necklace was like a brand against her skin. She had to get by him. Her hands shook as she snatched up the photos, muttered a quick sorry, and took the front steps two at a time. She slipped between Kyron's sedan and the truck Jimmy and Travis rode in, cut across the street, and beelined for Hattie Juniper Pickle's colorful house, the white pots like a beacon.

She raised her hand to knock, but the door flung open before her knuckles made contact. She lurched forward but caught herself. "I've been expecting you," Hattie said.

In the dark and in another voice, those words would have been ominous, but coming from this blue-haired eclectic woman, it was almost comical. Pippin stared. "You have?"

"Sure. You realized something, didn't you?"

Pippin fluttered the photographs in her hand. "Can I show you something?"

Hattie held the door open to let Pippin pass through. She checked the street, looking both ways, as if someone was out there watching them, before she shut the door, turned the deadbolt, and led her to the kitchen.

It's said that a house reflects its owner. That was definitely the case with Hattie Juniper Pickle—both inside and out. The walls were vibrant colors—green, blue, purple. The furniture was mismatched, yet somehow worked. Plaid upholstery on the couch coordinated with the massive floral print on the chairs. Solid yellow pillows tied it all together just as her clogs had done for her outfit.

The kitchen cabinets were painted a dark turquoise, while the walls were light coral. Even the small round kitchen table was painted—yellow again—with a busy geometric design stenciled on the top. Living in such a house would have given Pippin a permanent headache, but visiting it was fascinating. Hattie, with an outfit that was just as colorful as the one the day before, almost blended into the fabric of the house. She reminded Pippin of a character from Harry Potter who could morph into an armchair, or melt into the wall, becoming part of it.

Hattie sat at the table, leaning back in her chair and crossing her legs. "You found your daddy's killer," she announced matter-of-factly, as if she'd read about it in the newspaper.

Pippin sat down opposite Hattie and slid the photo of the three men to her. She pointed to the one with the hula girl tattoo. "Do you recognize him?"

"Looks like it was taken about a hundred years ago, by the looks of him, but sure I do. He's been here just about as long as I have. That's Shannon Gallagher, and he was in love with your mama."

Pippin's skin turned cold. She'd been right, but she needed to hear it again. "What did you say his name is?"

"Shannon Gallagher," Hattie repeated.

Pippin wrapped her hand around the pendant again and uttered the final line her bibliomancy had just revealed. "Iron has powers to draw a man to ruin."

Chapter 25

Irish Blessing

May the road rise to meet you,
May the wind be always at your back,
May the sun shine warm upon your face,
May the rains fall soft upon your fields,
And, until we meet again,
May God hold you in the hollow of His hand.

*I*t had been light when Pippin had crossed the
street to talk to Hattie. Now, on the way back to
her inn, she walked into the gloaming. All the cars were
gone. She heaved a sigh. Jimmy was gone, thank God. She'd
be alone. She'd have time to think.

With the photographs still in hand, she went straight to
her father's study. She grabbed the bookshelf and pulled
open the secret door, quietly slipping through it and closing
it behind her. She hadn't been up here since Jamie had told

her about the translation of the piece of papyrus. The first thing she saw was the family tree her father had created. The curse that had taken her mother and father. Leo had gone back as far as Siobhan O'Quinn and Artemis Lane, but if the piece of papyrus her father had hidden behind the clock had to do with her family, then their line...the Lanes... went back as far as the first century. "Morgan Dubhshláine," she said, repeating the name Jamie had said. "Dubhshláine." Which someone, probably her great-great-grandfather, Artemis, she realized, had shortened to Lane after leaving his homeland, crossing the Atlantic, and entering the United States.

Somewhere, she heard a faint beeping sound. A dying smoke detector battery probably. She made a mental note to add that to Grey's punch list. She ignored the sound and sat on one of the club chairs, everything she thought she knew careening in her mind. She'd interpreted the book magic, but had she interpreted it correctly? She couldn't very well go to Lieutenant Jacobs, tell him her theories, and hope that he'd believe her. She had circumstantial evidence, at best. A photograph showing Salty and Leo together the day before Leo disappeared didn't prove anything. The fact that Jimmy was also at the marina didn't prove that he'd pulled the plugs and sunk the boat. He'd been a kid, though, so the mistake of sinking the *Caterina* instead of the *Cassandra* made sense.

She couldn't prove that Salty had loved Cassie, though she knew it was true. Bev and Mick had said so. Hattie had confirmed it. Jealousy is an ugly beast, Hattie had said. Even though Cassie died, had Salty still wanted to hurt Leo? But for what? Because he imagined Leo had stolen Cassie from him? He may have felt that way, but was that enough for murder? And so many years later?

Or was it only about the necklace?

The weight of her mother's pendant was a comfort, but the air in the room seemed to change suddenly. A shiver ran up her spine. If she was right, Jimmy probably knew what his father had done. He hadn't been with the other two guys when Grey had first seen the room, but that didn't mean he didn't know about it. She shouldn't be alone here.

She took her cell phone from her back pocket. Just as she entered her passcode to unlock the screen, her head snapped up. She'd heard a noise. The quiet swinging of a door. Of the secret door.

"Grey?" she called.

No answer.

She thought quickly. It had to be Jimmy. She'd dropped the photos when she'd bumped into him. He had to have seen them, which meant he knew she'd made a connection between Leo and Salty.

She needed something to defend herself with. She scanned the room for something to use as a weapon. Books. All that was here were books. She dropped the photos and pulled a stack of hardcovers from one of the shelves. A second later, a head came into view.

"Stop," she said, summoning up as much force as she could. To her ears, her voice sounded scared. Shaky. She backed up against the shelf and waited, her heart nearly pounding out of her chest.

Finally, a head appeared. "Grey'll be back any minute, Jimmy."

"He won't, love. He went to visit the waitress," a man said. It wasn't Jimmy's voice.

Salty Shannon appeared at the top of the steps wielding a knife. It looked razor-sharp with a long, thin blade. Perfect for filleting a fish—or stabbing someone.

Pippin's mind raced. How would books fend off that knife in a killer's hand—because she knew without a doubt that Salty was a killer. Book magic had led her to the truth. "Is that the knife you used to kill my father?" she said.

Miraculously, her voice sounded stronger aloud that she'd thought possible. Confrontational, even.

Salty clucked as if she were a fool for asking.

Pippin stole a furtive glance at her phone clutched in her hand. If she could just tap on Grey's name...

"Put it down, love."

She played innocent. "What?"

His eyes shifted to her hand. "Put it down."

Pippin froze. If she relinquished her phone, she'd have no chance at getting help.

He thrust the knife in her direction. His eyes bulged large on either side of his bulbous nose. "Put it down!"

She jumped, hitting her back on the shelves she was already pressed against. "Okay." She turned just enough to have her hand out of his line of vision. Surreptitiously, she pressed the button before tossing the phone onto the chair.

Pippin had only one thought: Get him to confess. "Did you kill him to get back at him? Because my mother loved him and not you?"

He glowered. "You don't know anything, girl."

She bristled, her hackles up. "I know you killed him." She nodded to the knife in his hand again. "With that."

"Whatever blade killed your pops is at the bottom of the Sound."

His Eastern Carolina accent made everything sound hospitable and friendly, but Salty was the farthest thing from either. Pippin scrambled for an idea. A way to get past him. A faint sound carried up the stairs. A car door slamming? Salty darted a glance at the stairwell. It was quick, but it gave Pippin a fleeting opportunity. She hurled the first book from her stack at him. It fell short, dropping to the floor with a thump. Salty spun toward her, arm outstretched with the knife in hand. Pippin acted, grabbing another book from her stack and throwing it at him, harder this time. This time, it made contact, nailing him on the side of his head. The impact startled him enough that he sputtered. Pippin launched another volume. The corner of it got him smack in one of his eyes. He howled, covering it with one hand.

Like the Cyclops.

She hurled book after book at him, grabbing more from the shelf when she'd gone through the first stack. Every time he tried to come at her with his knife, another volume flew at him. *Bam! Bam! Bam!* She pelted him, one book after another until an entire section of her father's bookshelves was empty and Salty Shannon Gallagher had collapsed to the ground.

Pippin edged toward him, ready to smash him with the last book she held, but she stopped herself. He wasn't moving. She'd show him mercy, not that he deserved it.

She started to step back. Felt a hand curl around her ankle. The hand yanked. She fell back, a ragged scream catching in her throat as she went down on top of the books scattered all over the floor. The hand released her, and she scrabbled to stand up. She snatched up one of the books on the floor and launched it at Salty's head with all her might.

Rapid footsteps sounded on the steps. She sagged in relief. Grey! The twin connection. He'd known she was here. She turned and froze.

Not Grey.

Jimmy.

He looked from his father to Pippin. And then he

lunged. She dodged, but he was younger and quicker than his father. He caught her easily, locking her in a chokehold.

"Why'd you kill Max?" she yelled, struggling, needing answers.

They both looked at her. But no, not at her. At her chest. Cassie's necklace burned against her skin.

"For this?" she said, grabbing hold of the pendant in her hand. "Whatever you think it is, you're wrong. It's just a necklace."

"Don't say anything, Pops. Don't say a word." Jimmy's hold on Pippin's neck tightened.

Salty ignored his son. "I looked everywhere for that. All these years I thought it was buried with your mother, then you came back to town and I figured out Leo gave Max somethin'. He told Riordin at the last *Synkéntrosi* meeting. Said he'd finally be able to honor Leo's last request of him. We looked for it, didn't we, Jim?"

Max's ransacked house, Pippin thought. They'd searched Lorraine's jewelry.

"Pops!" Jimmy roared. "Shut up."

"She tried t' kill me." Salty ran the back of his hand over his bleeding mouth. He muttered under his breath. "Damn books."

Pippin struggled to draw in a breath under the pressure of Jimmy's hold. She coughed. Sucked in more air. Jimmy loosened his grip on her throat. She coughed again. Drew in more air.

"Take it," Salty ordered gruffly.

Pippin coughed, managing a mangled, "Why?"

"It's ours. The legend—"

Jimmy growled. Any nice guy demeanor he'd had working on her house had completely vanished. "Pops. Shut. Up."

But Pippin had to keep Salty talking. "The boat."

"Took longer 'n I thought for your pops to be found." Salty chuckled. "It was a good hiding place."

"At the marina?" Pippin asked, her voice hoarse from the pressure of Jimmy's hold on her.

Jimmy laughed. "I was a dumb kid. I sank the wrong boat."

"He was s'pposed to search Leo's boat, then sink it. A threat so he'd give up the necklace," Salty said, his hand cupping his injured eye. "Dumb ass. Both of 'em."

But Leo hadn't given it up, and now it was around Pippin's neck.

"I've more than made up for it," Jimmy grumbled.

Salty tried to nod. "You did, you did."

"M-Max?" Pippin croaked.

"Damn loyalty cost 'im 'is life," Salty said. "Jimmy tried every which way, but he wouldn't give it up." He looked at Jimmy now. "Take it."

Pippin panicked. She'd just gotten it back. She wasn't about to lose it again to these two. She fought harder, but Jimmy's sweaty hand felt around her neck. Fisted around the pendant. He gave the chain some slack, ready to yank it off her neck. "D-Did you r-really love her?" she managed to ask Salty.

"Sure, I did. I loved her. And I hated Leo for takin' her from me. Seein' him die was a bonus."

Before she could respond to that, a voice bellowed up the stairs. "Let her go!"

Finally!

The voice startled Jimmy. His hold loosened. Pippin thrust her head back, her skull colliding with his nose. He grunted and let her go.

She spun, stomping on his foot. "Shit!" He bounced on

his other foot and Pippin went in for the final blow. She heaved her knee up, right into the groin. Jimmy screeched, doubling over.

Pippin stumbled back, one hand clutching her throat.

It happened so fast, all before Grey made it to the top of the steps. Salty managed to roll over and get to his knees, but Grey put one foot on his back and shoved him back down.

Time seemed to slow as more footsteps pounded up the stairs. Pippin collapsed against the paneled wall as Lieutenant Jacobs rounded the corner. "How did you—" but Pippin stopped, a faint smile tickling her dry lips. Behind the lieutenant, panting and clutching her chest, was Hattie Juniper Pickle.

Chapter 26

Dogs and philosophers do the greatest good and get the fewest rewards.

~Diogenes

*P*ippin sat in the Adirondack chairs facing the pampas grass. She dropped the collar and leash she'd bought at the local pet store on the grass next to her. She was done waiting. This dog needed a good scrub, a good meal, and a good snuggle—in that order.

It was clear to her that the dog couldn't hear, so Pippin couldn't call to her. She'd tried to lure her with treats, but the poor thing was too skittish. She didn't know how she'd gain the dog's trust, but she was determined. If she could solve two murders—one of them twenty years old—surely she could win over a canine.

She'd brought a cup of coffee...ah, sweet caffeine...and her new copy of *To Kill a Mockingbird* with her. Nothing like trying to struggle through a book to kill time. She opened to the first page and slowly read, taming the mixed up letters into submission.

When he was nearly thirteen, my brother Jem got his arm badly broken at the elbow.

SHE'D SET TO READING, albeit slowly, and before she knew it, thirty minutes had passed. Then almost an hour. Her coffee had grown cold. Dark clouds hung over the Sound. The spring rain would make its way toward the island eventually, but for now the clouds were holding steady.

The dog had flitted in and out of Pippin's mind since she'd first laid eyes on her. Now, with a storm coming, Pippin was determined, once and for all, to make that pup a friend. Now here she was, alternating between reading a page from the book in her lap and scanning the base of the pampas grass.

A flash of light lit up the sky, followed by a clap of thunder.

A whimper sounded from somewhere in the foliage.

Pippin perked up. She put the book down and dropped to her knees, searching.

Finally, she spotted the dog's rosy nose poking out from between the blades of grass. "There you are," she said softly, only to herself since the dog couldn't hear her. She waved her hand to catch the pup's attention. Pippin had been afraid the dog would spook, but instead, she inched her way out until Pippin could see her coppery eyes.

Pippin dropped to her belly. She propped her chin on one fist, stretching her arm out in the direction of the pampas grass. She tilted her head as she looked at the dog, her heart melting a little bit. The pup's floppy ears hung down like ponytails on the sides of her head. Her hair was golden, but lacked the shine it might have if she were well fed.

Pippin patted the ground with one palm. The dog tilted her head to match the angle of Pippin's. Again, Pippin patted the ground. This time, the dog scooted forward until her body was out in the open.

Pippin bit her lower lip. She could make out the dog's ribs. Food might need to come before the bath. "Come on, sweetie," she cooed.

The dog never blinked. Never moved her gaze from Pippin's as she inched further away from the pampas grass and toward Pippin.

Another flash of light. Another faint whimper. Pippin glanced up at the darkening sky. "Come on, girl," she said, looking back at the dog army crawling toward her.

Bit by bit, they each crept toward one another, the gap between them closing. "Almost there," Pippin said softly. The dog couldn't hear her, but she seemed to sense the gentleness in Pippin. Another shock of light flashed across the sky. The dog whimpered again and laid her muzzle on her paws.

"It's okay, sweetie," Pippin said. She propelled herself forward with a push of her back foot, reaching her arm out until she could touch the tops of the dog's paws. She froze for a few seconds, not wanting to spook the dog. Finally, just as another bolt of light flashed in the sky, and another thunder clap echoed in the distance, Pippin moved herself to a cross-legged position just in front of the dog.

The dog's gaze never left hers. Slowly, Pippin beckoned her toward her with a simple rolling of one hand.

The dog's head popped up and the next second she was standing.

"Don't go!" Pippin said. She started to reach but stopped herself when she saw the dog was just standing there. Waiting.

Again, she rolled her hand.

The dog took a tentative step forward. Then another. She understood the hand movement.

"That's it," Pippin cooed. "A little more. Come on."

After the third step, Pippin could gently put her hands on either side of the dog's face, letting them slide down her neck, lightly scratching with her fingernails. "Are you hungry?" Pippin asked, knowing the answer had to be yes.

The dog's gaze shifted to Pippin's mouth, and once again, she tilted her head. Her invisible brows pulled together as Pippin spoke again. The dog knew something was happening, she just didn't know what it meant.

Pippin picked up the purple collar and slowly put it around the dog's neck, snapping the buckle together. She attached the leash, and still moving slowly, she stood.

The dog watched every move she made. She didn't fight, instead responding to the gentle tug Pippin gave the leash by walking with her. Pippin picked up her book, but left the chair, leading the dog through the gate and into the backyard. Beyond the fence, the water of the Sound lapped the shore.

"Do you want this to be your home?" Pippin asked the dog.

The pup tilted her head again, her big eyes somehow a little less sad then they'd been.

"I'll take that as a yes," she said. She spent the next thirty minutes bathing the dog, scrubbing out the dirt and the fleas. The dog lapped up half a bowl of water and an entire can of the dog food Pippin had bought for just this eventuality. A trip to the vet would be on her list of things to do tomorrow.

Later, Pippin sat in one of the club chairs in what she'd come to call the hidden room, the dog at her feet, looking up at her with what she could only describe as adoration. She spent an hour agonizing over a letter she wrote to her aunt, finally tucking it into an envelope she'd addressed to Rose Lane in Laurel Point, Oregon. Now it lay on the table next to her, ready to be posted in the morning.

It was a relief. She still didn't know what her father was after with the family tree and the bit of letter from Morgan to Titus. "I'm not giving up," she said aloud, wiggling her fingers. The dog tilted her head, her ears perking up. The pup was smart. They'd have to learn some simple sign language commands together to communicate. "I'm going to name you Sailor," she said.

EPILOGUE

D ear Aunt Rose,
        I hope this letter finds you, Cora, and Lily well. I am sorry to have been silent all these years. I only recently came across the name and address of your bookstore at Laurel Point.

I must share something with you, but I am still trying to sort out what it all means. I have been teaching myself our family's gift of bibliomancy and it helped me solve the murder of my father. Yes, murder. Everyone thought he went missing three years after my mother died. It turns out that isn't what happened at all. He was killed. Grey and I found his remains on his boat.

It turns out the man who killed my father—and another innocent man—had been in love with my mom. Shannon Gallagher. They call him Salty. A marine rat, my neighbor called him, which seems to fit, at least to my mind.

He hated my dad, but he killed him for her necklace. That's why he killed the other man—Max Lawrence—because my dad gave the necklace to Max for safe-keeping. It's hard to make sense of.

I'm wearing mom's necklace now. It must be valuable, but I don't want to know. I don't want to take it off. In a way, it's like she's still here with me, although I know that's ridiculous. But Aunt Rose, there's something else. The murders are solved but practicing bibliomancy has helped me to listen to my gut, and, well, I think there is more to the story.

There's more. My parents were researching the Lane family. My dad continued after my mom died. Grey and I think he was trying to figure out how to stop the Lane curse—you know, about the women dying in childbirth and the men being taken by the sea. Anyway, I found an ancient piece of a scroll written in old Irish. It was hidden in my dad's study. I had it translated and found that it is part of a letter written by someone named Morgan Dubhshláine. Aunt Rose, I think she may be our oldest ancestor. The letter is written to the man she loved. All I know is that he was named Titus.

Please, if you know the story of Morgan and Titus, I would love to hear it. Aunt Rose, I need to hear it.

With love, and awaiting your reply,

Pippin Lane Hawthorne

BOOK MAGIC MYSTERIES

Continue with the next Book Magic Mysteries:

Murder in Devil's Cove, by Melissa Bourbon

Death at Cape Misery, by Wendy Lyn Watson

Murder at Sea Captain's Inn, by Melissa Bourbon

RECIPES FROM THE DEVIL'S BREW

RUBY'S GINGER COOKIES

Ingredients
3/4 cup butter
1 cup sugar
1 egg
1/4 cup molasses
2 1/4 flour
2 tsp baking soda
1 tsp ground ginger
1 tsp cinnamon
1 tsp ground cloves
1/4 tsp salt
Sugar to roll the cookies in

Directions

Preheat oven to 350°

1. Cream butter and sugar until light and fluffy. Add egg and molasses.

2. In a separate bowl, combine dry ingredients.

3. Gradually add the dry ingredients to the butter/sugar mixture. Combine well.

4. Roll dough into 3 inch balls. Roll in sugar to coat and place on uncreased cookie/baking sheet.

5. Bake until cookies puff up slightly and are lightly browned, approximately 10-12 minutes.

RUBY'S GLUTEN FREE BERRY SCONES

Ingredients

    2 cups all purpose gluten free flour blend
    1 1/2 tablespoons baking powder
    1/2 tsp salt
    1 tsp xanthan gum
    2 Tablespoons sugar
    6 T butter
    1 cup fresh or frozen berries of your choice. Blueberries are Ruby's favorite.
    1 cup, plus 1 Tablespoon, if needed (oat milk works too)
    1 Tablespoon fresh lemon juice (optional)
    Zest from one lemon (optional)

Directions

Preheat oven to 400° and prepare a baking sheet by lining it with parchment paper.

1. In a bowl, whisk together dry ingredients.

2. Cut butter into small chunks. Using a pastry cutter, cut butter into the flour mixture.

3. Add the milk and lightly mix together until just blended. Add more milk if needed. If you are including the lemon juice and zest, add now.

4. Stir in berries.

5. Flour the counter and turn out dough. Gently press into a rectangle shape about 1/2 thick.

6. Divide rectangle in half. Divide each have into triangular quarters. You will have 8 equal triangles. Place on prepared baking sheet.

7. Brush each triangle with milk and sprinkle liberally with large granular or regular sugar.

8. Bake 15-20 minutes, or until lightly browned.

READ AN EXCERPT FROM
DEATH AT CAPE MISERY

Every book tells two stories.

There's the story written on the pages, with heroes and heroines, villains and valor, loves and losses, and occasionally a murder.

But beneath that text, there's another -- a story *in* the pages, woven in the warp and weft of the paper itself. It's the story of the hands that held the book and the hearts that skipped with each twist of the plot. It is also a story with heroes and heroines, villains and valor, loves and losses.

And occasionally a murder.

Most folks only see the story in black-and-white.

My name is Cora Lane, and I can read them both.

They say the Inuit have a hundred words for "snow." Oregonians should have at least that many words for "green." As the pale early-morning light struggled to find its way through the lush foliage, I could feel the verdant pulse of the forest contracting around me. A fairy tale forest of towering spruce and fir trees crowded up to the edge of the highway's black top, their trunks enrobed in emerald moss while lichen of the palest celadon dropped from the branches like enchanted cobwebs. Every now and then, we would pass a clearing, where either man or nature had taken down the trees and left fields that popped with sun showers of Scotch broom.

Next to me, Birdie had tipped back the passenger seat as flat as it would go. Every now and then, she muttered softly in her sleep.

I won't say Birdie McCoy is my better half, but she is definitely my other half. Birdie is a sixth generation Texan, with the oil money and big hair to prove it. Kissing six feet (her hair puts her over the edge), she towers over my five-three frame, but she wins the girly award every time: she never ventures out without mascara and earrings, she favors pink and glitter, and she worships her doting daddy.

While she is the apple of her papa's eye, she also possesses a titanium backbone and a keen desire to raise hell when she can. In a particularly dramatic act of defiance, she'd turned down full-ride offers at Baylor and Southern Methodist to trek across the country to attend Portland's Cedar Circle College, the hippiest-dippiest college in all of America. We'd met there in a first-year writing course and struck up an unlikely friendship, but a friendship that had lasted for a decade

I took the mountain turns of the road between Portland and the Pacific coast with more speed than was strictly safe, but I had driven the route so often that I could navigate by muscle memory. I had finished closing up my classroom just the day before, my hands still smudged with the ink of dry erase markers and my back aching from hauling calculus books to the supply closet, and I was eager to get home to see my Aunt Rose and celebrate her seventy-fifth birthday with her.

My phone, nestled in a holder on the dashboard of my little Subaru, began playing a tinny rendition of Fur Elise: Rose's ringtone.

I swiped my finger on the screen to connect.

"Cora!" Rose's voice sounded breathless, anxious. "Where are you?"

"I'm about thirty minutes out, just about to turn down the coast."

"Good. Good. Be careful, okay? There's a storm brewing here. I can see it rolling across the horizon now."

Rose had lived within spitting distance of the ocean her entire life, but our family's uneasy relationship with the sea came to haunt her whenever the weather picked up.

"I'll be fine, Aunt Rose. I have Birdie with me."

As if on cue, Birdie roused, righted the passenger seat of the Subaru, and rubbed her hands across bleary eyes.

"Oh good. I hate thinking of you making that trip alone."

I smothered a smile. If I went off the road or got a flat, I seriously doubted Birdie would be any help. Her eclectic knowledge base, gleaned from her liberal arts education and years as a bartender, worked well on trivia night or for chitchat over cocktails, but the girl didn't have a practical bone in her body. I wasn't bringing her along for her mechanical skills. I needed Birdie's solid pragmatism to keep me focused on the here and now, to prevent the books that cluttered Rose's home from drawing me into the morass of their stories.

"Is everything okay, Rose?" I asked. "You sound kinda off."

After a beat of silence, she sighed. "Thing have gotten a little ... complicated. Family stuff."

This was a surprise. Rose was the only family I had anymore.

"What's going on?"

"I'll explain when you get here. Over a nice cup of tea and some coffee cake. Right now, I want you to pay attention to the road and be safe. I'll be waiting for you when you get here."

"Okay. I love you."

"I love you, too, Cora. You know you and Lily mean the world to me."

I shivered. I always did when Rose referred to Lily in the present tense. I hated the thought that my sister was dead, but it had been fifteen years without so much as a peep from the family wild child. Alive or dead, Lily was tucked safely in my past where the memories couldn't do so much damage. Not for Rose, though. Rose, who was technically my great aunt, had raised Lily and me after our mother died in childbirth. She was the closest thing we had to a mother, and we were the closest things she had to children. Lily would always be alive in Rose's heart.

I let the sentimental comment fade in the ether. "I'll be there soon, Rose. Start the kettle."

"Wonder what that's about," Birdie said.

I took the turn south onto the highway that ran along the Pacific coast. "I guess we'll find out soon enough."

When we finally emerged from the woods, we immediately found ourselves on the outskirts of Laurel Point. The tiny town, snuggled between the coastal range and the Pacific, still slumbered. A few tourists shuffled along the sidewalks in search of breakfast from the Carousel Bakery or Ida's

Skillet, but the town's many art galleries wouldn't open for hours and, given the line of leaden clouds sweeping in from the horizon, it would likely be a quiet day in town.

As we wound our way through its cockeyed streets, the lighthouse on Cape Misery floated in and out of view through the morning fog. From a distance, the lighthouse looked like any other along the Oregon coast, its hard-candy reflectors gone still atop its whitewashed stone tower. But Cape Misery's lighthouse hadn't been abandoned. Unlike the other lighthouses that belonged to the state, Cape Misery belonged to the Lanes, the keeper's quarters built large enough to house a good-sized family. When the light itself had outlived its usefulness, my Grandpa Edgar had converted most of the first floor and the tower into Books by Bequest, a used bookstore specializing in rare and estate books. Despite its rustic front, the shop was high tech. It thrived mostly on internet sales. Books by Bequest put just the right volume in just the right hand, whether that hand was in Laurel Point or Shanghai.

As we drew closer, I could see the profusion of wild-flowers that clustered around the base of the lighthouse and provided small sparks of color to an otherwise gray and green world. Hear the popping of my tires on the pebbled road. Smell the astringent scent of the sea-salted air mingle with the loamy essence of the forest. I felt myself slipping body and soul into the landscape of my youth. Coming home.

"Welcome to Cape Misery, Birdie."

She peered through the half-light at the ghost-white lighthouse rising out of the rocky terrain.

"Wow," she breathed. "I still can't believe you grew up here. In the fog it's freaky. Why does your family live in this thing?"

"Simple. We own it. And getting rid of a lighthouse is a lot harder than you would think."

"But, I mean, why do you own it? I thought the state owned all the lighthouses."

"The state owns all the lighthouses in Oregon except for this one. One of my ancestors, Trevor Lane, captained a boat called The Merry Jack. It broke up on the rocks of Cape Misery during a summer storm. His father, Artemis, sorta fell apart, especially since Trevor's sister Ruth had predicted the wreck. Both men ignored her warnings, and the tragedy unfolded just as Ruth had said it would. Artemis sold everything he owned to build the lighthouse as a memorial to his son, and Lanes have lived here ever since."

"Wow," Birdie repeated. "Huh. There aren't any lights on. Are you sure your Aunt Rose is home?"

I looked more closely and, sure enough, there wasn't even a flicker of life from the lighthouse. But Rose had been waiting for me, and her dinged up red pick-up was parked on the side of the cottage.

"Maybe she fell asleep. She's starting to slow down a bit."

Birdie laughed. "Last time we were here she outlasted both of us and still managed to get up early enough to bake a sour cream coffee cake before we got out of bed. If that's 'slowing down,' I would have loved to see her in her prime."

She was right. Even though she'd spent more than seven decades hustling around, Rose still had the get-up-and-go of a woman half her age. She didn't carry a lot of spare flesh on her five-ten frame, but what she did have was pure muscle.

We pulled ourselves out of the Subaru, letting its heavy doors slam shut with nothing more than the momentum of gravity. The sound echoed in the mist. Morning lurked out there beyond the edge of the waves, but the fog cocooned the cape in cotton wool, making every sound louder and more resonant. As we approached the door to the Lane family lighthouse, our footfalls echoing in the moody air, it felt like approaching an altar.

The arched wooden door had been painted a candy-apple red, contrasting starkly with the whites, grays, soft blues, and muted greens that dominated the rest of Cape Misery. I pushed it open—not surprised to find it unlocked, as Rose never bothered with lock and key—and stuck my head in.

Immediately, the dust and leather scent of old books enveloped me, and I felt that first tickling of the books calling out to me.

Books always speak to me. I'm a bibliomancer. When I open someone's favorite book, it falls open to a page and my eye is drawn immediately to a sentence, a passage, a stain, a note . . . . some detail of the particular volume that tells me something of the person's past. I can read their life's story almost as clearly as I can read the story the author intended to tell. I did not develop this skill willingly. It's a gift the Lane women all possess, those of us of the bloodline. Ruth, who had predicted her brother's death, had the gift, though she could see the future as well as the past. My grandmother, Annabel, married into the family, but my Great Aunt Rose, my mother, and my sister Lily had the same ability. Now that my mother was dead and my sister disappeared from our lives, Rose and I had only each other with whom to share the burden of all the sadness and secrets the books held. I know it hurt Rose that I didn't come home more often, but while Rose was at peace with the muttering of the books, the bookstore unsettled me, drawing on some deep need I was afraid to explore.

I pushed the insistent voice of the books away and called out for my aunt.

"Rose? You here?"

Something thumped hard just to my left, and I let out a squeak of alarm, but it was only Rose's marmalade tomcat, Byron.

"Here puss," I called softly. Byron moseyed my way, pausing to lower his body into a long-limbed stretch. When he opened his mouth in a plaintive silent meow, I scooped him up and draped his heavy body over my shoulder.

With Byron purring like a rusty tug and Birdie keeping up a steady chatter about the quaint interior of the house, I made a quick circuit of the store and the living quarters. I hoped to find Rose snuggled beneath the storm-at-sea quilt my mother had made her or humming to herself over a pot of oatmeal. But other than Byron, the building was empty.

Thunder rumbled in the distance, the storm Rose had mentioned building over the ocean. Letting Byron slither out of my arms, I looked out the window in Rose's room to judge how long before it made landfall. A flickering of light at the horizon was followed a few seconds later by another low echo of thunder. Having watched many storms roll in, I estimated we had another fifteen minutes or so.

I was so focused on the horizon that I almost missed it, a flash of lemon yellow among the boulders on the leeward side of the cape, where its tip curled around to create a shel- tered tidal pool. Rose's Macintosh, maybe?

"What the holy heck is she doing out there?" I muttered.

"Where?" Birdie stood at my shoulder.

I pointed toward the rocks below.

"Huh," Birdie said. "Why is she standing so still? I heard thunder. Surely she'd head for shelter with a storm coming."

"I don't know." I felt a steadily increasing sense of unease. "I'm going to go find out."

"Not without me, you're not."

"Don't be silly. It's slippery out there. I'd never forgive myself if you broke an ankle or fell in the ocean."

Birdie waved a hand dismissively. "I'm wearing my sensible shoes." I glanced down to the pair of sparkling white track shoes on her feet. "Besides, it can't be any slipperier than horse pucky after an east Texas downpour. I'll be fine."

Together we went outside, where the wind was already picking up from the oncoming storm. Carefully, we wrapped around the base of the lighthouse to the southern side, where the relative shelter of the cape's angle met with the long stretch of beach running alongside Laurel Point's weathered boardwalk, and then crept between the larger rocks, the salt spray soaking our clothes.

As we came around one large boulder, I saw a lump of yellow on the shore ahead of me. My first thought was that a dinghy had washed ashore, but then I saw a denim-clad leg ending in a pair of crepe-soled black shoes.

My unease burst into full-fledged panic. I ran across the stretch of rock-littered sand that separated me from Rose, splashing through the rising tide to reach the rocks on which she rested, jutting up from the beach like a tiny island. Behind me, Birdie yelled at me to slow down, but I was past rational thought.

I stopped short when I got to her. Her delicate head hung over the edge of a tidal pool, long white hair swirling in the water like sea foam. Her face appeared ashen except for the swath of blood that ran from her temple, across her cheek, and disappeared into the collar of her coat.

I dropped to my knees, a strangled cry struggling to

break free of my lungs. Gently I reached out a hand and pressed my fingers to that paper-fine skin beneath the stark curve of her jaw, confirming what I already knew.

Whatever secret Aunt Rose had wanted to tell me, she had taken it to her grave. More...

ACKNOWLEDGMENTS

Sometimes writers need outside guidance from experts. With Murder in Devil's Cove, Laura Valerius, guided me through the ins and outs of a marina, Leo's boat, and general sea life. Laura, I bet you never knew those stories you told those nights on your houseboat at Lake Ray Roberts would end up in a book! Thank you for your infinite knowledge and your help.

Also, a big thanks to The Book Warriors for always being around to talk books, and to my Facebook readers who are always so creative and full of title ideas, names, feedback on covers, and daily conversation. Y'all are the best!

Revisions are a part of writing, but it doesn't take long before a writer stops seeing every single word. Copy editors are so important. My mom, Marilyn Bourbon, is my first editor. She may have missed her calling! Thanks, Mom, for your eagle eye.

A big thanks to Wendy Lester and Amy Brantley for your editing. You helped make this book better.

A special shout out to Finn, the inspiration for Sailor,

and his "hooman", Gwen Romack. Finn the cover model pup!

Finally, thanks to Wendy Lyn Watson. This book and series wouldn't exist if not for your brilliant mind. Creating this series with you has been more fun than I could have imagined. To enter into such an endeavor takes commitment, trust, and honesty. I wouldn't want to do this with anyone else. xxx

ABOUT THE AUTHOR

Melissa Bourbon is the national bestselling author of more than 20 mystery books, including the Lola Cruz Mysteries, A Magical Dressmaking Mystery series, the Bread Shop Mysteries, written as Winnie Archer, and the brand new Book Magic Mysteries.

She is a former middle school English teacher who gave up the classroom in order to live in her imagination full time. Melissa, a California native who has lived in Texas and Colorado, now calls the southeast home. She hikes, practices yoga, cooks, and is slowly but surely discovering all the great restaurants in the Carolinas. Since four of her five amazing kids are living their lives, scattered throughout the country, her dogs, Bean, the pug, and Dobby, the chug, keep her company while she writes.

Melissa lives in North Carolina with her educator husband, Carlos, and their youngest son. She is beyond fortunate to be living the life of her dreams.

VISIT Melissa's website at http://www.melissabourbon.com

JOIN her online book club at https://www.facebook.com/groups/BookWarriors/

JOIN her book review club at https://facebook.com/melissaanddianesreviewclub

ALSO BY MELISSA BOURBON

Book Magic Mysteries

Murder in Devil's Cove

Death at Cape Misery

Murder at Sea Captain's Inn

Bread Shop Mysteries, *written as Winnie Archer*

Kneaded to Death

Crust No One

The Walking Bread

Flour in the Attic

Dough or Die

Lola Cruz Mysteries

Living the Vida Lola

Hasta la Vista, Lola!

Bare Naked Lola

What Lola Wants

Drop Dead Lola

Magical Dressmaking Mysteries

Pleating for Mercy

A Fitting End

Deadly Patterns

A Custom-Fit Crime

A Killing Notion

A Seamless Murder

Mystery/Suspense

Silent Obsession

Silent Echoes

Deadly Legends Boxed Set

Paranormal Romance

Storiebook Charm